THE RIGHT BLOOD

Cris Pfeil

5 Fold Media
Visit us at www.5foldmedia.com

The Right Blood

Published by 5 Fold Media, LLC
www.5foldmedia.com

ISBN: 978-1-936578-36-8

Library of Congress Control Number: 2012937716

Dedication

This book is dedicated to You, Jesus, my Champion! My life marches on to the beat of Your great heart. Thank You for everything!

It is also dedicated to the heroes You have given to me: Norni, Norno, & Uncle Johnny, and to my newest champion, Brady McKay Manberg, my grandson, who came into my life on March 23, 2012.

Acknowledgments

I wish to acknowledge my partners in destiny that prayed for and gave me guidance in this project: Eleanor Sabean, the editor who saw the promise in my work and who encouraged me; Andy and Cathy Sanders of 5 Fold Media; my pastor, Rev. Dr. Chris Abhulime of King's Tabernacle Church; and all the people at King's Tabernacle in North Providence, Rhode Island.

Contents

Chapter One

⌘

Tracker

Mentor stopped on the bank of the river that flowed through the Tabor Forest and stared into the dark places between the trees. His undisturbed fishing nets still hung from the bridge. Although every report of enemy incursions placed the most recent Zaagote intrusions far away, he kept alert.

Like his grandfather, who stood beside him, he saw no visible signs of an enemy's presence but he felt one. He saw only trees in front of him. He turned in a full circle to search for an approaching adversary in another direction. He observed nothing unusual. Looking up, he appreciated the brilliant patches of orange sky that sparkled between the lofty branches of the giant cindar trees high above him. Their strong, icy perfume both invigorated and comforted him. The scent of the trees reminded him that they were both still alive, and that even if an enemy did seek them out, they were already deep inside of the forest that he knew so well.

There were many forests in his world, but none like the Tabor. He had been to this forest many times with his grandfather. His mother had told him that when he was only a baby, Ben Zarek had carried him here in his arms. Much had changed. On that first day, long ago, he had not known what it meant to be uneasy.

That first visit had been followed by wonderful hunting and fishing trips with Ben Zarek, so many that he had stopped trying to count them, but over the years he had not only learned what it meant to be uneasy, he had also learned what it meant to be afraid. There was no safe place in his world anymore. The Zaagotes had once dwelled peacefully within their huge empire on this planet, but their unwelcome invasions of New Earth, Tire Elween, and even into the unknown lands of the tribes, had made his world a dangerous one. Still, whenever he was with Ben Zarek, as he was today, his dangerous world was always better. He loved the Tabor almost as much as he loved Ben Zarek. Despite the danger this forest now held, it would always be his refuge.

He knew every inch of the Tabor. He knew every hiding place and every escape route. Knowledge was power. His grandfather had told him that. His old friend and teacher, Takal, had also told him that. He understood what they meant. Because he was aware of the hiding places and the escape routes in the Tabor Forest, he had an advantage over all kinds of enemies when he was here.

In spite of the advantage the forest gave him over enemies, he kept moving. He noticed that his grandfather had traveled some distance away from him, to the left, to search behind the tall bushes which grew there. Mentor stepped to the right to do his own inspection. He was determined to take no chances. He was always mindful of his adversaries. Some were human as he was; these enemies lived in the part of his world called New Earth. Some were Elweenian. These enemies were the humanlike beings who lived in Tire Elween, a vast territory controlled by an emperor who ruled the diverse races and somewhat civilized peoples native to his empire and to this world.

Some were more formidable foes. The tribes and the Zaagotes fell into this category. The tribes controlled the vast, uncivilized and unexplored areas of the planet, the unknown lands. Because the tribes were so hostile to humans, New Earth had formed an alliance with Tire Elween, whose emperor had enslaved or killed many from every tribe except one--the Ayan. In both the known and the unknown lands of Mentor's world, the Ayans were greatly feared. They were ancient and undefeated foes.

But the most dreaded foes of all were the Zaagotes and their trackers. He knew that he should be ready to face Zaagotes or trackers at any moment, but he had no real combat experience against them.

The distant sound of snapping branches whipped his gaze away from the river to a place beyond the huge trees. He wondered who or what was there. He wanted it to be an animal native to the forest, but he had trained himself to think otherwise. He pictured a human stalker, one of the many who hated his family, or one who opposed Ben Zarek's peace initiative.

Although all of the Van Ardens hated his family, Tal Van Arden, his rival for Adamis' affection, was the worst of these human stalkers. He pictured Tal behind one of the trees, poised to stab him in the back with the long knife that he was famous for using. He was ready to defend himself against Tal who had already tried to kill him several times. Tal was a brutal, but known, entity.

Zaagotes and trackers, however, were unknown entities. In a confrontation with them, Mentor did not know what to expect. When he heard the faint noise of another branch breaking, he wanted to believe that he would not have to confront a Zaagote or his tracker.

If a Zaagote warrior was the source of the sound, he understood that the Zaagote might or might not have to use a weapon. Zaagotes, slightly affected by the mysterious virus infecting them, still resembled people. In such Zaagotes, only minor physical changes occurred. These changes included sharper teeth, longer nails, coarser hair, and increased strength, but these Zaagotes still relied heavily on the weapons they carried. In those moderately affected, the body became taller, thicker, and heavier. It had a more muscular appearance, larger hands and feet, and sharply pointed fingers and toes. Coarse hair grew on their bodies in unpredictable ways and places.

These moderately affected Zaagotes were much stronger than those slightly affected, but they were still vulnerable so they also used weapons. However, in those severely affected by the virus, the Zaagotes themselves became the weapons so there were some who chose not to carry them. Serious cases of the virus transformed Zaagotes into beastlike warriors. With fang-like teeth and sharp claws, these Zaagotes were known to tear apart whatever they hunted. Because the virus was spreading and mutating, more were changing into this animal-like state every day. These Zaagotes were hard to kill.

On Mentor's secret expeditions to collect dead Zaagote bodies for his old teacher, Takal, who studied them, he had seen many horrifying examples of these hard-to-kill, fully infected Zaagotes. Such Zaagotes were as infamous for their fierce brutality and for their unpredictable behaviors as Tal was for his unbridled cruelty and blade inflicted deaths.

All Zaagotes in whom the virus had done its worst, were merciless, massive, heavily-muscled, and powerful beyond belief. All severely affected Zaagotes had extremely thick veins running through and over their wide necks and bodies. All had enormous eyes, oversized black-skinned heads with high ridges that peaked on top, and thick black hair that grew just past their shoulders, with a very thin layer of hair covering every other part of them. Some had heavy scales that grew on their chests, arms, and legs to protect their heavy bodies; but even more frightening than the outward physical changes that the virus caused, were the changes that the virus made within the Zaagote body.

In addition to studying Zaagote customs and language, the deepest changes in their anatomy were part of his daily lessons. Under Takal's supervision, he had dissected fully infected Zaagotes where these deepest changes took place. From these dissections, he had learned that these Zaagotes had two hearts. One was inside of the Zaagote's massive chest, in approximately the same place a human heart was found, but the exact location of the second heart within the chest wall was never the same. It was this second, harder-to-find heart that made this type of Zaagote almost invincible.

When he heard the faint noises of other branches snapping and leaves rustling, Mentor wished that he did not know as much as he did about how difficult it was to kill these two-hearted monsters. Although he realized how lucky he was that Takal, one of the wisest healers on his world, had been teaching him about Zaagotes for years, he understood that if he had remained ignorant, he would not be as intimidated by them as he was now.

The other dreaded foe, tribesmen, were also mysterious and intimidating. They looked human, but with tribesmen he did not know how he would be attacked or with what type of weapon. He had heard that they killed with their hands or hacked their enemies to pieces with things no one had ever seen before. The nature of the tribes was one of the few things that he and his father agreed on. Like his father, Mentor thought all tribesmen were ignorant, filthy savages—as bad if not worse than the Zaagotes—and he had no use for them.

If the noises were made by a Zaagote's tracker, he would face one of the beasts controlled by them. He had seen fewer trackers than Zaagotes. Each tracker was different from the others, but all were said to be as vicious and as powerful, if not more so, than their masters, and equally intimidating.

He hoped that the source of the noise would not be intimidating, that it was a familiar animal moving through the forest, but he began to notice a peculiar odor that he could not identify. He knew the way the forest smelled when familiar animals were close. He sniffed the air again. He did not recognize this smell. Its source was unknown.

Who or what was there? Was it human or Elweenian? Was it one of the tribesmen, a savage, or a Zaagote? Was it a tracker? Sometimes humans and Elweenians used masking scents to conceal their presence. Still, he had never experienced a masking scent as terrible as this one. Some of the savages in the tribes did have a distinct odor, especially the Ayans, but the odor had never been described as rotten, just different. If the smell did not come from an Ayan, the odor had to be from a Zaagote or a tracker. He knew how terrible fully infected Zaagotes and trackers sometimes smelled.

More often than not the Ayan tribesmen and the Zaagotes were silent killers. They did not make leaves rustle or snap branches even if they did smell. The sounds and the nauseating scent that corrupted the forest today whispered an unmistakable warning. There was someone or something else in the forest that did not belong there, and he did not know who or what that something was. Was it one of the many unidentified beasts who hunted for them?

Would his grandfather be able to deal with the unidentified intruder? He was not sure. Ben Zarek had been a formidable fighter when he was younger, but he had slowed down so much that he had been ordered not to participate in actions against the enemy. He could only direct them. His grandfather's hearing had also diminished, and like other warriors who had inhaled strange smoke during one of many skirmishes with the Zaagotes, his grandfather had lost his sense of smell.

Mentor turned around to warn Ben Zarek about the foul presence in the forest, but when he glanced at the spot where his grandfather had been, Ben Zarek was gone. He was not where he had been standing and studying the forest for signs of an enemy only a moment ago. His heart thudded against the wall of his chest. He darted to the place where Ben Zarek had been weaving in and out of the thick bushes. He pushed the heavy branches aside. He shoved his way through the forest.

While he searched, he blamed himself for not watching his grandfather more closely. Although there were no further steps they could have taken to prevent an adversary from following, they had done what they could to keep this trip private. They wanted to be sure that no one from New Earth, or from her ally, Tire Elween—especially the Van Ardens—knew about Ben Zarek's leave of absence, but *he* knew that he could have been more vigilant.

He had done a great job keeping the secret that Ben Zarek had taken a leave of absence from his duties as a general and an advisor to Tor Noc, the Elweenian emperor, but he had failed to take care of his grandfather here in the forest. Apart from Mentor, only Kor Elion, Ben Zarek's second in command, and the emperor himself knew about Ben Zarek's sudden departure. In spite of the well kept secret, he had failed to keep Ben Zarek in sight. He was furious with himself. He wracked his brain. Who or what had taken his grandfather? Where was Ben Zarek?

He crouched close to the ground and kept searching. He crept forward slowly. He remembered that he was alone. Now many sounds filled the tainted air. In front of him a herd of deer-like Elweenian musks stampeded through the trees. Around him fat, bristled seldacs scampered away. He inhaled the rotten air again. The faint odor had become a heavy scent that violated the forest around him.

He clasped the hilt of his sword, inched forward behind the massive trees, and tried to breathe through the odor. Another herd flew by. Rabbits, squirrels, and seldacs scurried over his feet. In his experience, those who used a masking scent never frightened animals away in such numbers. The sound of birds disappeared. Unnatural silence replaced chirping. Though he did not want to think so, he was sure that the stench came from one of two things: one of the fully transformed Zaagotes, or one of the Zaagote's hunters, a tracker. The sweat and the breath of a fully transformed Zaagote smelled like spoiled meat, but trackers sometimes marked the territories in which they hunted by depositing piles of dung all over it. It sickened Mentor to take another deep sniff, but he did. Was the smell the odor of spoiled meat or was it from newly created dung heaps? In either case, his first confrontation in combat would be exactly what he hoped it would not be—a battle with a Zaagote or his tracker. His heart pounded.

More animals thudded through the forest in a desperate attempt to leave. Still, Mentor did not see his grandfather. He kept moving. He crouched behind bushes. He wove in and out of the Cindar trees. He looked everywhere. While he scoured the area the noxious smell became a suffocating blanket. Under its leaden cover a Zaagote or a tracker, or perhaps even both, would soon attack.

To ready himself for the onslaught, he thought about the places where Zaagotes were vulnerable. He knew where to thrust his blade to destroy the first heart, but he realized that he would have to thrust quickly, probably again and again, to get the second. About trackers he did not comprehend nearly as much. He had dissected only a few and the ones that he had studied were all very unique. Because of the vast differences among trackers there was no sure way to kill one. Only one thing was certain when it came to killing trackers—because of their thick skins they were just as hard to kill as Zaagotes were, if not harder.

Mentor kept his hand on his sword as he squatted behind another tree and listened. Now he heard louder sounds—not the sounds of branches snapping. Whatever it was, it was thudding around him and moving fast. If he wanted to stay alive, he had to do the same.

In the past speed had saved him, but running was no substitute for combat skill or combat experience. Takal had taught him things to help him understand where and how Zaagotes or trackers might be vulnerable, but he had always prefaced his lessons by telling Mentor never to face a fully transformed Zaagote or a tracker unless he had no other choice. All of the seasoned warriors had given him the same piece of advice.

In a confrontation with a Zaagote or a tracker, chances for survival were minimal. How could he even try to defend Ben Zarek against either when he did not know where his grandfather was? If anything happened to Ben Zarek, it would be his fault. He hurried on while hoofbeats circled him. As he listened to them, his focus shifted from blame to survival. In order to survive he had to do what his trainer, Dex Argon, had told him to do during practice fights. He had to concentrate on the battle at hand.

The foreign odor signaling the imminent battle was heavier. It was harder to breathe. The leaves rustled. The unknown predator was approaching. The hoofbeats that had begun in a wide circle around him shrank into a smaller circle and then to a noose. When the pounding stopped abruptly, Mentor peered into one of the few spots where the late afternoon sun lit the dark forest floor. There he saw the huge stag trapped in the noose with him. He was glad to see the stag instead of a Zaagote or a tracker, but he was sorry that the exhausted animal was as trapped as he was by the unbelievably fast predator circling them.

Crazy with fear, the stag started to dart in every direction in an attempt to escape, but it did not know which way to go. Its beauty reminded him that his world was worth fighting for. Of all of the specimens that Mentor's ancestors had brought to New Earth from Old Earth, he loved the stag more than any other creature.

Many creatures from Old Earth had survived its destruction and escaped to this world where they had multiplied and mated with creatures native to this place, but the stag was significant to him. In it he saw what he wanted to be—a creature of speed and grace. Beyond that he saw its incredible will to be free, a will that he understood and shared. He was free when he was swapping stories with his grandfather around a campfire in the forest, or when he listened to Adamis laugh at her own jokes, but those times of freedom were rare.

Now, in this moment, the stag was as he was most of the time—trapped by circumstances. The stalker had robbed it of its freedom. Its helplessness tortured Mentor. As it ran around within the invisible barrier created by the circling hunter, he understood that the unseen predator had chosen to torment the animal with a prolonged and deadly game of chase before the kill.

With the hunter's perimeter tightening around him, Mentor sprinted silently from tree to tree, searching for Ben Zarek. He wondered if the unknown assailant had already played the same game of chase with his grandfather, if the predator had already killed Ben Zarek. Had the hidden hunter also sensed Mentor's presence within the circle along with the stag? Was the stalker about to play the deadly game with him? His throat tightened and closed. He could not swallow. He could not take a deep breath. It was only when his fear had almost convinced him that Ben Zarek was already dead, that he recalled his grandfather's familiar habit of quiet, unannounced withdrawals to secluded places where he could pray.

One of these secluded places was a ledge in this part of the forest. He had seen Ben Zarek kneel there many times. He knew how to find it. In spite of the suffocating air, he ordered himself to inhale and headed for the ledge. He told himself that the hunter was focused on the stag, not on him. Keeping as close to the ground as he could, Mentor hurried toward his grandfather's favorite place of prayer and hoped that the noose around them would not become a lethal knot while he was on his way.

He hugged the forest floor. He wove his way through the tall, thick bushes without a sound. He inched his way toward a small outcropping of rocks. As he approached the hill, he lost sight of the spot where he had often seen Ben Zarek praying. The hill was so completely covered with impenetrable shrubs; he could not see if Ben Zarek was kneeling somewhere behind them.

He reached the hilltop. Hand over hand he climbed the tree next to him. When he finally spotted Ben Zarek, his heart soared. While he collapsed in the fork of the tree, his breathing slowed. No matter what hunted them—a man, a monster, or something in between—Ben Zarek was still alive.

From his perch in the tree, Mentor surveyed the surrounding greenery while Ben Zarek talked with God. As Mentor kept his quiet surveillance of this part of the forest, he studied the possible approaches to the hill and wondered what Ben Zarek and God said to each other, but he knew he would not ask.

Mentor's father had repeatedly said that there was no God. Kan had told Mentor that every man was his own god, that his grandfather's beliefs were wrong. He did not know who was right, but when he glanced to his left and saw a shadow slide between trees, he knew it was not the moment to decide.

The shadow moved around the stag and him. The stag jumped and landed on the other side of the hill where his grandfather knelt. Although Mentor was relieved to see his grandfather completely motionless, in a kneeling position where he was totally hidden from the predator's eyes, his fear increased. The shadow was close. As long as Ben Zarek stayed in the kneeling position, he would remain in the tree and maintain his silent vigil. He held his bow in readiness, positioned an arrow, and waited.

Each moment that his grandfather knelt in pra er was another moment of life, but he was surprised to see his grandfather praying so ardently. Never during any of Ben Zarek's prayer times, had he seen his grandfather press his forehead against the ground. The fervor of the prayer astonished him.

But the enormity of the shadow and the speed with which it moved astonished him even more. Not once during any of his travels as a runner had he seen such a huge shape move so fast.

Stay down, Mentor thought. *Stay down. Stay down.* He repeated the words over and over in his mind, wishing that he had the tremendous telepathic power that some in his world had. He was afraid that his grandfather would get up, but he did not move. Like Ben Zarek, Mentor kept still, but the black shape did not.

The dark form slid in and out of the spaces between the surrounding trees. When it finally darted away from the stag and from his grandfather, Mentor expected the stag to see its chance and try to escape. It did not disappoint him. It leapt to its feet. In a formidable jump it shot into the air, but the shadow shot after it. Mist sprayed through the leaves and blinded him. He wiped the moisture from his eyes with the back of his hand. He shook when he saw that it was covered with blood, that *he* was covered with blood.

With clearer vision, he peered through the blood-spattered leaves. The shadow was gone. He heard it dragging the stag away, but he knew that it would return and wait for a chance to kill again. He inhaled the slightly improved air around him with relief, until the sound stopped abruptly. He did not hear the shadow coming back, but he kept his body motionless and turned only his head. In that instant he saw the shadow dart back in his direction and slide behind some trees close to his hiding place.

He jumped when it shot through the sky in an arc and landed in the huge tree to his right. His heart skipped a beat. Then it thumped wildly. He was fast but he understood that he could not outrun the shadow anymore than the stag had. During his days as a courier, he had once outrun a tracker, but the creature next to him was a different breed. He had never seen any hunter move as swiftly, as fluidly, or as unpredictably as this one did.

Even if he managed to fire off a round of arrows and hit the creature before it reached him, he knew that some would bounce off the animal's thick hide, and that those which did manage to penetrate its tough skin might not take it down. He slid the arrows back into his quiver.

From his close observations of the few other trackers that he had seen as a scout, he realized that his best hope for survival was not a weapon. To stay alive he had to remain unnoticed. He felt helpless. He wanted to fight the shadow. The stag's death angered him. The relentless hunter angered him. The threat to Ben Zarek angered him, but he did not budge. If he wanted to live long enough to help his grandfather, he had to stay where he was.

In silent stillness he watched and waited. He wanted to act, but there was nothing he could do. If he climbed out of the tree to warn Ben Zarek, he would lead the shadow to his grandfather. If Ben Zarek stood up, Mentor decided to jump from the tree and try to lure the hunter away.

His grandfather still knelt on the other side of the hill. The shadow bounced from tree to tree around them. Mentor could not see it through the heavy leaf covering that rose above him, but he saw the branches shaking as the unknown predator jumped from limb to limb. Unaware of the approaching killer, Ben Zarek continued to pray. Mentor was determined to save his grandfather's life, in what he believed would be the last run he would ever make, but when the animal climbed down from the tree and Mentor took his first long look at it, his resolve weakened. He wanted to save his grandfather's life, but he did not want to die with the talons of this tree-climber buried deep inside of his body.

Though not much was known about the Zaagotes or their servants, one rumor about the origins of their race was that they had come from a faraway planet, and that the animals with which they hunted their enemies came from this other world as well. The longer he stared at the creature, the more he believed the rumor was true. The hunter was repulsive. Four limbs powered its enormous, muscular body. Its large head, huge cheek pouches, and long, naked, dog-like muzzle gave the creature a bizarre face, but its powerful limbs, its extensive canines, its size, and its ferocity gave it panther-like strength. The black animal was a natural killing machine.

He wanted to turn away from the killer, but he forced himself to watch its approach. The hunter crawled toward the top of the hill. When it reached that spot, it would attack. Mentor readied himself for its ferocious onslaught. He wriggled between the two heavy branches in the fork of the tree and stood in a jumping position. He was determined to hit the ground running and draw the tracker away from Ben Zarek.

Suddenly a loud, droning sound reverberated through the forest. Instantly the creature disappeared from sight.

Mentor did not know how close or how far away this hunter's summoner was when it darted away in response to this call. He was only sure of one thing—for now the animal's master had called it and ordered it to hunt in another direction. He wiped the perspiration from his brow, swallowed hard, and took a deep breath. Then he jumped. He landed on the ground with a thud and flew over the uneven terrain until he reached Ben Zarek.

From the surprised expression in his grandfather's eyes, Mentor could tell that he had startled Ben Zarek, but he wrapped his left arm around his grandfather's shoulder and pushed him gently back toward the ground. Kneeling beside Ben Zarek, he chose not to speak or even whisper. Uncertain about whether or not his grandfather had heard the droning noise, Mentor pointed in the direction of the closest hiding place. Using sign language, he communicated the only word he needed to say before he led his grandfather to it—tracker.

Chapter Two

⌘

Fade

Mentor hurried toward the hiding place; Ben Zarek followed. He slid through the narrow, vine-covered cave entrance and held the thick, stringy vines apart while his grandfather stepped inside. Then he pushed the vines back in place to camouflage the entrance to their refuge.

Through the darkness of the cave passage, he moved quickly and silently. He grabbed his grandfather's hand and pulled him forward. He did not stop moving until they were deep within. Although his grandfather was winded from their escape to the cave, he did not look worried. In spite of the unwelcome presence of this new and deadly tracker and the master who had summoned it, Mentor did not see the same anxious look in Ben Zarek's eyes that he had seen before his urgent prayer. His grandfather looked peaceful when he spoke.

"When it comes to scenting potential prey, this new tracker is no match for the forest. No Zaagote or tracker has ever been able to smell well enough to locate its prey with great accuracy in here. Our hunter seems to have lost us. Let's hope that its master cannot follow our scent and has ordered it away."

"The fragrance of the cindar trees continues to be our friend," Mentor said. He felt relieved that the tracker and its master had probably left their immediate area, but he was uneasy. He knew what his grandfather was about to say.

"Now, for my sake and for your mother's, you must return to the fortress. You cannot go with me the rest of the way."

Though he hated to agree with Ben Zarek, he knew that he was right. He had never been so torn in his life. No matter how much he wanted to go with his grandfather, he could not protect his mother while he remained with his grandfather.

He wanted Ben Zarek to know two things before he left. "No matter what you do," he said, "I will support you, and while you are gone, I will take care of my mother. Now tell me where you are going and what you are going to do so I will know where to look and how to help if you do not come back." When his grandfather shook his head, began to pace back and forth, and changed the subject, Mentor was not surprised.

"Where I am going and what I am doing are not as important as the conversation you were supposed to have with your father. Did you talk to him about the danger that Van Arden poses to him, to your mother, and to you?"

The way his grandfather's skin reddened against his white hair reminded Mentor that although he controlled his anger well, he was furious. Over the years Mentor had seen this happen many times when Ben Zarek was trying to convince his father to take action on some issue and his father had refused to listen. As he watched his grandfather's skin change from a light shade of pink to a fiery red tone, his own face grew hotter. He was as furious with his father as his grandfather was. He was so angry that it was hard to get the next words out.

"The way Faxes Van Arden stares at my mother makes me sick to my stomach, but my father chooses to ignore the danger to her, to all of us."

He knew why his father chose to remain blind to the danger. Nothing was more important to Kan or to Kan's family, the Fallels, than power. He had perceived his father's plot to use Van Arden's infatuation with his mother to bring his grandfather's family, the Zareks, his father's family, the Fallels, and the Van Arden family together.

Before he had fallen in love with Adamis Kor Elion, it had been impossible for him to understand how any woman, even a woman as beautiful as his mother, could have such a strong effect on a man. Adamis Kor Elion's beauty rivaled his mother's. Because Mentor adored Adamis, he could fathom what feelings a male could have for a female, but he hated his father for using his mother's peril to bring about his own ascension to glory.

He had tried to be like his father to gain Kan's approval, but he was glad that he was different when it came to using a woman in a way that would threaten her safety. If someday Adamis became his wife, he would never use her as a pawn in a dangerous game. Just the thought of her made him quiver. They had grown up together, and though he could not have put his true feelings for her into words at an earlier age, he was sure now that he had loved her from the beginning.

Faxes Van Arden's attraction to Mentor's mother, Mia, was very different from his love for Adamis. His grandfather had told him the whole story. Van Arden's infatuation with his mother had begun with his grandmother, Ellana. It reminded Mentor about the Old Earth story of *Helen of Troy*, a woman so beautiful that she had a face that launched a thousand ships. Ellana's beauty was also legendary; she was the woman with whom both Ben Zarek and Faxes Van Arden had fallen in love, but she had chosen his grandfather. Ellana was dead now, but Faxes was determined to have her the only way he could. That his mother, Mia, was another man's wife did not matter to Faxes. Only one thing mattered—Mia was her mother's mirror image and Faxes wanted to look upon her every day.

The more Mentor thought about Faxes Van Arden's insane obsession with Mia, the more incensed he became. His furious words spilled out. "My father took me aside," he said. "He tried to joke with me about Van Arden and mother, and about all the times the Van Ardens tried to kill us. He told me that if he could manage to end the hostilities between the Van Arden family and ours, the emperor would reward him by making him more powerful than any Van Arden could hope to be. Kan is so sure that he can make this happen, he even invited Van Arden to have dinner with us at Kan Fallel. My father knows how uncomfortable my mother is around Faxes; he doesn't care." Ben Zarek's face was a furious crimson color. He did not want to further enrage his grandfather, but he had to air his feelings. "You should hear the tone that Van Arden uses around my mother. When he says my mother's name, he lengthens it until she cringes. 'Meeeee--ah,' he says. When he bends over to kiss her hand, he almost drools on her. It's sickening. I never leave her side when he's anywhere around."

"Nor should you," Ben Zarek replied. "Your mother must not be there when he arrives; you must not be there when he arrives. His recent overtures of friendship cannot be trusted; his intentions are evil. How can your father be so blind? It is up to me to protect you and your mother and I have taken the necessary steps to do so."

When his grandfather reached into his pocket and took out the famous ivory colored parchment, upon which all proclamations were elaborately written in the emperor's large and flowery script, Mentor knew that it was a royal decree.

"Along with this declaration, Emperor Tor Noc has given me his word to protect your mother and you. I've told him everything. Your father forgets how long the Zarek family and the emperor's family have been friends, and how loyal I have been to the emperor. He forgets that our ancestors were the people who saved the emperor's predecessors when they first arrived on this world so many years ago. When Tor Noc's family gave New Earth to the survivors of Old Earth, the emperor's family became our first ally. Tor Noc has not forgotten any of this, nor has he forgotten my faithful service. He has also heard about you, the promising young courier." He was so happy that his grandfather was proud of him. He did not know what to say so he did not try to interrupt.

"And you are promising in every way," his grandfather said. "You can learn and understand things at which sages marvel. Beyond the favor Tor Noc owes me, one he plans to repay by helping you and your mother, he would enjoy having you by his side as a trustworthy subject. So from here you must go back to the fortress immediately to rescue Mia and join the emperor." He did not want to be separated from Ben Zarek; but for his mother's sake, he understood the separation had to take place.

"Take your mother to the emperor's palace on the secret path," Ben Zarek said pausing only long enough to take one breath. "Leave without telling your father. Your mother is now part of the emperor's court as you are. You will serve the emperor by becoming one of his personal runners. You will live in the palace until I return. When you are both under the emperor's protection, you will be beyond Van Arden's reach. Your father will be powerless to change this."

His mother had tried to conceal her fears of Van Arden from him, but he was sure that she had confided her terror to his grandfather. He realized that his father would never forgive his mother, his grandfather, or him for refusing his dangerous plan. He understood that by taking his grandfather's side against his father, he was ending his relationship with his father for good. He took a deep breath and wiped the perspiration from his forehead.

Though he had always felt closer to Ben Zarek than he had to his father, Mentor had always longed to be close to Kan. He had always wanted his mother, his father, and him to stay together, but he could see that the family he had known was coming to an end. His heart started beating faster. He was also in danger of losing his grandfather. He refused to let this happen.

He could barely speak but somehow he forced the words out in a whisper. "Tell me where you are going, what your mission is." He knew there was a good reason why his grandfather was not going to the fortress with him. He wanted to know what his destination was and what he had to accomplish.

"Why do you keep asking when you know I cannot tell you?" Ben Zarek said quietly.

"*Can* not tell me or *will* not tell me?" Mentor replied. He could not keep the anger out of his voice. No matter how resistant his grandfather was to his questions, he was determined to make him answer.

"I *can not* tell you. I am sworn to secrecy. The emperor has many enemies. All of them would like to know my place in his plans. I refuse to let them see it. More importantly, I must protect *you.* To quote an Old Earth expression, 'What you do not know will not hurt you.' "

Out of frustration, Mentor approached his grandfather, stood at arm's length from him, curled his arms into a wrestling position, and spread his feet for his attack, but he did not expect his grandfather to give in.

"If I win you have to tell me," he said. Maintaining his wrestling posture, he gave his grandfather an angry look, but he was not mad. He was fearful about where his grandfather was going, about what he was going to do, and about the possibility that he would not come back.

"I do not have to tell you," his grandfather said as he raised his arms, ready to defend himself. Mentor lunged, but Ben Zarek wrapped his arms around him and hugged him so tightly that he could not do anything. They finally rolled to the ground.

In spite of Mentor's determination to appear furious, he hugged him back. When they sat up, Ben Zarek embraced his grandson once more. After a long pause, during which neither of them said anything, his grandfather stood up to say goodbye, but before either of them could speak terrible shrieks punctured the silent forest.

"Stay here," Ben Zarek said as he squeezed Mentor's shoulder. He forcefully pushed his way back through the heavy vines that hid the opening and headed toward the penetrating cries. Knowing how useless it was to argue when Ben Zarek became the general and gave orders, Mentor waited until his grandfather disappeared behind the trees in front of the opening before he followed.

He tried to keep Ben Zarek in sight, but it was impossible. Even though the moonlit night was bright and stars sparkled above, the forest was so filled with cindar trees that it was dark even during the day. Everything was black, but he knew that his grandfather would go towards the awful sounds. He would find Ben Zarek if he also moved towards them. The cries were penetrating, so piercing that Ben Zarek would have no problem finding his way to the source.

Mentor moved quickly and silently towards the shrieks and hoped that he would not step on anything that would also cry out to draw attention to his presence. No hint of moonlight pierced the forest floor. He inched closer to the struggle. His eyes strained to see through the blackness. He wondered if anything hostile was moving closer to the sounds, to his grandfather, to him. He saw and heard nothing apart from the animal-like noises that told him the fight was not between humans. He finally spotted Ben Zarek and gripped the handle of his sword.

He was shocked to see his grandfather in the only clearing lit by the bright light of the twin moons. There an enemy could so easily spot him. Mentor hurried to him. Ben Zarek was hovering over the bodies of two Zaagotes side by side on the forest floor. Blood covered the ground. The sword that Zaagotes called a claveg had completely severed the dead Zaagote's head. The other Zaagote groaned in pain from another sword that was slightly embedded in his neck.

He wondered why they had fought. Realizing that the unconscious, but living Zaagote posed no threat to his grandfather or to him, he sheathed his own sword and put his hand on Ben Zarek's shoulder. His grandfather did not turn to look at him.

"I told you to stay where you were; it was a direct order," his grandfather said. Though he expected his grandfather to sound angry, Mentor could tell from the tone of his voice that he was not. He seemed to be intent on something else. Following his grandfather's gaze, he realized that he was not staring at the Zaagote's wound, but at the handle of the jewel-encrusted blade that belonged to the living Zaagote. He understood the significance of the glittering gems.

Ordinary Zaagotes carried simple, black handled clavegs not jewel-encrusted ones. Also, most clavegs with jeweled handles only had three stones. The first one identified the royal house or family to which the bearer belonged. The second one identified what part of the Zaagote Empire each Zaagote came from, and the third identified the Zaagote's position in that world. Each additonal jewel in the handle indicated a great accomplishment or a special honor received for a successful mission. Certain shapes carved into the claveg's handle indicated an extraordinarily high ranking Zaagote.

From the half moon shape in the central part of the handle around which other precious stones were arranged, Mentor already knew what his grandfather had not yet put into words. This sword was unique, and this Zaagote was unlike any other of his kind.

The jewels clearly indicated the survivor's special status. The half-moon shape carved into the handle indicated the victor's unique place in the Zaagote royal family. He was Oliphar, the emperor's brother. Oliphar also distinguished himself in one other way that made him unlike any other Zaagote that Mentor had ever seen. Unlike most Zaagotes, his blood was red.

He had never seen a Zaagote with red blood. He took one of the vials that Takal had given to him and placed it next to the open wound until it was full. Then he put the vial inside one of the many tiny pouches that his mother had sewn on the inner pocket of his battle vest. Next to other small pouches where Mentor carried critical herbs and rare medicines that he never traveled without, it would be safe. Thrilled with his discovery, he forgot about the dangerous situation until his grandfather broke the silence.

"You know who he is, don't you?" Ben Zarek hesitated. "His brother, Vorg, the Zaagote emperor, wants war. Oliphar came here against his brother's wishes to negotiate a truce. The second part of his plan was to convince the rest of his empire to accept it. I have been planning to meet him here for a long time, but he was not supposed to arrive in this part of the forest or at this time. He was supposed to meet me in an underground cave long after you were on your way back to the fortress. I did not want you to be involved in what the empire has declared to be an act of treason. I did not want to risk your safety or your future."

"Risk my safety or my future? What about your safety and your future?" Mentor said incredulously; he could not believe what he was hearing. "Why would you break the law of the emperor you have served for so long and so well? Why commit an act of treason with someone who came here to kill you? All Zaagotes are killers."

"I did it because the emperor asked me to do it. He knows all about my meeting with Oliphar, but if outsiders find out about it, he will not be able to help me. He cannot openly break his own law. You know what the law says —contact with an enemy is a treasonous act punishable by death. Too many of the emperor's lords still favor war. If his opponents find out that he sent me on a peace mission before he can gather enough support to change the law, his enemies will try to kill him and put another in his place."

Ben Zarek stood up. He started to pace back and forth. Before Mentor could say a word, his grandfather grabbed his shoulders and looked into his eyes. "I'm sorry you do not agree with what I have done. Agree or not, you have to leave now, and I have to stay. If the dead one knew that Oliphar was coming here to meet with me and tried to kill him because of it, then others know he came here and will follow. There are just as many against peace in the Zaagote Empire as there are in the Empire of Tire Elween and in the territory of New Earth. Oliphar's brother, Vorg, the Zaagote emperor, is only one of them. If Oliphar's enemies find him before his friends do, these war mongers will torture him before they execute him. I must help him."

Even though he finally understood why his grandfather had refused to tell him where he was going, he still did not understand why Ben Zarek had broken the law and risked his own life to meet a killer. When he did not budge his grandfather shook him and repeated the command.

"Go now! I made the decision to come here; the risk is mine." His stare spoke the silent order once more.

Mentor did not care how many times his grandfather ordered him to leave. He knew that he was not going anywhere without Ben Zarek, just as he knew that his grandfather was not leaving this place without Oliphar. He loathed this Zaagote and every other Zaagote. They abused or killed every living thing that was not like them. He wanted Oliphar to die, but he had to save his grandfather's life. To help Ben Zarek he had to use the knowledge that Takal had given to him. He had to revive Oliphar and help him escape from the forest. If he didn't, his grandfather would stay here with this Zaagote and be captured when other Zaagotes came.

As soon as Oliphar was able to travel, his grandfather would be willing to leave this very dangerous place. Instead of letting the Zaagote die, he swallowed his loathing, knelt down next to Oliphar, and placed his hand on the scaled, blood-soaked skin around the sword still embedded in his neck.

"If you want me to go away from here quickly, please help me," Mentor said. He had always been respectful of Ben Zarek, even when they disagreed, but he realized that his use of the word please did not hide the anger in his voice.

When Ben Zarek knelt down beside him, Mentor remembered what Takal had always told him about anger. It interfered with the ability to make good decisions. It was hard to put his fury aside, but he did what his teacher had trained him to do in life and death situations. A critical decision had to be made. Ben Zarek's life, as well as his own, depended on what he chose to do next.

"Let's get him back to the cave," Mentor said. "I can care for him there. Then we can all get out of here." He started to lift Oliphar, but when he saw the seldac inspecting a nearby log, he stopped and lowered the Zaagote back to the ground. The bulky black and brown seldac was curled into a furry ball. Its large paws covered its eyes and its long ears were folded over its round body like a blanket. Only its large black nose and its even larger black and semi-open mouth were exposed to his view as it sniffed away.

"This fat fellow can help us," Mentor said. Tearing a branch filled with sela berries from a nearby tree, he sniffed the potent leaves and smiled as he inspected the large folds of ample skin around the seldac's plump neck. "No seldac can resist sela leaves," Mentor remarked as he reached into his pocket, took out a small pouch, and poured a little bit of finely ground powder from it on top of each leaf. After the seldac ate them and snored loudly, he tore a small piece of cloth from Oliphar's cloak, opened his vest pocket, and pulled out a needle and thread.

"The powder I poured on the leaves has a numbing effect. The seldac won't feel a thing while I stitch this Zaagote scented cloth into the extra skin around his neck. If someone comes looking for Oliphar or for us, he may end up chasing this substantial decoy instead."

Obviously pleased with Mentor's diversionary tactic, his grandfather nodded his agreement.

Also satisfied with this strategy, Mentor completed the sewing procedure. Then he turned to his grandfather, put his hand on his shoulder, and smiled. He remembered his love for his grandfather, why he was doing what he was doing. While he nudged the seldac awake with a long branch, his smile became an even broader grin.

Totally unaware that he had Oliphar's scent on him, the groggy seldac shook his head furiously and sat up. He collapsed on his stomach a few times before he staggered away and disappeared, but he was going to be fine. Mentor stood on one side of Oliphar and his grandfather stood on the other. While they dragged the Zaagote back to the cave, he wondered if Oliphar would recover as well as the seldac did.

On the floor of the cave, Mentor knelt down close to Oliphar and studied him. Ben Zarek crouched behind the vines that covered the cave's entrance to watch for an approaching enemy. As he bent closer to Oliphar's thick neck, Mentor saw that the sword had only partially severed one of the four huge veins that powered his massive body.

Placing both of his hands on the blade, Mentor jiggled it slightly and pulled it towards him until he had completely removed it from Oliphar's neck. Then he reached for the sac that hung from his belt. He knew that he would have to use one of the precious healing lotions that Takal had perfected. He removed the cork from the vial, allowed the liquid to fall directly onto the deep slice, and rubbed his index finger over the long gash. He massaged it by moving his finger lightly up and down over its length. Following this procedure, he circled the wound with his lotion-soaked fingers in feather-like motions.

While he completed the massage he compared Oliphar's features with the features of some of the dead Zaagotes that he had dissected with Takal. Although he noticed a few similarities between Oliphar and the others, he also noted many things that made him very different. Some of the Zaagotes that he had seen had hairless, scaled, and oversized black skinned heads formed in high ridges that peaked on top. Oliphar had thick black hair that covered his entire body. Many Zaagotes had heads that were only slightly bigger than a man's head. Oliphar had an enormous head which sat on an enormous, muscular body.

No two Zaagotes possessed the same degree of superior strength or incredible agility, but each seemed to have sensory abilities that extended beyond the normal range. Oliphar's gigantic form and fully developed muscles convinced Mentor that he was exceptionally powerful among his own kind. His huge eyes were shaped the way human eyes were shaped, but his thick black lips, his long brown nose, and his scaled cheekbones made him appear bestial.

Whether or not Oliphar's hidden traits were even more memorable than his physical characteristics, he did not know. No matter what abilities Oliphar had, no matter how intimidating his hidden powers might be, Mentor had to help him heal. Oliphar's outward appearance was frightening enough, but when he considered the possibility that this Zaagote might have unseen powers more daunting than his physical prowess, he decided that it was better not to think about it. He had to focus on the work he was about to do.

Oliphar's beast-like form revolted Mentor more than the appearance of the most mangled, bloodied cadaver that he had ever worked on. In spite of this revulsion, he put his hand over the thick blood that covered the Zaagote's neck and kept it on the heart spot to check for any vibration that would signal signs of recovery. He jumped when he felt one. At that moment Ben Zarek crept up beside Mentor, put his hand on his shoulder, and whispered in his ear.

"Can you do anything to speed up the process? Someone or something is coming this way." Not waiting for an answer, Ben Zarek was already on his way back to the vine-covered opening to watch at the entrance to the cave.

Pulling leaves from the vines that grew over the walls, Mentor soaked them in water that dripped from one of the cracks. Then he spread the leaves on a flat rock in front of him. From the inside of his battle vest, he took out some herbal powder, sprinkled it onto one of the large wet leaves, and rolled the leaf into a poultice. When he pressed this poultice against the wound in Oliphar's neck, he jumped again. There was another beat and another.

Understanding that these beats, these vibrations in the heart spot on his neck, meant there were only minutes before Oliphar woke up, Mentor hurried to the cave entrance and crouched next to Ben Zarek. Side by side they peered through the small openings in the vines, stared into the forest, and listened to the silence until they heard a single word spoken loudly in a high form of the Zaagote tongue.

"Idiot," the voice said. Mentor pressed his face against the vines until he found a wider hole to improve his view. Something was coming towards them. Branches snapped and bushes rustled. It crawled toward the opening. In the bright moonlight illuminating the small clearing in front of the cave, Mentor saw an extremely small tracker.

This tracker hobbled out from behind a huge jagunda tree on the fringe of his viewing range. He was surprised by it. He knew that trackers came in all shapes and sizes, but he had never seen one the size of a small man. Behind it was another creature. In the moon glow that lit another place in the dark forest, another silhouette of tremendous proportions appeared. At first this enormous creature looked like a shadow, but when the shadow stretched its long arm out, seized the smaller creature's left arm, and twisted it behind him, he realized how real the shadow was.

The tracker cried out. The giant released him, but only long enough to ram a booted foot into the tracker's back. With its face in the dirt, the tracker stayed where it had fallen until its master lifted his foot and held it over the tracker's neck. When the tracker saw this, it scrambled for a claw-hold and tried to drag itself forward with its right arm.

Mentor hated trackers, but the longer he watched the cruel giant beat his injured animal, the more he wanted to help the tracker end its master's life. He thought about immobilizing the Zaagote by slashing the veins in his neck, but the Zaagote was too tall. He could not reach the tormentor's neck unless he stood on something or jumped on him from above.

He wanted to drive his sword into the Zaagote's chest. He considered what might happen if he did. He knew that he might miss. He could also see that this Zaagote was fully transformed; this brute had another heart buried deep inside of his huge body. If he pierced the first heart but missed the second, his attack would be disastrous; he would only succeed in wounding the bully.

In any failed assault, a wounded Zaagote or tracker would alert others to a human presence in the forest. This would greatly reduce the odds for a successful escape. He cared nothing about what would happen to Oliphar if the Zaagotes found the cave before he woke up. He was ready to slip away unnoticed as soon as the opportunity came. In spite of his burning desire to leave Oliphar behind, he knew that Ben Zarek would not abandon Oliphar any more than he would abandon Ben Zarek.

While the tracker sniffed the area a short distance away from the camouflaged opening to the cave, Mentor considered another option. With each valuable moment that passed, Oliphar was gaining strength. If Oliphar did recover enough of it, he would not slow them down too much when the chance to escape came. All three of them might make it, but for Ben Zarek's sake as well as for his own, in this moment, he had to keep still. Their current best hope for survival was to stay where they were and do nothing. Gripping the handle of his sword even tighter, Mentor exchanged an encouraging glance with his grandfather and listened.

"Don't get up, Pel," the giant said to his tracker. "Since you can't walk without stumbling, I prefer that you crawl anyway." Pel rolled to his side. He tried to aid his progress with his good arm while he kept his injured arm clear of the ground. Time after time he tried to get out of his master's way, but the giant kept his huge legs on each side of his tracker. He straddled his slave to keep him from moving too far away. It was clear that the brute relished his position of power.

From this straddling position, the giant delivered sharp kicks to Pel's right or left side. With each blow Pel changed direction. When the task master shoved Pel forward by kicking his rear end, Pel tried to speed up.

He also lifted his head to see where the next blow was coming from, but the giant finally put his foot on Pel's back and shoved him to the ground.

As Pel's tormentor held his foot above his neck and arched his own head back in what appeared to be a state of sadistic rapture, Pel did not move. When the massive torturer glared down at him once more, Mentor thought that the Zaagote was about to kill his tracker. He was surprised when the giant put his foot back on the ground instead of using it to break Pel's neck. He was even more stunned when the giant pointed toward the opening to the cave and said "Try that way." As soon as his tracker wiggled forward, the Zaagote's rolling laughter reverberated in the forest.

Pel struggled towards the cave opening. The giant continued to laugh and strike Pel intermittently. During the beating the tracker and his Zaagote master inched closer to the cave's entrance. Each time Pel moved, he lifted his nose from the ground and sucked the air in as if he was taking his last breath. His flaring nostrils became gaping holes when he got ready to press the flat end of his nose against the ground; he desperately wanted to catch the scent of prey before he slogged on.

This tracker's sensitive nose was its most prominent feature. Though it resembled the shape of a human nose where it connected to the body, the tip of it looked like a giant fan. Pel's nose covered so much of his face that his lips were hidden under it. It was the biggest part of Pel's yellow and brown striped body. It was also the only feature that stood out apart from his webbed, pointed ears. In all the reports that Mentor had read, he had never seen any description that matched the appearance of the tracker before him. This was not the case with Pel's master.

When Mentor looked at this giant, a list of distinguishing characteristics for key enemy leaders came to mind. The longer he stared at him, the more details he remembered about one Zaagote warrior in particular: scarred upper lip, left ear higher than the right, extremely rare brown eyes flecked with specks of yellow, and a reputation for extreme cruelty.

In addition to the physical description of this giant, there were unforgettable comments. He recalled one comment especially: "*Wears a three-strand necklace of human teeth and hair that he never removes.*" During the many hours that Mentor had spent studying descriptions of key enemies, he had paid close attention to unique details. He recognized the necklace covering the Zaagote's massive chest, the jalar; its disgusting details set its owner apart from the rest.

To be certain that this particular jalar matched the one unique neck piece spoken of in the profile of one particular Zaagote, he inspected it more closely. The three-stranded necklace was composed of different colors and thicknesses of human hair. From this hair, human teeth of various shapes and sizes dangled conspicuously. Between the strands of hair and teeth held in place by tightly fastened knots, remarkable jewels glittered.

According to the reports that Mentor had read, only one Zaagote warrior chose to include teeth in his jalar to remind himself of favorite victims. Inhaling deeply, Mentor closed his eyes and tried to remain calm. He knew who the giant was.

Although he had never seen this Zaagote before, he had no doubts about his identity. He was Vorg's deadliest assassin. His identity made Mentor sure that the giant had come to the Tabor Forest to kill Oliphar and Ben Zarek before they could discuss the truce they hoped might lead to peace.

Stopping the peace process before it had begun was why this assassin was in the Tabor. About that there was no question. He felt the fight for survival that was about to ensue here. He did not know if he and Ben Zarek and Oliphar would survive the battle. Only one thing was certain. The most violent Zaagote killer of all, Vorg's personal and unrelenting butcher, had come to the forest. His name was Fade.

Chapter Three

⌘

Oliphar

Fade stood just outside the cave. Thoughts of revenge filled Mentor's mind. He remembered the night that he and Takal had gone to Treleba to retrieve a Zaagote body after a battle there. He remembered his friend, Gal, the runner who had been sent to find out which way the Zaagotes had gone after the massacre.

He swallowed hard whenever he thought about Gal. At first he had not found Gal when he went to search for him. He gagged each time he recalled how he had finally discovered his friend—in pieces placed carefully in a pile on the path by which the Zaagotes had left the village. He also recalled the old man, Gal's neighbor, the only survivor of the massacre, and the shock on the elder's face.

One survivor-- it was the pattern. It was Fade's trademark, his way of telling others what would happen to them if they did follow. With one survivor from each slaughter left behind to provide a living witness of horror, fear of Fade had quickly spread throughout all lands not controlled by Zaagotes.

Though the old man would have to live with the horror of the massacre that he had witnessed, Mentor thought the sole survivor was luckier than those who had been cut into pieces or taken captive. Captives were another part of the pattern. Some were always taken away alive. A few became living experiments for Zaagote healers who searched for answers about how and why the virus was transforming them and leaving other races on the planet unscathed. Others became slaves. The unluckiest survivors, selected by Fade himself, belonged to the Zaagote emperor. Some of these captives entertained Vorg by losing their lives in The Ring of Glory. There they fought opponents that they could not hope to beat. Others of exceptional rank or beauty were chosen to appease the blood lust of strange Zaagote gods. According to Zaagote law, only perfect sacrifices provided the satisfaction that Vorg's gods demanded. Fade's reputation for finding these perfect sacrifices in return for lands, titles, slaves, and other favors, was well known.

Mentor wanted to kill Fade. He willed Fade to come closer to the opening in the thick vines. He visualized his sword slashing the dense veins that powered his gigantic body. He wanted the monster to suffer before he died. He saw himself stabbing his sword into Fade's chest over and over until he found and destroyed the second black heart beating there.

As he gripped the handle of his drawn sword, he thought about his friend, Gal, who had not survived the massacre, and about the old man who had survived. Then he asked himself how many more might live if they could somehow kill Fade and his tracker, Pel, before Fade summoned other Zaagotes to this part of the forest, but when he turned to his grandfather to suggest an attack, disappointment wasn't the only thing he felt.

One claw-like hand closed around his neck and pierced his skin. Another hand with claw-like fingers punctured his battle vest and the black tunic under it. Sharp points pressed into him. Before he could turn away from the cave opening to defend himself from the attacker behind, he thought he would be dead. Then the hands suddenly released him; Ben Zarek's sword was already at Oliphar's neck.

Oliphar withdrew his taloned hands as quickly as he had extended them, but in the next moment he raised his own sword as if he was about to strike at them both. While Ben Zarek and Oliphar faced each other with drawn blades in the semi-darkness of the cave, Mentor understood how right he had been to hate Oliphar. He was more certain than ever that the arranged meeting between Ben Zarek and Oliphar was part of an elaborate plot that Oliphar and Fade had designed to kill his grandfather.

He held his own sword in readiness. He waited for his grandfather's signal. Now Ben Zarek could see that Oliphar was not to be trusted. He expected Ben Zarek to attack. He was shocked when his grandfather did not. While Oliphar used the same sign language that he had been taught to use when silent communication was critical, Mentor watched in disbelief.

"I meant no harm," Oliphar said, "but I read the boy's mind. I had to stop him. If he attacks, Fade will summon others and we will never get out of the forest alive. He is too young to die."

Angry that Oliphar had called him a boy, and that he had grabbed him from behind, Mentor squeezed the handle of his sword until his knuckles turned white. He was furious. He could not think of enough insulting words with which to reply to Oliphar's lies.

When Oliphar cupped his huge hand to his ear and pointed outside the cave to indicate that they should pay attention to what Fade was saying, Mentor could still barely control his anger. He did not like taking orders from a Zaagote, but he decided to listen.

"Find Oliphar," Fade commanded. "Find Ben Zarek and find my dinner. Keep your nose to the ground." Each time he issued an order he placed his boot against Pel's slightly raised furry behind and pressed down on it. Pel coughed spasmodically, but kept going. While Fade's tirade continued, Mentor studied the strange pair hunting for them. Fade kept talking to the tracker as if Pel had the ability to speak. The tracker said nothing, but there was an intelligent look about Pel. Mentor was sure that he could speak, even if he chose not to.

"Zarek will pay for the victories he stole from me," Fade said. "I will tear his loved ones to pieces in front of him before I take his life," he added without pausing for a breath. "Perhaps you'll be better at scenting Zarek than you are at scenting Oliphar. Perhaps the reward will be greater, but I could be wrong. After all, Oliphar is Vorg's brother and Ben Zarek is a stranger." Pel still said nothing. Fade muttered on angrily talking to himself. Mentor absorbed every word.

"Vorg really hates his traitorous brother. Oliphar defied him by coming here secretly to make peace. Vorg lives to make war, and we can't forget that Oliphar could become more powerful than Vorg if enough Zaagotes chose to support him, so some jealousy is involved. Still, I have heard Vorg vent his hatred for Zarek many times more than he cursed his brother, so who do you think he would enjoy killing first, or more?" This time when Pel failed to reply to his master's questions, Fade kicked his behind hard. Pel opened his mouth to speak because he knew his life depended on it, but Fade held up his hand to silence him.

"Relatives should come before friends, acquaintances, or strangers when it comes to killing," Fade said only stopping long enough to watch Pel agree. "You do not expect relatives to fail you. I always keep this in mind. I never forget you are my cousin's favorite tracker. It is true that I want to watch Ben Zarek and Oliphar die together on the Zaagote high day of sacrifice more than I want to kill you; but if you do not find them, you will die before they do." Pel quickened his pace. He smelled anything and everything until he found the exact path over which Mentor and Ben Zarek had traveled to reach Oliphar. If Pel kept looking for Ben Zarek and Oliphar the way that he was looking for them now, there was a good chance that Fade's dreams for Ben Zarek and Oliphar's executions would come to pass.

As Pel scrambled through some bushes and disappeared, Fade approached the cave entrance and started to sniff the branches that hung over the tangles camouflaging the opening. Mentor held his breath. Would Pel find the body of the Zaagote they had left behind before the giant found them? Would he draw Fade away from the cave long enough for them to escape on the river?

Ben Zarek fingered the get ready signal. Oliphar bowed slightly to show that he understood. While Fade pulled a large, bug-covered branch toward his mouth and picked the lizards off one at a time, Mentor waited for the inevitable cry from Pel. He knew it would be a gut wrenching sound. Ben Zarek squeezed Mentor's shoulder. Oliphar nodded again to indicate readiness. Resting his right hand lightly on the vines just inside the cave's entrance, Mentor waited for the moment when he would push them apart and race toward the river.

Finally the shriek of discovery pierced the air. Fade pivoted in the direction of Pel's alarm, leapt over the bushes in front of him, and landed with a thud on the other side. In an instant he was out of sight. In that same instant, Mentor pulled the thick vines out of the way and stepped outside of the entrance. He stood there just long enough to watch Ben Zarek and Oliphar follow. Then he tore through the narrow strip of forest between him and the river.

The first time he looked over his shoulder, Ben Zarek and Oliphar were right behind him. In the second glance, they were nowhere in sight. He stopped running and waited until they appeared again.When they caught up with him several moments later, they collapsed.

Ben Zarek forced the words out between gasps. "Oliphar is as old as I am and he has lost a lot of blood. He needs more time to fully recover and we're slowing you down. If we make it, we make it," he said breathlessly, "if we do not, our time has come. Get to the river. Run!"

Instead of running he sat down beside them and said the only thing that came into his mind. "Stay here and fight then. I will stay with you. I will not leave you behind." When they stood up, Mentor turned and walked rapidly towards the river, pleased that his strategy had worked. At the slower pace that he was setting, Ben Zarek and Oliphar kept up. It would not be long before Fade finished inspecting the body of the dead Zaagote and started searching the area where the body was for another clue, but Mentor hoped that clue would be the seldac moving away from them.

If the seldac with the piece of Oliphar's cloak wrapped around its neck led Fade and Pel astray long enough for Ben Zarek, Oliphar, and him to reach the river, they would escape.

Again he looked back, but when he spotted the seldac to which he had stitched the piece of Oliphar's cloak trotting along next to Oliphar and Ben Zarek, his hope for escape without a heart-stopping chase were dashed. Fade would not be far behind his failed decoy.

He turned abruptly and hurried down a shorter—but far more dangerous—approach to the river. Ben Zarek and Oliphar followed. Breaking through the cover of the thick trees and the heavy bushes that bordered the rushing water, he climbed down the cliffside. He stood on a small precipice overlooking a whirlpool. Here water from several powerful tributaries thundered into one raging river.

He pulled a boat which he and Ben Zarek had made and hidden there long ago from its secure nook under the thick moss that covered the precipice. He was glad now that he had listened to his grandfather. Ben Zarek had told him that they needed to make as many boats as they could and camouflage them in various places along the river in case they ever needed to make a speedy departure. His heart skyrocketed when he saw that its paddles and poles were still inside.

The heavy spray from the turbulent connection pounded him. In the swirling collision where the tributaries met, the shooting whirlpool soaked and blinded him. He held the small craft steady until Ben Zarek got in, but before Oliphar could join them Fade exploded through the trees above and dove into the water. Leaping from the precipice, Oliphar landed in the water near the boat, swam towards it, and climbed in. Fade surfaced in the pounding water and swam towards them in long, powerful strokes.

In eye-stinging spray, Mentor maneuvered the boat towards a small opening between the sharp rocks and the high cliffs. He tried to direct the boat towards the narrow spot that would take them down the river, but the whirlpool turned the boat in a circular spin that prevented them from making any progress. Still splashing closer with powerful strokes, Fade stretched his long arm towards them and tried to grab the rim of the boat, but he missed. Again he stretched his long arm towards them. This time Oliphar smashed a paddle against Fade's hand until he lost his grip. When the swirling water hurled Fade against a partially submerged boulder, the giant finally went under and was out of sight.

Keeping his eye on the place where Fade had disappeared, Mentor steered the boat towards the only exit to the wide river by pushing his pole away from the rocks on each side. Ben Zarek and Oliphar aided him with their own poles until they lost their balance, fell against each other, and landed on the floor of the boat.

Barely managing to hang on to their poles, they tried to stand up but fell again. The whirlpool spun the boat in a circle once more. Then, suddenly, unexpectedly, Fade surfaced. This time he did not swim towards the boat still spinning in the middle of the whirlpool. Instead, he swam towards the rocks beyond the opening through which they had to pass, pulled himself onto the tallest boulder, and howled.

While Fade summoned his subordinates, he threw something towards the boat. The instant the heavy rope covered Mentor, he knew it was a net; but before Fade could yank Mentor out of the boat with it, Oliphar grabbed the net and pulled Fade into the churning water. Fade tugged on the net again, but Ben Zarek had already pulled it off of Mentor and thrown it over the spot where Fade was. Fade could not swim through the thick net to reach the boat. With the boat spinning in yet another endless circle, Pel and three of Fade's subordinates appeared on the precipice that bordered the whirlpool. One by one they jumped in. Fade surfaced again, but the net was spread over the water on top of him and he was tangled in it. Splashing forward against the strong current, the Zaagotes who had come to help Fade could not make any progress.

This time when the whirlpool threatened to send the boat into another circular spin, Oliphar jammed his paddles into a crevice between the rocks and shoved the boat toward the opening that led to the rushing river. They shot through the exit point over frothy whitewater and went down.

Ahead of them the raging river thundered into a long, narrower channel that funneled between rocks, precipices, and high cliffs on both sides. Using their poles, Ben Zarek, Oliphar, and Mentor pushed against the rocks to keep the boat from crashing into them. As the boat turned, twisted, and banged into the sharp stone outcroppings that bordered the channel, Mentor saw the results of Fade's summons.

Above them more Zaagote warriors stood on top of the cliffs and looked down. At the same time more Zaagotes rappelled down the sides of the cliffs until they reached the narrow, rocky path that bordered the river. They tried to run over the treacherous path, but they stumbled and fell repeatedly on the sharp rocks that covered it. They could not keep up with the boat.

The boat flew down the river on the powerful, bone-chilling current. Mentor glimpsed other enemy warriors along the banks, but when he wasn't observing these new Zaagote threats, he was watching Oliphar—the Zaagote in the boat.

With more adversaries surrounding them, Mentor eyed Oliphar's every move with suspicion. For now, Oliphar wanted to keep Ben Zarek alive, and acted as if Fade was his enemy. Oliphar had even saved their lives by pounding Fade's hands until he released the boat. Still, Mentor did not trust Oliphar any more than Oliphar trusted them. He knew that sooner or later Oliphar would betray them. As the channel tightened further and the churning water engulfed them once more, he tried to concentrate on the enemies above them and along the river while he waited for the expected betrayal.

Suddenly, above them, Fade crashed through the thick bushes and stood on one of the higher precipices surrounded by more Zaagote warriors. The powerful giant had survived the watery death that had threatened him and climbed to the top of the cliff to get above them.

Mentor tried to shove the boat away from the place where he thought the Zaagotes might jump in, but when he saw the boat heading towards one of the many rocky pinnacles that punctuated this part of the river, he focused on avoiding the sharp stone outcroppings until he could propel the boat safely down the river again.

With tall, pointed rock shards protruding everywhere in the water around the boat, it was easy to see why the Zaagotes who had appeared on the precipices above had disappeared as quickly as the Zaagotes who had jumped in and tried to swim after them. The treacherous current was smashing their pursuers against the rocky spikes. The large stone pinnacles sticking up everywhere in this section of the river made one thing very clear. If any Zaagote was considering jumping into the dangerous whitewater, this was not the place to do it.

Mentor could no longer see Fade or the other warriors, but he knew they had not given up. The path that ran parallel to the river along the cliffs above them was where they would be until they found a place where they could climb down, jump into the water, and capture them. For now the boat was smashing through the whitewater making such a capture impossible. The incredible volume of water squeezing into the gorge through the narrow passage pummeled the boat forward and thrust it down the river. From what Mentor had heard about Fade, he knew that he was fast, but he did not know if the Zaagote legend could keep up with the rushing river.

When the giant looked down on them again from a precipice above, Mentor realized that he really was that fast. Now, even though Mentor could not see Fade, he realized that Fade was catching up with them over the path at the top of the cliffs. In spite of this disappointing realization, Mentor was hopeful. The sun was setting. This would make it harder for Fade to see them.

While the sun sank lower still, Mentor watched the cliffs above them for another glimpse of their adversary. In the dimming light he maneuvered the boat away from the stone shards. When the sun finally disappeared behind the cliffs and mountains, the orange twilight became a deep purple, but this quickly turned to black. Now nature would keep Fade from observing any more of their treacherous river ride by covering their progress with the darkness of the night.

Thankful that the night had blinded Fade, Mentor relaxed until a sudden jolt rocked the boat; then he remembered that he also could not see. The boat turned on its side. The current engulfed him and pushed him out. Smashing into one of the rocky shards, he swallowed water and started to go under. Then in an instant, just as instantly as he had been swept over the side, a strong arm wrapped around him. In the darkness the arm held him and pulled him through the icy water until he felt the ground under him once more. When he opened his eyes, he was shocked. It was not his grandfather who had saved him. It was Oliphar.

Chapter Four

⌘

Too Late

Exhausted from his near drowning in the river, Mentor managed to keep his eyes open long enough to realize that he was lying down inside of a dimly lit rock tunnel. Only a moment passed before he closed his blurry eyes again. In spite of his intense desire to know exactly what had happened and his precise location, he kept his eyes closed. His head was aching.

When he opened his eyes again, he saw Oliphar leaning over him. Where was Ben Zarek? He tried to sit up. He could not move. Again his eyes blurred. Sharp pains shot across his forehead. Once more he was forced to shut his eyes. He was powerless to defend himself from Oliphar. He panicked.

What has happened to my grandfather? He wanted to scream the all important question, but when he opened his mouth to speak nothing came out. Had the betrayal that he had been expecting already taken place? Had Oliphar already killed his grandfather? When Oliphar reached towards his face with his claw-like hand, he wanted to jump up and run away, but he could not budge; he was too dizzy.

Each time Oliphar touched Mentor's forehead, he cringed. Each time the Zaagote dipped what appeared to be the tip of one finger into a small vial that he held, Mentor was sure that it was a touch of poison. Oliphar's dark brown finger felt like the tip of a human finger, but he knew that he had to be hallucinating. He felt drowsy. His head was pounding. Orange and white lights kept flashing in front of his eyes. He didn't know if he was seeing things or not.

He tried to speak his grandfather's name, but he could only whisper. He tried to focus, but all that he could see was a dark creature with enormous yellow and black eyes staring down at him. As Oliphar rubbed the liquid from the vial into his temples and the sharp pains in his head began to diminish, his vision improved. He was amazed by what appeared to be a gentle, concerned look on Oliphar's face. Oliphar did have one very human finger, of that he was now certain, but a concerned look on his face—or on the face of any Zaagote—was impossible to believe.

In spite of his disbelief, Mentor could not deny what he felt. Oliphar administered the salve in a gentle manner. The long, soothing strokes with which the Zaagote applied the ointment told him that he could trust Oliphar, but he was more determined than ever not to trust this Zaagote or to let down his guard whenever he was around him.

The pain disappeared, but he remembered the reason for the pain—the river. Once more panic rose inside of him. *The river!* Had his grandfather perished in the river? This time when he opened his mouth to speak his grandfather's name, Ben Zarek rushed to his side and helped him up. He felt Ben Zarek's strong arms lift and hug him in a brief, but powerful, embrace. Before he could say anything, Ben Zarek started to guide him forward. He spoke breathlessly while they inched ahead.

"The boat split in two when it crashed into the rocks. Oliphar pulled us both out of the water. Then we managed to find this tunnel. He carried you deeper inside to take care of you while I guarded the entrance, but we have no time to lose. We have to leave this place now. Be as quiet as you can."

At first Mentor felt shaky as his grandfather guided him back through the tunnel, but as they moved closer to its rock-covered entrance, some of his strength returned. Oliphar followed them.

At the entrance, Ben Zarek stopped in front of a pile of rocks and pointed to a place where Mentor could kneel by his side. Oliphar knelt on the other side of him. Mentor felt uncomfortable, but when his grandfather removed one of the rocks and Mentor looked outside, he knew that being uncomfortable around Oliphar was the least of their problems.

In the moonlight that illuminated the rocks and the river in front of them, two Zaagotes passed by. As soon as they disappeared, two more came along. Without a sound, Oliphar put the rock back in place while Ben Zarek led Mentor back along the way they had come. When they were a safe distance from the cave opening, Ben Zarek pointed to a flat rock where Mentor could rest and sat by his side. Facing them, Oliphar slid to the ground, rested his back against the rock wall, and listened intently while Ben Zarek spoke.

"Fade's scouts are all around us. When daylight comes, they will notice the pile of rocks that Oliphar and I used to disguise the tunnel entrance. If we stay here they will find us, but I've been watching them for a long time now. They are searching in timed intervals. As soon as the next two pass by, we take our chance. Remember our plan. Time is running out for your mother just as it is for us. Get her out of the fortress before Van Arden arrives. I will guide Oliphar safely out of the gorge and put him on a safe path back to Zaeg. If we leave this place before Fade finds us, Oliphar will be home before his brother can prove that he was ever gone."

As Ben Zarek spoke, he strapped Mentor's weapons belt around his waist. Mentor tried to help his grandfather by standing up, but he had to sit down when a sudden tide of dizziness, pain, and nausea passed over him. When the sickening wave did not pass, he stretched out on the rock where he had been sitting.

He was surprised when Oliphar came to his side. While he watched, Oliphar drew a stick back and forth between his sharp white teeth until he had shaved it bare. Mentor was sure that he was hallucinating again, but after Oliphar rubbed more salve into his forehead and turned his head to the side, he knew he was not.

As the horrible feelings began to leave him yet again, he could see the pile of bark that Oliphar had shaved from the stick on the flat rock near his nose. The soothing aroma from the bark made him feel better. He understood that Oliphar was helping him, but when Oliphar reached into the pile, took a piece of the bark, and held it in front of Mentor's mouth, he became suspicious and clamped it shut.

"Eat this," Oliphar said in a quiet soothing voice. "It will give you incredible strength for the journey,"

Although Mentor did feel much better because of the things that Oliphar had done so far, he did not open his mouth until Oliphar opened his own mouth, chewed a piece in front of him, and swallowed it. While Mentor chewed, Oliphar wrapped the rest of the bark in a cloth and handed it to him.

"If you feel sick or tired," Oliphar continued, "chew more bark along the way." When Mentor took the bark from Oliphar, puzzling questions filled his mind. *How does Oliphar know so much about medicines and treatments for humans? Why is he really helping me? Why does he have one human finger? Is the truce that he says he has come to discuss a trap?*

All of these questions were important, but the biggest question of all was whether or not Oliphar was really an ally? Was he? Or was he here to spring a trap that he had set in place with Fade? Perhaps their entire pursuit and Oliphar's aid were part of an elaborate plan to get his grandfather to trust Oliphar with more important confidences. If so, Oliphar and Fade could spring this terrible trap at any time and they would be caught in it.

These questions tormented him, but he would not get the answers today. When his grandfather hugged him, he knew it was his way of signaling that the time for goodbye had come. How could he say goodbye when he knew that he might never see Ben Zarek again?

He expected his grandfather to say goodbye in the general's way by barking orders, but he didn't. To cover his own feelings, Mentor tucked the bark-filled cloth inside his belt, chewed another piece of wood, and put his hand on his grandfather's shoulder where he allowed it to rest before he pulled it away. Then he followed Ben Zarek and Oliphar back to the stone covered entrance.

"When you step outside, you'll know where you are. As soon as the next two walk by, you'll be on your way," Ben Zarek said stretching his hands out in front of him with his palms up. This sign of victory was the one he used when he sent warriors into battle, but as abruptly as he had extended his hands to make the familiar palms up gesture, he changed his mind. He threw his arms around Mentor and hugged him hard before he pulled away.

"Remember the bark," Oliphar said. "The bark is healing and strength giving. Eat it whenever you need it. It has saved my life many times."

Near the entrance, they spoke no more. They crouched behind the camouflaged opening. Oliphar removed one of the rocks. They peered outside. While Mentor waited for the two Zaagote scouts to pass by, he found it hard to believe that he was crouching behind some rocks watching these Zaagotes with his grandfather to his left and another Zaagote on his right. As soon as the scouts were out of sight, he scrambled to help his grandfather and Oliphar remove the rest of the camouflage. Then he stepped outside.

Directly in front of him he saw the twin gray peaks that marked one path back to the fortress. While Ben Zarek and Oliphar disappeared between the large boulders that marked the way back to Zaeg, Mentor darted between two smaller ones. This was the quickest way to reach his mother.

When he turned to look back, he thought that Ben Zarek and Oliphar had departed safely. In the next instant, he heard how wrong he was. As he crawled toward the sounds of a struggle, he looked up and saw several large shadows on top of the boulders above him. He finally reached a niche between some lower rocks where the Zaagotes above could not see him. From here he could watch what was going on, but there was nothing he could do. Tightly wrapped in heavy nets that their hunters had thrown over them, Ben Zarek and Oliphar struggled helplessly. Their Zaagote captors were dragging them away.

Their capture paralyzed him. He did not know what to do. There were at least fifty Zaagotes and only one of him. He could not think, but he forced himself to listen to the Zaagote commander. "Don't hurt them. They are to be unharmed and unblemished for the high day of sacrifice."

Saved for the sacrifice meant they were to be killed, but not right away. Overwhelmed by confusion and more head pain, he took out another piece of bark, chewed it, and tried to think of a way out of this mess. He was too greatly outnumbered to sneak in at an opportune moment and free them. They were heavily guarded, but they would be alive until the Zaagote day of high sacrifice. If he could survive now, he would find a way to save them later.

In studies with Takal, he had learned that the day of sacrifice came only once a year. That day was still far away. He knew how to get to Zaeg. After he had taken his mother to safety, he would go there to rescue Ben Zarek and Oliphar before that day came.

While he hurried back to the trail that would take him to the fortress and to his mother, he promised himself that he would do whatever it took to save them. He believed that there would be enough time to get into and out of the prison where he was sure they would be kept, but there would be no escape for his mother if he did not reach her before Van Arden arrived. Against his better judgment, he took a dangerous shortcut to recover some of the time that he had lost. Behind him he heard the sound of gravel and small rocks being crushed under heavy feet. Something was following. Perspiration broke out across his forehead. Streams of sweat trickled down his back. Had the Zaagotes spotted him? He wiped his brow and tried to think clearly.

With the number of Zaagote scouts that Fade had summoned to the area, he surmised that his pursuer was either a Zaagote or a tracker—perhaps a more formidable tracker than the one which had killed the stag in the forest. His head ached again. His legs felt weak. He took another piece of bark out of the pouch and slipped it into his mouth. While he sucked on it, the sound of stones crumbling on the path behind him grew louder.

If he was going to survive, he had to put distance between his pursuer and him. There was a way to do it, but it was even more dangerous than the shortcut. In spite of the risk, he increased his speed and ran towards the ledge.

If he failed to jump across the space between the ledges on each side of the narrow canyon, he would fall into a deep chasm, but he told himself that he could jump across it and land safely on the other side. He convinced himself that the hunter closing in on him could not. The loud, constant sound of pebbles and larger rocks crumbling or rolling was nearer, but he refused to look over his shoulder to see what was pursuing him. He flew over the rocky ground.

Though he could not see it yet, he pictured the jumping spot in front of him. He ran faster. The ledge came into view. Now, his pursuer was right behind him, pounding towards him, ready to reach out in a fatal grip. He kept going. He increased his speed again. He had jumped great distances before, but never this great.

Breathe, he told himself. *Just breathe*. He could feel something closing the final gap between them. His heart pumped harder. He gulped the air. Now, in the moonlight, he saw the ledge just ahead. In the moonlight it was white. He charged toward the spot he would leap from. He thought about what would happen to Ben Zarek and Oliphar if he failed to make it. Then he thought about the terrible light that he had seen in Van Arden's eyes when the man looked at his mother.

What would happen to her if he didn't keep going? He approached the ledge. His feet were barely touching the ground. Hot breath seared the back of his neck, but he flew across the chasm and landed with a thud on the other side. After he finally rolled to a stop, he looked back. He saw a large form hurtle into the empty space between the ledges, but before he could determine what it was, it plummeted soundlessly and hit the bottom with a shriek and a thud.

Sitting down on the edge of the ledge, he looked into the black chasm, tried to catch his breath, and listened. While he stared into the blackness and sucked air into his lungs, his breathing gradually returned to normal, but when he stood up a cramp in his left leg took his breath away again.

He stepped away from the ledge and pressed his foot against the ground to relieve the cramp, but as he was doing this, he thought he heard the sound of something moving below. He told himself that he had imagined the sound, that nothing could have survived such a fall.

Still rubbing his cramping leg, he limped back to the ledge and looked into the blackness of the chasm a second time. Again he heard a noise below, followed by another noise, then the continuous noise of crumbling rocks. In spite of the terrible fall, his pursuer was crawling upwards, back towards him from the terrible depth below. In spite of the cramp, he started to run again. He did not look back. His hard-to-kill pursuer would catch up with him unless he was much further away before it crawled out.

He did not know what this predator was. He did not want to know. He tried to put it out of his mind. He pictured Ben Zarek and Oliphar covered in Zaagote nets, locked in a Zaagote prison. He pictured his mother's face as she stood on the tower and watched, anxiously waiting for him to come home. These images encouraged him not to give up. They were the things that Takal would have told him to fix the inner eye of his spirit on. These visions motivated him to press on to achieve his goals.

"God has not given you a spirit of fear," his friend had always told him, "but of power, of love, and of a sound mind." Although he didn't believe in God or in all of the things that Takal had told him about God, he was amazed at the power that the words had. He focused on these words. They were helping him. As he listened to them, he was able to turn his spiritual eye away from the nameless fear that moved behind him and focus on the path ahead.

In the moonlit shadows of the unmarked path to the fortress, he sped toward Kan Fallel. Realizing how much of a delay his unplanned trip down the river had caused, he increased his furious pace. He had to reach his mother before it was too late.

Chapter Five

⌘

Thunder

Mentor approached the fortress from the forest. It rose from the solid rock mountain on which it was built. Through the trees he saw a continuous stream of Van Arden's men moving towards it. Then he noticed another group of men leaving the fortress. Their faces were battered and bloodied, but he recognized them. They wore the same dark blue uniforms that all the soldiers under his father's command wore. They walked between the men who wore Van Arden's red and black uniforms—men who carried weapons and prodded their prisoners forward when they could no longer walk.

As Van Arden's men kicked and hit their already badly beaten prisoners, it was obvious to him that these men were cruel like the master they served. In the instant that his thoughts turned from the task masters before him to the brutal lord they served, Mentor's heart sank. Was he too late to save his mother?

He was sure that his father did not understand why Ben Zarek had told him to stay away from Faxes Van Arden, and why he should keep that man away from his family. His father had never understood the man's evil nature. How often Ben Zarek had said never to underestimate the lengths to which Faxes would go to acquire power or anything else he wanted! But Kan had always ignored his grandfather's counsel about the kind of man he was befriending.

Ben Zarek had also told his father how many times Van Arden had lied. His grandfather had spoken at length about his dishonesty and about his cruelty, not only toward his prisoners but also toward his own men and some members of his own family. In spite of the things that Ben Zarek had revealed to Kan about Van Arden, Kan gave little weight to his father-in-law's words about this liar's malignant personality.

Mentor's mother had also spoken to his father about Van Arden's foul intentions. She had told him how many times Van Arden had tried to see her when his father was not around, and how he had sent "secret" compliments and gifts and asked her to meet him in isolated places, but Kan had put her feelings aside. Because Van Arden had made empty promises to his father about wealth and about giving his father the rank and privileges of the highest of lords, her distress no longer counted. Because such a promotion could be opposed by the objections of Defense Minister Faxes Van Arden, who was by birth one of these lofty lords, his father was doing everything he could to please the liar.

As Mentor watched his father's beaten men leave the fortress, he realized just how right Ben Zarek had been when he'd said that people who made friends with snakes always got bitten by them. In his father's beaten men, he could see the high price that Kan had had to pay for welcoming this viper into their home. Swallowing hard, he wondered if his parents' lives were part of it.

Were his mother and father still breathing? He did not see them among the prisoners. If they were alive, they were still inside the fortress with Van Arden. Short of death itself, it was the last place he wanted them to be.

By the time the last horse and rider had passed the place where Mentor stood hidden in the trees, his mind was already traveling through the hidden passage that he would use to get into the fortress and out again. The situation was grim, but he had an advantage that Van Arden and his men did not have. He knew the fortress as well as he knew the Tabor Forest, far better than they did.

In many ways the fortress was similar to the forest. They both had many hiding places. The fortress, especially, had tunnels, passageways, entrances, and exits that only he had discovered. No one was more familiar with the fortress than he was, not even his father. Kan had not spent hours playing in those secret passageways or exploring them the way he had. Like the forest, the fortress really was Mentor's home. He knew all of the ways to get in and out of it.

He entered the tunnel that began at the bottom of the rock mountain and ended inside the fortress itself. As soon as he emerged in the storage cellar, he pressed his hand against the white stone in the wall. It slid aside to expose the secret stairway that led to his room. When he got to his private chambers, it sickened him to see his maps and charts spread all over the place. He was furious when he saw that his golden messenger owl had been taken from its cage and that a chest full of treasures that Ben Zarek had given him was missing. Curling his hands into fists, he promised himself that he would recover what Van Arden had taken from him and make him pay for violating his home.

Filled with anger, Mentor ran to the window and looked below. What he saw there was no better. The courtyard was filled with Van Arden's men. The only good thing about the repulsive scene before him was that these men were leaving in great numbers, both on foot and on horseback. He raced to the door and peeked into the corridor. He saw no one, but he heard the sound of a man's voice coming from his father's study. Silently he moved to his father's door and turned the handle gently. He wanted to open it just wide enough to look inside, but the door was locked. Tiptoeing now, he slipped inside the adjacent room and removed a loose stone which slid in and out of the wall. This moveable stone allowed him to see and hear what was going on inside.

He started to choke when he saw his father's body lying in a pool of blood. Waves of nausea gripped him. To keep sounds from coming out of his mouth, he covered it while he watched Van Arden roll his father onto his back. When he saw the handle of a knife sticking out of his father's chest, he shook until he was transported to a faraway place; a place where everything was dark and dead. As Van Arden pulled the knife out of his father and sliced his own arms with it, he watched in horror.

In spite of his shocked state, he realized that Van Arden was trying to make it appear as if his father had attacked him. From the black fog where he was, he forced himself to listen. He heard Van Arden talking to Kan as if his father could hear him.

"What's that? Did you say something, Kan?" Van Arden said. "I could not hear you," the evil man chided. "Are you asking about these plans?" he added holding a scroll in the air. As he stood over Kan who bled profusely and appeared to be dead, Van Arden laughed diabolically before he went on. "There are stolen plans of every major fortress in New Earth and Tire Elween by your side, and the Zaagote jewels with which you were paid for stealing them. Of course, you intended to sell these plans to the Zaagotes, but I will eventually sell them all, one at a time, as the Zaagotes give me more of what I want. *Be alive,* Mentor ordered his father. *Breathe, so I can get you out after he leaves the room,* but he saw no sign of life. Once more Van Arden's voice filled the room.

"With stolen plans and Zaagote jewels near your body, there will be no mistake about what you have done. There will be plenty of witnesses who will testify to your family's guilt. You attacked me, you know, when I discovered your treasonous plans. I saved Tire Elween and New Earth from the Zaagotes. I am the hero; I shall always be the hero. Your family is finished, and your wife will agree to be my wife. In return I will ask the emperor to show mercy to her father and to her son. Mia is locked in her room; she has been there all day waiting for me. I think I should go there now—to tell her the good news about my proposed mercies."

When Mentor thought he saw Kan's lips moving, he wanted to rush into the room to help him. He wanted to thrust his sword through Van Arden's evil heart, but when Van Arden picked up the key to his mother's room, Mentor realized that her best chance for survival could only be secured if he remained hidden and launched a surprise attack.

Before he left Kan's study, Van Arden took one final look around. Then he knocked over everything that he could push. He purposely stained the floor with blood from his self-inflicted wounds. Mentor watched the deceiver closely. He made it appear as if there had been a struggle between Kan and him instead of the premeditated murder that had taken place.

Closing his hand around the handle of his sword, Mentor started to draw it out of its sheath. He wanted to cut Van Arden in half, but he knew that he was no match for this man with this weapon. He realized that he could not help his mother escape if he died fighting him that way today. Shoving his sword back into its sheath, he put both hands around the heavy statue next to him and lifted it from its place.

As Van Arden came out of the study, Mentor brought the statue down on his head as hard as he could. Van Arden landed on the stone floor with a thud. He did not move. Mentor turned towards his mother's chamber, but before he could leave the study, he heard his father muttering. When he knelt beside his father, Kan opened his eyes.

"I am sorry," his father whispered in a voice so raspy that Mentor could barely understand him. The words sounded strange. His father had never said he was sorry about anything. In that moment, Mentor realized that he had also never told his father how sorry he was for the things he had deliberately done to hurt him. He started to say the words, but his father could not hear him. Kan was dead.

Mentor could not help his father now, or help himself by apologizing so that he would feel less guilty, but he could still make things right for his mother. He remembered Ben Zarek's words—get your mother out. He took the key from Van Arden's hand, ran down the stone corridor to his mother's room, and unlocked the door.

His mother was huddled on the floor with her arms wrapped around her shoulders. When she threw her arms around him, Mentor wanted to cry with joy. Although it had not been that long since he had seen his mother, it seemed like years. He hugged his mother harder than he had ever hugged her before. Then, holding her away from him, he put his finger to his lips and drew her back into the corridor. Tightly grasping her hand, he started to lead her back the way he had come.

A moment later someone tore his mother's hand from his and hit him hard. The blow sent him reeling head first to the stone floor. He tried to stand. He felt only an instant of pain before he saw black. When he opened his eyes, he saw Van Arden grab his mother's hair and pull her toward the head of the long, curved stairway that led to the main hall.

Unable to stand he crawled towards the stairway, but he made little progress. His vision became fuzzy. Then it cleared. He saw Van Arden trying to wrap his arms around his mother. She was twisting and turning to get away from him. When she finally kicked him where there was no defense, he pushed her away. She lost her balance at the top of the stairs.

His mother spiraled and tilted backwards. *Mother! Mother!* His lips had formed the word. He thought that he had said it twice, but he heard no sound. Her arms twirled around her in a circle. She continued to spiral and fall. As she tumbled down the long stairway, he could no longer see her. He heard the thud of her body as she hit each step, but on the last step the sound of her body crashing against the stone floor was louder than thunder.

Chapter Six

⌘

The Hunt

It was Mentor's first time in the Imperial Chamber. He stared at the high golden walls that rose around him and met in towering arches above. He fixed his eyes on the circle of light in the middle ceiling. There the sun poured in through a transparent dome. He wanted to become a bird, smash through it, and fly away.

On his way to the front he passed a savage. This barbarian had come to the chamber to secure the release of the women and children who had been captured during a raid in the borderlands. He tried to look straight ahead, but he was curious about the bold chief he had heard so much about.

As he listened to Kor Elion explain what the chief had said to convince the lords to give up their captives, he wondered how long it had taken Elion to interpret his ignorant grunts before he could put the chief's proposal into intelligible words. He was surprised that the merciless rulers had agreed to release their slaves and grant them and their chief safe passage to the unknown lands in exchange for the life-saving medicines they would receive when they arrived. He had to take a closer look at the man who had risked his own life to save his people.

Out of the corner of his eye, he saw an eagle carved into the chief's heavily muscled right arm. Though he did not know what the chief's name was, he knew that he was part of the most dreaded tribe of all. The eagle clearly identified him as an Ayan.

Before Mentor knew what had happened, he found himself face down on the floor. Someone had trippped him. He eyed the chief who was staring down at him, but his feet were tied together. When the Ayan grabbed his arm to help him up, Mentor tried to yank it away and pushed against him in an effort to break free. He also gave the savage a look of disgust, but he could not wrench his arm out of the chief's grip until the Ayan decided to let go.

By the time he reached the stone bench reserved for the accused, the distinctly Ayan scent had faded, but the chief's penetrating golden eyes and his fiery expression were impossible to forget. So was his iron grip. That the chief's hold had only grown stronger while he tried to twist his arm free spoke volumes about his intractable nature when it came to giving in. He did not like to admit how ineffective his efforts had been until the chief decided to release him, or how stunned he was. There were many civilized people close to the place where he had been tripped and fallen, but the chief was the only one to show any mercy.

Still shaken from his encounter with the Ayan, Mentor tried not to look toward the high gallery on each side of him. There two rows of darkly robed figures with bowed heads were chanting the same black hymns that they always chanted when they wanted the judges to declare the accused guilty. "Condemn him, condemn him," were always the first two words of the chant.

He knew the words because his grandfather had told him what they were. The words were supposed to summon the spirit of death whenever anyone they considered to be an enemy was brought to trial. Because his grandfather had refused to embrace their religion—The Religion of the Many—and because he had openly declared his belief in the one true God that his ancestors had brought with them from Old Earth, these chanters wanted his grandson to die.

He tried to ignore the chanters, but he could not keep his eyes away from the mysterious figures known to all as the Hoods. Because of the lengthy caps that formed the top part of their robes, caps that completely hid their faces from view, no one knew who or what they really were. The emperor allowed the Hoods to be present when the fate of an accused person was to be decided in the Circle of Judgment for two reasons. The first was obvious; their chanting stirred the crowd's emotions. The second was unspoken; the emperor feared them and their curses.

His fears were well-founded. In the past the Hoods had made many predictions about the lives of their opponents. In these predictions, they always prophesied destruction, disease, and painful deaths for their adversaries. As these prophecies came true, the power of the Hoods continued to grow.

Mentor did not believe in Hood curses, but he realized they could influence the Royal Council to condemn him. Angry with himself because he had given the Hoods more attention than they deserved, he turned to his only two supporters, Kor Elion, Ben Zarek's second in command, and his daughter, Adamis Kor Elion. They were the only ones who had accompanied him to the judgment chamber on this critical day.

When he looked at Adamis he saw far more than her long golden hair, her deep hazel-colored eyes, and her strong, but exquisitely-curved body. He saw the girl he had grown up with, his lifelong friend. Since his parents' deaths and Ben Zarek's capture, she had treated him like a sister would treat a brother, but his feelings for her were no longer those of close friendship or those of a sibling. He was in love with her. In her, he saw the woman that would someday be his wife.

Out of respect for Kor Elion, he hid his true feelings for Adamis. He respected Elion too much to declare his love for her without seeking permission to court her properly. Until he could prove his innocence, he never would ask for that permission; he had nothing to offer. When he looked at Kor Elion sitting beside him on the stone bench, the one advocate who would be allowed to speak on his behalf before his fate was decided, his confidence in an innocent verdict grew.

By petitioning the emperor to be his advocate, Elion was risking his promotion as commander-in-chief of all of the armies of New Earth and Tire Elween. He was also risking his popularity with the people, but that was not as important as openly declaring his belief in Mentor's innocence. In the days since his parents' murders and Ben Zarek's capture, Kor Elion had become a wise counselor and a tower of strength. He heard that strength in Kor Elion's voice now as he quietly advised him.

"Keep your eyes on the members of the Royal Council," he said, "and remember that you are not alone. Adamis and I are your family now. We will find a way to help you."

Though Ben Zarek was not related to Elion, he had always told Mentor that Elion was like a son to him as well as a younger best friend, and that if anything ever happened to him, Mentor should trust Elion for help.

To everyone else, Kor Elion's face was like a smooth stone tablet—impossible to read—but not to Mentor. Each time the Hoods finished one chant and started another, Elion's mouth hardened to a thin line that indicated his disdain for them.

Mentor had often been jealous of the close relationship that Ben Zarek and Kor Elion had shared. Today he felt ashamed of his jealousy. Today he could see that Kor Elion was as much of a father and a friend to him as his grandfather had been to Kor Elion.

While Mentor waited for the Elweenian emperor and the members of the Royal Council to file in, he remembered how Elion and Adamis had come for him after his parents' deaths. They had taken him back to their own fortress and brought Takal there to heal him. Though Mentor had drifted in and out of consciousness for days, Elion had often been by his side, holding his hand, while Adamis sang softly to him. He remembered how Elion would stay with him after nightmares and tell him stories about his adventures with Ben Zarek until he fell asleep.

No matter what the outcome of the judgment was, he was proud to have a man like Elion speak for him. He did not know what Elion would say, but he knew that he would speak eloquently and from his heart.

Inside the golden box, Emperor Tor Noc sat behind the ten members of the royal council until he stood to initiate the judgment proceedings. When he held up his hand to silence the chanters and the crowd, Elion stood up with Mentor. Together they bowed deeply before the emperor addressed them.

"Mentor, your grandfather, Ben Zarek, is accused of treason. Being of the same family and household, you are also accused. Your grandfather is not here to answer the charge. Therefore, on this day, you alone will be judged. Your accuser will speak first. Then your advocate will address us. Only then will you be permitted to say something on your own behalf."

Kor Elion squeezed Mentor's shoulder the way Ben Zarek used to do. From the bench where he sat next to his grandson on the opposite side of the judgment circle, Faxes Van Arden smiled arrogantly. Then he stood up, stepped into the circle, and walked to the middle of it. From the center he glared in their direction and spoke.

"Ben Zarek is a traitor as is his grandson. He stole the defense plans from the commanders of the cities and fortresses, had them copied, and sold them to the Zaagotes in return for the power they promised to give him when they took over all of New Earth and Tire Elween. Mentor's father, Kan, and Mentor himself were his puppets. They helped him. I had hoped to save Kan and his son by changing Kan's mind before they completed their traitorous plans, but when Kan realized that I knew everything, he tried to kill me. I killed Mentor's father in self-defense."

Shaking with fury, Mentor started to rise with a clenched fist, but Kor Elion wrapped his arm around Mentor's shoulder to make him sit while the liar continued.

"When Kan's men found out that their lord was dead, they attacked my warriors. I did what I had to do. I took over Kan's fortress and made his warriors my prisoners. Mentor's mother killed herself. When she found out what her father, her husband, and her son had done, she threw herself down the stairs. The only crime of which I am guilty is failing to stop her."

When he finished speaking Van Arden stepped out of the circle. Then he bowed to acknowledge the applause of the crowd and the cheers of his supporters. After this, he nodded politely in Elion's direction to impress the council with his manners, bowed deeply in the direction of the emperor's box, and took his seat in front of the other members of the Van Arden family.

Elion's arm tightened around Mentor's shoulder to remind him to stay calm. From that point on, Mentor glared at Van Arden but remained expressionless in every other way. He felt his face growing hotter as Van Arden's lies repeated themselves in his head, but he controlled his anger. Elion also betrayed no emotion. As he stood to speak, Mentor recalled his grandfather's words, advice that Ben Zarek had repeated to both of them countless times: "Never let the enemy see what you are thinking."

Elion cleared his throat and prepared to speak. Mentor knew how proud Ben Zarek would have been of him as he practiced his advice. He spoke calmly and clearly.

"Ben Zarek was on a mission when the missing defense plans were found at Kan Fallel, a reconnaissance mission from which he has not returned. His absence does not indicate guilt. He is a true hero of New Earth and Tire Elween. Have we forgotten the many victories he has won? Such a hero would not leave his grandson to face charges of treason alone. If he could be here, he would be. He is not here because he has been captured by the Zaagotes and is now their prisoner.

I have known Mentor all his life. There were no stolen defense plans at Kan Fallel. The only defense plans that were there were those planted by Faxes Van Arden to discredit the Zarek family. It is Faxes Van Arden who is guilty. He is the one who committed treason and killed Mentor's parents. It is Van Arden who should be condemned. This judgment is not about stolen plans. It is about who is telling the truth and who is lying. There are no witnesses who can tell us what really happened at Kan Fallel that day—no witnesses except Van Arden and Mentor. Let your judgment be based on the answer to this question. Who is telling the truth and who is lying? If you answer that question correctly, Mentor will be free."

After Elion finished, the emperor nodded. As Elion took his seat the emperor held up his hand to stop the proceedings. While the emperor conferred with his advisors, Mentor stared at the Van Ardens and waited for his chance to speak.

He wanted to call Van Arden every foul name that came to his mind, but he knew that he would be removed if he did. *Liar, traitor, murderer!*

Van Arden was all of those things. Mentor wanted to shout these words now, and to shout them over and over again, but he knew that he would be dragged from the room with no opportunity to speak at all if he did not wait for the proper signal. He stifled the impulse.

Tal Van Arden sat smugly by Grandfather Faxes and stared at Adamis Kor Elion. Mentor knew that Tal was involved in the treachery against the Zarek family. During the proceedings, Tal moved his fingers over the handle of his knife to remind Mentor about the way his father had died, about the way Mentor would die if he didn't step away from Adamis. Tal had been casting admiring glances at Adamis for as long as Mentor could remember, but she had made it clear to Tal that she wanted no part of him.

Adamis was not allowed to approach Mentor in the Circle of Judgment where he stood, but she smiled at him from her seat whenever he turned in her direction. That Tal had noticed her smile was for Mentor and not for him was obvious now. Tal stabbed his knife into the wooden table in front of him each time she gave Mentor an encouraging grin. When the emperor finally nodded to let Mentor know it was time to speak, he ignored Tal's implied threats and spoke with the new confidence her smiles had given to him.

"I am innocent. My grandfather is innocent. My parents were innocent. Kor Elion, my advocate, has placed the guilt where it belongs. Let the judgment be against Faxes Van Arden, not against me." Mentor felt as if the last drop of energy had left his body with his last spoken word. At the end of his brief statement, the members of the royal council stood up.

In front of him the council formed a circle. Each member held a black stick half the length of a man's arm in his left hand and a white stick of the same length in his right. Holding these high above their heads, the council members bowed before the emperor when he stood. They waited until the emperor raised the royal scepter above him and opened his mouth to speak before they resumed their normal standing posture.

"Let the sticks decide," the emperor said calmly. Then he sat down.

Each member of the council tossed a stick into the deep white porcelain bowl. Each stick made a chiming sound when it hit the bottom. When the last of the ten chiming sounds reverberated throughout the massive chamber, the emperor nodded his head to accept the judgment. Two servants hurried to the chiming bowl, removed it from its place, and put it on a high table in front of him.

As Tor Noc pulled the first stick out, Mentor took a deep breath. The emperor held the stick high above his head. Because it was black, the emperor pointed to one of the ten girls robed in black who stood to his left. He waited until she took the black stick and carried it to the top of the stairs that flanked one side of the judgement circle. She stood on the left side of the wide steps with the stick in her hand. There she remained. She held the black stick high above her head. Van Arden's supporters cheered.

The next four girls dressed in black ascended and stood on the four steps below her. They also held black sticks high in the air. Cheers from Van Arden supporters became jeers funneled in Mentor's direction. With only five out of ten sticks left, he understood that if the next stick was black his guilt had been declared and death was his fate.

He held his breath until the next stick was removed from the bowl. When the emperor pointed to a girl in a white robe, he felt blood rush to his face. As the next four, white robed maidens took their places on the right side of the judgment steps and held white sticks in the air to declare his innocence, the crowd went wild.

Although no one he had ever known had survived the test that this judgment demanded, the only way he could search for Ben Zarek, restore his family's honor, and be with Adamis, was to live through it.

The emperor pointed his judgment scepter at Faxes. His accuser approached the royal box first and bowed low before it. At the emperor's second signal, Mentor bowed and took his place next to the liar. When the sticks were evenly divided the outcome was always the same. Before the emperor spoke, Mentor already knew what he would say. Holding his own golden spear high above him, Emperor Tor Noc uttered words that hung in the air. "Prepare for the hunt."

Chapter Seven

⌘

The Tribes

Five of the emperor's imperial guards escorted Mentor to a departure point on the north side of the city. Five others escorted Faxes Van Arden to a departure point to the south. Adamis and Kor Elion were somewhere in the crowd. Circled by guards whose job it was to keep him in custody until the emperor's hunters were released, Mentor tried to look beyond his keepers to see them but he could not spot his new family.

Adamis and Kor Elion could never take the place of his old family, but they had given him two new reasons to go on. He was desperate to catch a glimpse of them before he began the contest which would decide his fate, but he was not desperate himself. He was not the same person he had been before his parents' deaths and his grandfather's capture.

He had changed. In some way the terrible things that he had been through had made him stronger. He was determined to survive, to find Ben Zarek, and to clear his family's name. He was also determined to honor Adamis and Kor Elion. He had to prove how right they were to put their faith in him when so many considered him to be a traitor.

By taking his part against their world, Adamis and Kor Elion had become targets for the Hoods and other factions who had opposed his family. He had always thought of Elion as a good friend, but in choosing to take Mentor's side, Kor Elion was risking everything the way a good father would do for his son.

By remaining loyal to Mentor, Adamis had also put her own life in danger. She had always considered him a best friend when they were younger, but in choosing to support him before the emperor and the council, she had made it clear that she really thought of him as the brother she never had. Now, because of him, it was highly likely that those who were his enemies were now hers.

For their sakes as well as his own, he was already visualizing the day when he would prove his innocence. On that day they would no longer be in danger because of their devotion to him. On that day he could reclaim his family's lands, ask Kor Elion for permission to be his daughter's suitor, and express the depth of his love for her openly.

Anxious to get a glimpse of Adamis, Mentor inserted himself into an opening between his two closest guards. When a rock struck him, he hit the ground hard. He rolled onto his side and tried to get up before another rock found its mark, but before he could move another sharp stone hit his face.

Someone from the crowd shouted the word traitor over and over again. More rocks flew through the air. Mentor saw Tal Van Arden trying to shove his way past the guards around him with another stone in his hand; he wasn't surprised. Tal raised his arm to throw it and taunted him, but the guards knocked the rock out of his hand and pushed him away from their prisoner. In spite of the shove, Tal kept yelling at him from the crowd.

"Forget it, Mentor," he shouted. "Traitor's blood can never be the right blood. You have to have the right blood to win this kind of a race. My grandfather has it and I have it. My grandfather will survive the hunters, but you will die." Tal grinned viciously, held up his knife, and ran his finger along the edge of the blade. In a fit of rage, he tried to pry himself free from the guards who wrestled him to the ground and took his knife, but they tied his hands and led him away.

He put his hand on the place where the first rock had hit him. He thought it was ironic that Tal had reopened the gash that Faxes had inflicted on him the day that his mother was killed. Blood from the wound dripped into his eyes, but before his keepers could pull him up, someone held a damp cloth to his face.

"The prisoner deserves a fair chance," the familiar voice said authoritatively. "The emperor will not be pleased if he discovers that you did not give it to him, that you failed to protect him and allowed him to be wounded. You will form a tighter circle around your charge and stay in place." He could not see the speaker's face, but her voice was unmistakable.

Although Adamis rarely exercised her authority as the emperor's niece or the daughter of the man who might be the next commander-in-chief of Tire Elween, when she did give an order, the tone that she used left no doubt that she was to be obeyed. As she knelt down next to Mentor, she slipped a small pouch into his pocket and pointed to a place in the crowd where Takal stood.

"From your friend," she said gently. "In spite of the blows, your wounds will heal quickly. Now swallow the contents of the pouch. The medicine will revive you. Then run the way I know only you can and meet me at our lake."

Before he could argue with her about meeting him, she withdrew. As soon as she did, the commander in charge pointed to the top of the hill and led him towards it. Holding a signal torch above a prepared pile of dry wood placed on a high platform on the summit, the commander dismissed the guards. After they withdrew from the hill, he spoke to Mentor.

"From here you can look across the city. On the other side my counterpart is holding another signal torch in front of your adversary. When the torches start the signal fires, you are free to go just as he is. At sunset tomorrow the emperor's hunters and anyone else who wants to kill you will come.

If you are never captured by the royal hunters or other pursuers, you will be free. You will never be innocent and you will never be guilty, but you will always be an outcast and an outlaw, a hunted man. If you are caught before Faxes Van Arden is, you will be condemned and you will be killed. If he is caught before you are, your innocence will be proclaimed and he will be killed. Wait until I light the signal torch before you go. Do you understand?"

While he waited for the signal fire to start burning, Mentor nodded yes and looked across the city to the other hill where Faxes Van Arden was to be released. He did not have nearly as much experience as his treacherous opponent did, but he had two obvious advantages over Van Arden in this race. He was younger and faster. In spite of these advantages his chances of staying alive were slim. Imperial hunters would not be the only ones trying to kill him. The Van Arden family would also come. Tal Van Arden would be leading the murderous pack, but he could not think of them now. As the two warriors who were to run with him took their places on his left and right side, they pointed to the short swords they carried with a warning look. He understood the implied threat; he and Van Arden would run in opposite directions on pain of death. For now they would not be allowed to kill each other. No one had ever been allowed to interfere with the hunt.

In one quick movement the commander thrust the burning torch into the pile of wood and the hunt began. The moment the dry branches burst into flames Mentor was off. Until sunset the next day his warrior escort would run by his side. Until sunset the next day, the escort would follow his lead, run where he ran, and keep the pace that he set; as long as he continued to put distance between himself and Van Arden, the armed runners would not touch him.

As the sun dropped from the horizon the next day, Mentor finally left his escort behind. When he glanced back and saw them standing against a brilliant orange sky in the exact spot where they had stopped, he felt confident. Though they knew where he had left them, they were not allowed to follow, to tell anyone else where they had last seen him, or to participate in the hunt at any future time. Their lives and the lives of their families depended on their silence. From now on the two runners who had been with him until this second point of departure would be like everyone else. They would be unaware of the path that he would take.

After a second quick look over his shoulder, when he could no longer see his guards, his confidence in the integrity of the hunt grew. He knew the two men who had run with him. They could not be bribed. They were men of honor and they loved their families. Their enforced silence, their neutrality, and their non-participation in this hunt would keep them and their loved ones safe and well provided for by royal coffers. Certain that he was not being followed, he forced all thoughts about his protective escort from his mind. For a time these warriors had been with him to make sure that he and Van Arden would not run into each other, but now he had to run alone over the most difficult and least traveled paths. Now he was a hunted man.

He recalled the last time he'd been hunted—right after he had almost drowned in the river and Oliphar had pulled him out. He remembered the terrible feeling that he had had when he was running away from the pursuer who had fallen into the chasm behind him. He also thought about the comforting feeling that had grown inside of him as he had approached the destination that he knew so well—his own home.

Now he was fleeing from pursuers once more, but this time there would be no comfort because he could not go home. Now he had no home and his destination was unfamiliar. To have any real chance against the hunters, he had to go to places that he had never been before, places in the vast unexplored lands of his world.

Though he had never been to these unexplored territories, he had heard that these mysterious lands had many secret locations where a hunted man could hide, dangerous niches where those who were hunting for him would fear to go. As Mentor ran he knew that his legs were carrying him to the most feared locations, to the places the rumors he had heard were all about, to the unknown lands and to the tribes.

Chapter Eight

⌘

Adamis

Before he reached the tribes, he would see Adamis at the lake, at the special tree where they had carved their names so long ago. She would be waiting for him there. For her sake he made up his mind to say goodbye quickly and to tell her to go home.

Where would he go after he saw her? What would he do when he arrived? He had no firsthand knowledge of the vast and unexplored regions inhabited by the tribes, but he did not regret his decision to go there. For the hunted, the unknown lands were the best place to be.

In the unknown lands, the tribes were made up of many distinct groups labeled as one. The practices of each tribe differed greatly from one another, but he had heard a rumor that might help him survive. This rumor was that the tribes were trying to unite under one great chief who would lead them in the fight against the Zaagotes. If it was true, such a leader would have the power to grant sanctuary to someone hunted by those who lived in the civilized lands—a fugitive like him. If the whispers had any veracity, if such a leader existed and Mentor could find him, he knew that he might live.

As he approached the tree he stopped thinking about this rumor. His heart was pounding. Though she was nowhere in sight, he knew Adamis was nearby. He decided not to tell her about his plan to go to the unknown lands. She would try to follow him. Sitting down in front of the spot where they had carved their names, he traced the letters of her name with his index finger. When she stepped out of the shadows, pushed the long black hood away from her face, and lifted her long black robe, a tingling sensation rippled through his body. He could not move.

In addition to the tingling and the fits of paralysis that her beauty sometimes caused, the weapons that she had managed to put into the heavy belt and the provisions that she had strapped to her back made him speechless. While she unhooked the weighty clasp that held the belt in place and let it fall to the ground with a thud, all he could do was stare. He forced himself to pick up the belt, and fastened it across his chest. Then he inhaled deeply, and tried to act like any good brother would act, but it was impossible. She was breathtaking.

"You look beautiful," he said. He wanted their first kiss to be in front of their tree, but this was not the right moment. In this moment, he had nothing to offer her but the life of a fugitive traitor. For now it would be better to remain what he had always been in her life, her best friend, and what he had become in more recent days, her only brother. Instead of kissing her he smiled and hugged her affectionately the way a good brother would.

"There are medicines from Takal inside some of the pouches," she said. "He told me to tell you that he is praying for you," she added as she put her hand on his shoulder.

Though he was not sure he believed in those prayers, he felt grateful for them and hoped they would help. He stared at his bow and arrow, his sword, and his knife. These weapons would not keep her safe if they were surrounded and outnumbered. He could not believe the terrible chance that she was taking by coming to the lake to meet him. Her courage astounded him.

"How did you manage to get out of the city without being seen?" he said trying to keep his voice from showing how much her courage meant to him him, how much she meant to him. "How did you get here so fast?" he added, but as soon as the words were out of his mouth he knew that he had made a serious mistake by asking her.

"You are not the only one who can run," she said glaring at him in a sudden flash of anger. He had not meant to imply that Adamis was slow, but he understood that she had interpreted his last question that way. He hated the way she was looking at him. He knew the look. He had seen that haughty stare many times.

While he sat in silence and tried to think of a way to apologize for implying that she was not a fast runner, she drew him to his feet, laughed, and pulled her horse out of the heavy bushes behind her. Adamis had always been strong willed, fiery, and extremely sensitive about being able to do everything as well as he did, but she never stayed mad for very long. He loved that about her.

"Of course I rode here," she said smiling while she patted the horse. He smiled back. She relished a good joke, especially if it was hers, and he appreciated her humor. "With all these weapons and provisions, I had to ride if I wanted to get here before the snow flew. I left the edge of the city from the servants' quarters of a close friend. I changed my clothes in their hut near the edge of the forest. Your family still has many supporters you know. There are many who believe in your innocence. These friends of mine are among them. They will say nothing. Even if they didn't believe in you like I do, they would do anything they could to oppose those heartless chanters. They hate the Hoods. I knew if I dressed like one of them, I would not be approached."

Though he wanted to know how she had managed to get her hands on the billowy garment worn by the highest ranking order of the Hoods, the Black Prophets, all he could think about was how beautiful she looked even dressed as one of them. While he was still admiring her, she tapped him on the head with a map.

"Another gift from Takal," she said. On the map she pointed to the lake where they were. "If we take this route," she said moving her finger over the path that she traced, "we will soon be at the edge of the rain forests and uncharted areas. Here the map actually apologizes for being unreliable in some ancient tongue. Only Takal can really read these markings well."

He was amazed that she knew exactly where he was going, but he was determined not to let her go with him. There was no way he could force her to go back, but he had to protect her. The unexplored territories of the tribes were too dangerous and too unknown. He wanted her with him, but he did not want her to go with him there. He wanted her to be safe. For her own good, he had to do it. He had to make her so mad at him that she would not want to go.

"I am sure Takal did not tell you what this map was," he said. "You opened this seal against his instructions and snooped into something that was not your business, so *we* are not going to take any route," he said as convincingly as he could.

Instantly her face turned red. His plan had worked, but he decided to go on to the point where he would fulfill the Old Earth cliché that Ben Zarek had often used. "By putting the frosting on the cake" he would make sure that she would not forgive him later on and try to follow.

"And even if *we* chose a route, you would have to forget this trip," he said as arrogantly as he could. "You could never keep up with me." Spinning around, she stomped away from him and disappeared.

Now that she was completely enraged, it was time for him to leave. He turned around and ran up a ledge that was so narrow a rider could not travel on it. He ran at a furious pace. This pace only became faster when he saw that she was running after him. Hours passed. In spite of the speed that had qualified him to be one of the emperor's couriers, she was only a short distance behind. When he finally stopped, he was shocked that she had enough breath to speak.

"Surprised?" She gasped and coughed. Her chest moved up and down in giant shudders. She bent over to rub her legs, but she had a smug expression.

"Surprised at what?" He really was shocked that her speed had increased so dramatically since the last time they had run together, but he was careful not to show it.

"Surprised that I saw through your flimsy attempt to make me mad, and that anyone could keep up with you—especially me!" He tried not to grin, but he could not stop. She went on. "I have been practicing."

When a distinct sound came towards them without warning, Mentor swallowed the compliment that he was about to give and pulled her into the bushes adjacent to the path. He waited for the whirring noise to pass by again, but it did not pass by. It flew over.

Dropping the animal that it held in its beak, a creature with bat-like wings dove at them. Mentor reacted quickly. He did not have enough time to grab his bow and position his arrow. He drew his sword and shoved Adamis to the ground. Covering her with his own body, he held the blade straight up in the air to keep the huge creature from landing on them.

The creature swept over them just above the drawn sword. Then it turned unexpectedly and dove at them again, but missed. Mentor stood up, but he stepped into a hole and fell before he could fire any arrows. Adamis was quick. She crawled out from under him, pulled the bow strapped to her back into a firing pose, and notched an arrow. Before the mysterious hunter attacked again, Mentor had notched his own arrow and taken his place by her side, but as he aimed, her arrow hit the creature's wing. It flew away in defeat.

"Your skill as an archer is unbelievable," he said, "but you are dangerously stubborn. You insist on risking your own life to help me, but I cannot let you do it anymore. Besides, you are a lady of the court. You should not be living like a fugitive."

"Tell me the real reason you do not want me to come," she replied. He could see how angry she was again. "You do not think I can take care of myself, do you? Well, I just proved that I can take care of myself *and* I can also take care of you."

The way she strutted around when she put her bow away let him know that she was still determined to stay. She went on before he could protest. "Swallow that male pride of yours. You need my help. Now sit down and show me exactly where we are going."

When he opened the map to point out the markings of an ancient trail, the only one that led to the Odo Abadu Ridge, his hand touched hers. He could not resist the urge to close his hand around her wrist and squeeze it. He could barely hear his own words when he spoke.

"The real reason I do not want you to come is because you and your father are the only family I have left. I do not want anything to happen to you." When she covered the hand that held hers with her free hand, tears came to his eyes, but he blinked them away.

Releasing him, she waited until he pointed to the ridge again. "I will be as safe with you as I would be with my father," she said. "Now that we have taken your side, the Hoods will try to have us killed or they will try to kill us themselves with one of their curses. They will be able to find my father, but he is well protected. He can take care of himself. If I go with you, they will not know where I am. So," she said putting her finger on the ancient marks, "we are going there?"

He nodded. "To quote an Old Earth Star Trek expression, 'Where no man . . . or woman,' he said catching himself quickly before she got mad again, "'has gone before.'"

"I love the Old Earth expressions and all the stories you have told me about Old Earth," she said. "I wish I knew stories to tell you. If I could remember Elweenian history the way you remember everything about your ancestors, I would tell great stories and I could quote one of them to you. But I do not know my planet's history like you know the history of yours, so I'll just amuse you the best way I can." She smiled. When he did not smile back, she went on. "Do not be afraid, Mentor. I know what I am getting into."

He wanted to smile, but he was afraid for her. Though her stubbornness had always amused him as much as it sometimes made him mad, today it made him crazy with worry.

With all of the geography lessons that Takal had forced upon him during their times together, lessons that included this ridge, the landmarks on it, and its dangers, he realized that he knew a lot more than she did, but he did not know if he had learned enough to guide her over the ridge and keep her alive while he was doing it. When he started to explain some of its treacherous features, she stopped him from explaining any further.

"I know enough," she said pulling him up. He could feel his temperature rising.

"No, you don't!" he said. He knew he was shouting. As he held the map in his hand, he was so furious that he started to shake.

"You think you are the only one who knows anything," she said haughtily. "I know a lot more than you think I do. And there are plenty of things I'll never need to know. Let's go."

When she walked away from him he remembered how accustomed she was to giving orders and how much she loved to give them, but he didn't budge. She was almost out of sight before she stopped, turned around, and gave him *the look.*

His anger subsided as she walked back toward him. He remembered the comments that he had made each time Takal had forced him to study something he did not think he needed to know. He remembered his own words exactly. "I know enough! Why am I studying these ancient texts? I will never need to know any of the things that are in them." He also remembered Takal's no-room-for-negotiation response. "If you want to be my apprentice, you will study whatever I require and you will need to know about everything. Knowledge is power. Someday your life may depend on remembering something that you thought was not important."

That there was a reason for learning what you thought you never had to know was something it had taken Takal years to impart. He glared at her to let her know this. She glared back to let him know she disagreed. They were about to have a major fight. They both had tempers, but he knew they could not take time to quarrel now. The hunters were coming. Again he thought of his teacher. Takal had never lost his temper with him even when he had been the most obstinate of pupils. Recalling his patience, Mentor realized how important it was to be patient with her now. Mindful of this, he controlled his words.

"You never listen to me," he said. "Even when I am telling you things that you need to know for your own good."

Her furious look softened immediately at his carefully chosen words. Stretching her hand toward him, she grabbed his and held it. "I am sorry," she said. "I do not want to know anything else. I am going along no matter what, and I trust you. If you believe in what you are about to do," she added gently, "that is enough." She surprised him with a hug.

He did not know what to say or do. A pat on the back was not enough, but a kiss on the lips would be too much. When she started to pull away from him, he pulled her back and kissed her cheek.

"You should lead," she said gently.

Her smile melted him. "No," he said. "You take the lead for awhile. The trail is straight for a long time. You will be fine. I will let you know when I want you to stop."

"Ready?" she asked.

"Ready," he said, but he knew that he was not. The ridge on the map was the last place he wanted to go with her. Although part of him wanted to think that he was ready to face the challenges of the unknown lands, he knew that he would never be ready for her to face these dangers with him, or ready for her actions or reactions. She was and always would be the stunning and unpredictable Lady Adamis.

Chapter Nine

⌘

Close Behind

Adamis walked at a brisk pace and kept up with Mentor. Each time he saw a good place to set a trap he whispered, "Here." During these moments they hurriedly fastened the branches of smaller trees to whipcords and attached these ropes to foot ring traps they carried. He studied the forest behind them while she studied the forest ahead. They looked in every direction for enemies.

In those moments of scanning the forest for predators he always wondered how long it would be before one of these enemies attacked, how that assault would come, and what type of enemy it would be. He listened for the whir of a whipcord closing around the ankle of a common hunter or a bounty hunter and the shriek that would follow.

Common hunters and bounty hunters usually cried out when they were caught in traps. Like Zaagotes, imperial hunters were known to endure great pain without making a sound. Because of their great strength and training, imperial hunters and Zaagotes were also known to free themselves from the most terrible of traps. As strong as these more formidable hunters and escape artists were, only some were more intimidating than Zaagote trackers.

If their first hunter turned out to be the kind of tracker that he had seen in the forest the day the stag had been killed, or some eerie type of tracker that he had never seen, the traps would be no good. Imperial hunters and Zaagotes were powerful, but Zaagote trackers were often more powerful still. These predators were frightening beyond belief because there was no set way to kill them.

On their rigorous climb up the ridge he was grateful for each moment that he did not hear a sound, for each second that something did not devour them. While they walked he considered how different this experience was from the many imaginary adventures that he and Adamis had shared when they were little. On those playful trips they had done whatever they'd wanted to do and stopped frequently to rest. On this journey they did what they had to do and only stopped to rest when they were ready to drop from exhaustion.

Mentor did not remember dropping until he opened his eyes. While the first glimmer of dawn reflected on the small stream where they had camped for the night, he stared at Adamis as she slept. Her face drove all thoughts of snaps, traps, and approaching enemies out of his mind.

She was a matchless beauty. Her loosened hair circled her head in a golden halo. Her delicate eyelashes rested against her exquisitely high, round cheekbones. She took his breath away. She made him forget the pain of his parents' deaths, of Ben Zarek's capture, and of the false accusations that had been brought against him. In this moment of just being with her alone in the dawn's early light, his joy was so intense that he felt no pain at all.

The longer he looked at her face, the more certain he was that he was experiencing what his grandfather had talked about. Something that, since his grandmother's death, Ben Zarek had told him he only felt in the presence of God. It was a moment that his grandfather had called the state of grace.

Did she ever enter a state of grace when she looked at him? He doubted it. What did she see? He had yet to attain the height and ruggedly athletic shape characteristic of the men on both the Zarek and Fallel sides of the family, but he was already tall and lean, and his physical training had given him heavy muscles. His mother had often told him that the thick, wavy, dark hair that he habitually swept from his forehead would conquer any girl, and that his hazel eyes were so striking that every girl would fall in love with him. In spite of his mother's remarks about how good looking he was, and how lucky any woman would be to have him for her husband, he was not confident about his chances as her suitor.

Because of her royal rank as the emperor's niece, her great beauty, and her outgoing personality, she had many suitors. Even if she did think he was incredibly handsome, a very funny friend, and a loyal brother, he wondered if she would ever think of him in a romantic way, if she could ever be his. In the days following his parents' deaths, he had often opened his eyes to find her staring at him. Still, he understood that he was only one of many who would want to marry her.

When she woke up without warning, he pulled the map out of his belt, pretended that he had been looking at it instead of her, and hoped that she would not see the words, *I adore you*, written all over his burning face.

"You look tired," she said as she sat up next to him, smiled, and yawned.

"I am tired—tired of reading the map. I am having trouble interpreting some of the symbols and landmarks. Want to try reading it for awhile?" He gave her the map. Then he got up and walked down to the stream. He needed to cool off and recover from the feeling of wanting to kiss her.

"I can do that," she said with a naughty grin, "and maybe I'll even do it better than you did."

Part of him wanted to snap back with, "We will see," because when she was angry she looked even more stunning, but he didn't think his heart could take it. Instead, he bent close to the water, took a sip, and turned to warn her about the rugged path ahead. "From here it gets steeper," he said. "I'll go in front. You read the map and point the way."

With the map in her hand, she directed him confidently along the path during the steady climb. The heat was oppressive. He saw nothing on their route that reminded him of any of the places referenced on the map. If *he* had interpreted the ancient symbols correctly, *she* had not.

They stopped several times to argue about which way the nearly unreadable markings were telling them to go. Finally he could stand her directing no longer.

"Let me have the map," he said in a disgusted tone. He knew that it was not what he had said, but the blaming way in which he had said it that infuriated her. She shoved the map into his hand.

"Think you can do a better job?"

He went on in the same nasty tone. "Obviously, you think you can do the better job so go ahead," he said handing the map back to her. "You can lead and read at the same time. Just don't expect me to follow you when you step off the side of the cliff."

When she threw the map at him, he scrutinized all of the symbols again. He also reviewed the choices that she had made in all of the places where the trail forked, or where the vagueness of the ancient symbols and the landmarks made the route unclear. He quickly saw that she had made the same choices that he would have made. He could not have done a better job. The words printed in the special legend on this part of the map reminded him just how difficult reading a map like this was.

The descriptive words that he could read in the ancient legend made him cringe: "*Relief data incomplete, steep, rocky terrain, treacherous forest covered cliffs, significant discrepancies in landmark details.*" He wanted to forget these words and the way that he had criticized her. He felt like a fool. He stared at the next junction on the path and tried to think of a way to apologize.

Unable to find adequate words to say he was sorry or to admit that he was wrong, he decided to wait for a good opportunity to make peace. It came when she tripped hard on a branch, caught her foot in its arch, and could not get up. He stretched out his hand to pull her off the ground, but she refused to take it. He tried to brush a strand of hair away from her sweaty face. She pushed his hand away. When he put his hand under her arm to steady her after she started to rise, she shoved him so hard that he lost his balance. As he sat facing her, he knew he was where he deserved to be. The hot silence between them burned his foolish pride until he could stand it no longer. He had to speak to her even if she refused to speak to him.

"Adamis," he started to say. "I am . . ."

She cut him off. "Sorry? Sorry? You do not know what it means to be sorry."

He decided to try again. "Adamis . . ."

When she cut him off again, he knew it was better to keep silent and let her rage on. He understood that he could not say anything until she was ready to hear it.

"You are a fool," she said. "A fool, fool, fool."

No further words passed between them until they came to a place where the path forked yet again. Here the markings on the map indicated landmarks that were no longer there. They turned right. At the next questionable place anyone's guess could have been the better selection. They turned left. In yet a third spot where another choice had to be made, the rain forest had eaten up all the recognizable spots which the markings had indicated were once there. A little further on, the trail itself disappeared. At each of these places she said the same thing, "Lead on, fool."

While her tired groans mixed with the high-pitched whistles and shrieks of the forest, he kept hearing the word fool, even though she was too hot and tired to say it anymore. His skin was burning. His eyes watered. As he stared into the mist that blanketed the rain forest, he was edgy. He could only see a foot or so in any direction.

During the continuing climb, the discomfort became even greater. Sweat bees swarmed over them. Black leeches clung to their arms and legs. Clawing his way up another steep slope, he inched forward. His hands and feet were moving over thorny vines. The bees and leeches were making him crazy and miserable. Though he had been trying to save the bark that Oliphar had given to him for emergency situations, he decided there couldn't be a better time to give it to her, but she refused to take it.

"It's medicinal," he said. "If you chew it, you'll feel better and you'll have more energy," he added, trying again, but she wouldn't listen. She threw the bark he handed to her in his face.

When he picked the bark up, he did not chew it. He put it away. He did not want to feel better unless she felt better with him. He did not feel sorry for himself. He deserved to be miserable, but his heart ached for her. And through it all he hated himself for being so unfair about the map when she had risked her life to help him. Plagued by guilt, he watched her suffer during the terrible ascent and blamed himself for the mess they were in. Her suffering made the situation unbearable.

"Ouch," she cried out.

As soon as he heard the word he turned. She was caught in a prickly bush. Every time she moved, the thorns tore at her. Each time he tried to pull the thorny strands on the bushes gently from her clothes, she became more entangled. Finally, he pulled his sword from his weapons' belt. He was determined to hack her out of the thorny prison. It was then that he heard what he had hoped not to hear, the sounds of rustling branches jostled by something not too far away.

What was it? Something was moving along the path behind and towards them. Mentor hacked away at the tangled branches. Whatever it was came closer while he struggled to free her.

When he disentangled the last of the branches from her hair, he pulled her free and stepped in front of her to keep his body between her and whatever was following. The mist and the rock wall seemed to rise everywhere around them. He knew they had to hurry to find a way around the wall. It looked impenetrable, but he recalled a series of rock walls that Takal had told him about. These rock walls marked the beginning of a cave system that they had studied together. He remembered the spiral of ramps and passages that rose and splayed beneath the mountainous spine on the southwest side of the ridge.

Falling rocks cascaded down the ridge just behind and below them. The continued rumbling told him that they were still being followed, but his memory was sharp. He remembered what he had learned when he had studied the geography of this area with Takal. He recalled how the passages roiled unendingly inside the mountains, but remembering these things about the cave system was not the same as finding a way to disappear inside, to survive it.

He felt desperate. If he could not find a way to get past the rock wall, they would be trapped between it and their pursuer. Then he heard it, not the sound of another falling rock, but a whistling sound that Takal had once described in detail, a sound that his teacher had said came from a hidden tunnel inside of the ridge.

"This way," Mentor whispered to avoid giving away their exact position. In spite of the whispering, their stalker was closing in. In moments their hunter would leap out of the mist and fall upon them. He pointed to the bottom right hand corner of the rock wall, to what appeared to be a pit clogged with rocks. He crawled towards it and put his ear to the odd shaped stones stacked there.

As soon as he heard the whistling sound again, he started rolling the loose rocks away from the pile. The ease with which the stones moved only made him more certain that he had found the right place. When he had rolled the last rock away, she peered inside.

"It looks like a low, narrow rock tunnel a little further in," she said. "I think it's big enough for us." Taking off her pack she squeezed inside the crevice and dragged the weapons belt in behind her. He quickly followed, but when he was only a short distance inside he heard loud grunting sounds behind them. Looking back toward the entrance from the dark space inside the tunnel, he saw the huge shoulder of a large form silhouetted in the light outside. He did not know what it was.

Judging by the number of grunting noises that followed the shoulder sighting, he decided the large form had not come alone. That was not good. What was good was that whatever was there was too big to squeeze through the narrow opening at the bottom of the rock wall. It and those who were with it could not crawl into the tunnel after them. He did not know how many others were with this unidentified leader. He only knew one thing. Pursuers had arrived. They were close behind.

Chapter Ten

⌘

The Cave

Mentor crawled into the rock tunnel after Adamis. She scrambled forward, but he was not optimistic about their chances of leaving their hunters behind. Takal's teachings about the geography of the ridge had indicated that many tunnels wormed through this area. Their pursuers would soon find a tunnel big enough to allow them to track their prey.

As they twisted their way through what had become a winding rock passage, other details that he had studied came to mind. The cave system had been created by rainwater trickling through the rock here for eons. This water had eroded the interior of the peaks and turned the ridge into a sprawling system of voluminous grottos and uncharted pits. As he thought about this, he noticed the tunnel widening, but nothing could have prepared him for the sight ahead. When he crawled out of the narrow passage behind her, he saw an enormous cave lit by a rainbow-colored, phosphorescent glow.

"Now that we have some light, we should be able to find one of the features indicated by the map markings and pick up the trail again," he said as he searched for the best way to exit the breathtakingly beautiful grotto. "We have to keep moving through the tunnel system. If we go back into the dark and try to follow a branch in another direction, our hunters will be waiting for us."

"Over there," Adamis said. She pointed to the opening of another tunnel. Above it was one of the eagle shaped etchings they had seen on the map. "Look."

Mentor traced the engraved stone above the entrance with his finger. "It's a tribal symbol. It's Ayan."

"I hope it is light in there," Adamis answered. Without waiting for him, she crawled into the tunnel. Though some of the light from the grotto filtered into the beginning of the new tunnel, it darkened quickly and there was a stench that made it hard to breathe.

Finally they collapsed on the floor of a very black cave. He knew that she was afraid. She had always been frightened of the dark. Without saying a word, he reached for the wall, leaned his back against it, and drew her closer. With the back of her head against his stomach and chest for a pillow, he knew that she would feel more protected. When she stretched her legs out between the comforting V shape that he had created around her, he saw how right he was.

"Sleep," he said as he wrapped his arms more firmly around her. "I will take care of you."

While she slept fitfully, he listened to water drip from the ceiling into a muddy pool. It was dimly lit by a few phosphorescent rocks close by. So much for the beautiful cave they had passed through. They had found the cave system, but they were wet and the smell was horrendous in this terrible place.

They were coated with thick mud from crawling through the watery tunnel. The air reeked of bat guano. He felt sick, but he was relieved that Adamis was sleeping. He reached inside his provisions sac,took a piece of the bark Oliphar had given to him, and chewed it. When she woke up he decided to give her some. Then he wondered about the same thing that he always thought about whenever he had time to think. Were Oliphar and Ben Zarek held prisoner in the Zaagote citadel where he thought they would be? What kind of dark holes held them prisoner?

When something crawled over his hand, thoughts of Oliphar and Ben Zarek flew from his mind. He had hoped that he and Adamis would not encounter any of the venomous or flesh eating spiders that Takal had told him often inhabited these caves. As a hairy body brushed over his hand for the second time, he banged it against the stone wall that he was leaning against until he was sure that it was dead.

In the clammy darkness he listened to the chuggle of slow moving water. He heard the occasional cheer—eep of a bat on a flyby. Perhaps the large, hairy body that had moved over his hand was nothing to worry about. With that thought he dozed until she shook him awake.

"Something crawled over my hand," she said, shaking him furiously. "Something big and hairy."

He tried to sound calm when he answered her. "Stand up, now," he said. He pulled a piece of bark out and put it in her mouth when she opened it to scream. "Chew it. We have to move fast and this bark will help you do it."

It was too late for calmness. He was not sure what was crawling around in the cave with them. It was too dark to see. Takal had told him that dangerous spiders frequented the ridge in packs. He took out the powder that his old friend had given to him for situations like this and sprinkled it in a thin circle around them. Then he reached inside of his pocket, took out two firestones, and rubbed them together near the powder until they created a spark.

When the ring of powder became a ring of fire that lit up the circle, he caught his breath. Not one, but several clusters of hand-sized gat spiders scuttled toward them on the floor of the cave. They were coming from every direction but one. Looking toward the clear spot, he noticed a small opening on a ledge. He pointed to the opening and cupped his hands to form a step. As soon as she jumped on, he lifted her. She leaned over the ledge, grabbed it, and with a great heave pulled herself up. Then she reached over, grabbed his hands when he jumped, and pulled him up behind her.

The spiders began to climb the wall after them. He navigated the narrow ledge as fast as he could. She hurried after him. As his head collided with a long thin stalactite that glowed in phosphorescent light in that part of the cave, he tried not to imagine what would happen if the spiders caught up with them. *Just keep moving,* he told himself. They clawed their way forward until the roof of the cave lifted in front of them.

The passage was higher, but it tilted relentlessly upward. The floor was slick from dripping water above. She slipped. He pulled her up. She fell again. Again he lifted her and drew her forward. Ahead the passage flattened into a narrow, mud-covered shelf that ran against the cave wall. Next to the narrow shelf was a dark pit.

How deep the pit was or how far it extended he could not see, but the gat spiders were right behind them and he knew they had to go forward on the narrow shelf or be bitten, injected with venom, and eaten alive. He squeezed her shoulders and pointed straight ahead. "You go first; I will be right behind you," he said in his most encouraging tone of voice. She inched forward. Sprinkling a little more of the powder behind them to slow the spiders down, he ignited it and followed her. He felt the slickness of the mud on his own boots as he took each step, but he was more concerned about her. In some places he had to press his entire body against the cave wall to move forward because the ledge was so narrow.

In front of him she took careful steps until she stopped and asked him to lead. He held her firmly by the hand and went forward. She took one small step at a time after him, but her steps were as unsteady as his. He was terrified for her and for himself. If they had to die he did not want them to die the slow, painful death that the flesh-eating spiders would give them.

He turned back to see if the powder was still burning. It was, but for how much longer he did not know. As long as it was, it would keep the spiders from reaching them. In the same instant that he looked away from the flickering flames and back at her, she slipped. He grabbed her foot with his right hand, threw his left arm around a rock, and held on. Below him, she cried out. There many razor-edged pinnacles stabbed the air and threatened to stab her.

He felt his arm slipping. Her weight was pulling him down. The sharp point of a stalagmite pointed to the center of her body, threatening to impale her, but he refused to let go. He scanned the wall under him. He saw another ledge wider than the one he was on.

“A ledge next to you —- wide, wide, swing over,” he shouted. Using every drop of strength that he had left, he swung her towards it. Finally, she landed on it and started climbing the short distance between them.

“Keep coming, keep coming,” he said. He tried to sound calm but he knew he spoke in short gasps. She grabbed onto a thin rock formation just as she reached him, but it snapped off. As she ricocheted off the wall and crashed against other formations, he managed to grab her arm, hold it, and stop her fall. Though he knew that the spiders paid no attention to noise, he realized that others searching for them might have heard the clanging sound of the broken pieces very well.

The spiders were coming; the fire from the burning powder was going out. Now others who had heard the clanging would be coming as well, but he refused to give up. For her, he would find a way to get out. He was determined to escape from the cave.

Chapter Eleven

⌘

Alive Again

Ahead the narrow ledge in the cave widened. It also descended, but it was still wet and slippery from water dripping down. Adamis was shaking. As he pulled her through the muddy channel between the rock walls that rose on each side of them in this part of the tunnel, she shook harder, but he leaned forward and pressed on.

In the forward press, he heard the sound of running water. He looked down at his feet. There water trickled downward in a steady path. Though many passages of the cave network under the ridge ended on cliffs outside, and there was no way to go up or down, he followed the stream until he saw a light ahead of him.

They emerged from the dark tunnel on a small but sunny precipice that clung to the mountain. Below was a bottomless gorge. The light and warmth of the sun felt good on his face, but their surroundings were daunting. In front of them, above them, and below them were jungle-covered mountains made of rock. She startled him when she grabbed his arm and pointed wildly to a bald spot on the closest one. It was a short distance above them on the adjacent peak.

He knew this bald spot was referenced on the map, but before he could feel good about this realization, he heard the clanging sounds of icy profusions cascading down the rock walls and ledges they had just crossed. When he looked at her face and saw her alarm, his thought was the same. *Spiders don't make noises like that.*

The hunters who were making those noises were much bigger than spiders. Though he had counted on the spiders to eliminate some of them and slow others down, some would still come after them. He searched for a way to escape. He saw a good spot directly across from them, but the only way they could get there was to cross over the endless drop. He gave her an encouraging look when he spoke.

"Jump with me," he said, determined to appear confident. "And when you land throw your weight forward." He could tell that she was petrified when she agreed. When they hit the ground safely on the other side after the daring plunge, she hugged him wildly. He hugged her back. Then he yanked her to her feet and started climbing without a pause.

"If we made this jump, whoever is chasing us can make it too," he said breathlessly as they ascended. "Hurry," he added urging her on.

Above them the bald spot shimmered in the hot sunlight. They climbed as fast as they could, but their progress was slow and painstaking over the rugged terrain. As they worked their way toward the bald spot, he became aware of the sound of running water once more. It grew louder and louder as they ascended. When they finally reached the bare rock, he saw that it had been marked with the eagle that was on their map. He also recognized the funnel-like opening from which the sound of the thundering water came. It was one of the landmarks that Takal had spoken at length about. They were close to finding the Ayans.

While they inspected mysterious markings next to the eagle engraved on the bald spot and admired the pounding waterfall just inside the funnel-like opening, a swarm of giant bees buzzed by. Startled, he lost his balance and fell to the ground. She tumbled down beside him. When he grabbed the branch above his head with one hand, and the rock adjacent to it with the other, he did not see the nest lodged between the stone and the branch. This time the swarm inside did not fly harmlessly by. This time hornets attacked.

In spite of the pain from the hornet stings, he kept his arms wrapped tightly around her. Thinking the hornets would not follow, he rolled into the gushing waterfall inside the funnel. Instead of going through it, they plunged. In the seemingly endless fall, the chilling water pummeled them and pushed them into a raging subterranean river below. There the icy river ripped her away. Someone yanked him out of the bone-chilling current and tossed him onto solid ground. Then the ground disappeared.

He was above the ground, but not too far above it, when he realized that he was floating and that she was lying on the ground below. He hovered over her. Her eyes were closed, but he could see her chest moving up and down. He was sure that she was still breathing, but when he floated above his own body, he saw no sign of life.

Around their motionless forms a group of mud-covered men spoke in an unknown language. When the tribesmen carried their bodies to a wide shelf of rock above the river, he knew that he was dead.

Suddenly he was a baby again and Ben Zarek was holding him. As his grandfather cradled him in his arms he heard him saying, "I'm not going to let you go." He knew that this scene had happened on a night long ago because his mother had told him about it. On that night he had mysteriously developed a high fever and the healers had said he was going to die. During those terrible hours Ben Zarek had stayed awake, holding him in his arms, telling him how much he loved him. His mother had remembered her father's exact words to him after the healers had made their dire predictions.

"They are faithless," Ben Zarek had said, "but I am not. It is not time for you to leave. You have too many things to do and God will see to it that you live long enough to do them."

Then he saw another image of his grandfather. He saw Ben Zarek kneeling in a dark prison. He could hear his grandfather's voice clearly. "Let him live, God. Let him live out Your plan for his life." At that moment he felt Ben Zarek's hand on his shoulder. He did not understand this, but he remembered what Ben Zarek used to say to console him whenever they were going to be separated. "There is no distance in the spirit. God keeps the spirits of those who love each other together."

When Ben Zarek's voice faded, he saw his mother's face and felt her embracing him. There was light all around her. Behind her he recognized the tall cindar trees of the Tabor Forest. He smelled their icy fragrance and saw the bridge where he and Ben Zarek had always fished. Then he heard Ben Zarek's voice once more. "Help my grandson; God, help him." It was the last thing he heard before he flew back into his lifeless form.

Inside this body he had never felt so cold. His eyes were closed, but he could see dirty men. He did not know how he could see them, but he could. Only two were not covered with grime. He heard them speaking to each other perfectly in his own language. He was shocked, not only by the skill with which they spoke it, but also by the subject of their conversation.

"Why did we help them? Why did we pull them out of the river? Remember how disdainfully he looked at you in the imperial courtroom? I do not care whose grandson he is. He is not like his grandfather. He has no respect for us. He thinks that we are mindless savages," the first one said.

"We helped them because we are warriors, not killers. Warriors help people in distress," the other replied.

Mentor thought there was something familiar about this second one. While he watched, the first one rubbed a white salve over Adamis' forehead, massaged it into her temples, and put a dab under her nose. The second one sprinkled green powder on her tongue, but when they performed the same procedure on him the first one shook his head.

"I think that he is past saving," he said.

In truth, part of him wanted to be past saving. Above the savages he saw the Tabor Forest again.

This time his fishing pole was propped against the wooden railing where his mother stood and waved to him, but his grandfather was not there, and Adamis was not there waiting for him. She was lying on the ground beside him. She was still breathing. Suddenly, he was desperate to stay alive, but he was floating again, right above his body and moving toward a white light.

The light was so bright! He could not see its source. In spite of his fierce desire to return to his body to rescue Ben Zarek and be with Adamis, he felt himself hurtling towards it. "Back," he heard himself say. "I want to go back." However, the more he wished himself back into his body, the closer to the light he came.

Back, please send me back was his thought and it was very clear. In spite of his intense desire to return to what he was sure was his frozen corpse, he could not. Then, although he could not see a face in the brightness that surrounded him, he felt a hand on his shoulder. It was not Ben Zarek's hand, but he was glad that he was not alone. The voice that came with the hand sent a vibrating energy pulsing through every part of him.

"Back?" the voice said, but in that one syllable word another bolt of energy shot through his core. "Most people do not want to go back, but you do not really know Me yet, so I will send you back. I want you to know Me well before you come here again."

It was a voice unlike any he had ever heard. He could still feel the comforting hand on his shoulder and strength from the mysterious presence that surrounded him, but the voice which had started in a whisper was now booming inside of him and growing stronger.

"Back!" the voice said again, but this time when he heard the word he started to tremble. Then he shook. An arc of lightning shaped like a spear hit his chest. Waves of white light from the point of the spear shot right through him, but he felt no pain. Then he heard the booming voice once more. "This is the sword of the spirit," it said. "It is My word, My power. Hear it and live once more, and remember this: Those who truly come to know Me never taste death."

When Mentor opened his eyes, the trembling from the energy blasts intensified. The words about never tasting death were still repeating themselves in his mind, but he was back inside his body—alive again.

Chapter Twelve

⌘

The Ayans

He was alive! Air rushed into his lungs, but his body continued to shake uncontrollably. Someone put a stick in his mouth to keep him from choking on his tongue. When the seizure ended, the savage who had pulled them out of the river knelt by his side and took the stick out.

He didn't want the savage. He wanted Adamis. He tried to call her name, but he could not speak. Then he turned his head slightly and saw her motionless body. He started to choke again. Once more the stick was back in his mouth, but this time while it was there, his rescuer spoke to him in his own language.

"She is not dead and you are not dead although *you were*," the savage said. "Now your lives belong to me. I am Ipec." Before Mentor could respond splashes echoed in the river below.

"Zaagotes! Hurry!" Ipec said and yanked him to his feet. Mentor's legs folded under him when he tried to walk, but Ipec pulled him up. "Walk," Ipec commanded as he shoved him toward an opening at the top of the rocky path. In front of him another savage carried Adamis. She was suspended over his shoulder, sprawled over his back, and unconscious.

"Zaagotes, hurry!" Ipec said again, but Mentor's legs buckled under him once more and he fell to the ground. This time he expected Ipec to leave him behind because he could not keep up, but his Ayan keeper amazed him. He knelt down, lifted Mentor onto his own broad back, and carried him toward daylight. Other savages flew past them. A moment later they disappeared in the blazing sunlight that poured into the cave from the enormous aperture just ahead.

Ipec emerged from the dark cave and raced after his companions. Adamis' body was bouncing against the wide back of her transporter. The Zaagotes were right behind them. When Mentor lifted his head and looked back, he saw one enormous Zaagote after another coming out of the cave they had escaped from. He could hear their angry curses. When he turned to look ahead again, Adamis was gone. She had melted into the jungle with her carrier. A moment later arrows flew from a dense wall of trees around them.

Three Zaagotes fell. Others followed. Another wave of arrows flew from the trees. More Zaagotes thudded to the ground. He fought to remain conscious. He wanted to stay awake until he saw Adamis again, but his eyes blurred and kept closing. He heard Ipec speaking to him.

"Hold on. You can do it," Ipec whispered. He lowered Mentor to the ground, pushed some branches out of the way, and turned toward another savage. "The first scout is yours, Yola, but the others are mine. Your job now is to carry this foreigner away from the battle."

"I want to stay and fight," Yola said. Mentor could hear, but his vision was still blurry.

"Yola, you are my little brother," Ipec said, "but I promised our father that I would take care of you. Ganta will never forgive me if I break that promise. Now go. I stay to discourage any other scouts from following you."

Ipec was a fearless defender. As Yola and another savage lifted Mentor up and started to carry him away, Ipec knelt in the thick ferns that covered the forest floor, notched one arrow after the other, and fired at the Zaagote scouts to cover the retreat of his companions. He was unbelievably fast and accurate. Apart from Adamis he had never seen anyone with such a steady arm.

Yola flew through the forest carrying him, but the jarring motion made him so nauseous that he had to keep his eyes closed. When he finally did manage to open them long enough to focus on anything, Ipec was coming towards them, still firing one arrow after another while he was running. As one Zaagote after the other dropped with one of Ipec's arrows in his neck, Mentor appreciated his deadly aim.

In spite of the undeniable admiration he had for Ipec, he wondered what would happen now. Would he and Adamis survive? He did not know. For now, all he knew was that he had found what he was hoping to find, or rather that those he was hoping to find had found him. He was indebted to these mysterious people. They had saved his life and hers, and though they had not identified their tribe, he knew which one it was. He recognized the head of the massive eagle that each one had carved into his arm, the same eagle that he had seen on the bald spot of rock, and on the arm of the chief who had tried to help him up the day that someone had tripped him in the imperial courtroom.

His eyes closed again. He wanted to stay awake but he could not keep his eyes open any longer. His last conscious thought was that these strange people had to be taking them to the unknown lands. They were the Ayans.

Chapter Thirteen

⌘

Warrior

Bound and gagged, Mentor woke up to the clashing sound of spears smashing against the stone floor of a very large cave. Also bound and gagged, Adamis sat next to him. Around them savages danced feverishly. He could smell their sweat. Suddenly something hit his face. He did not know what it was. In the next instant something hit hers. When he saw the skinned, bloodied animal carcass sitting on her shoulder and her bloody face, he tried to break free but he could not move.

More carcasses flew in their direction and landed around them. The howling grew louder. The jabbing became fevered. Finally, a large black man with a green feathered crown on his head put his hand up and silenced the crowd. During this hushed silence Ipec stepped into the middle of an enormous white ring in the center of the stone floor. There he bowed before the crowned man.

"I, Green Feathers, the High Chief, speak for the tribes today," the feathered man said. "My ruling is that we will speak in the tongue of the captives," he continued. "Since their lives are at stake, I want them to know what we are saying about them." Then he lowered his hand and pointed to Ipec. "You may begin."

"Zaagote hunters chased these strangers onto tribal lands and I saved them," Ipec said calmly. "Their lives belong to me."

When Ipec finished speaking, the crowd howled again, but the din was not as loud as it had been the first time. For a moment Mentor felt hopeful about their chances for survival. That hope faded when a huge savage with a black feather sticking through his nose approached. As this towering brute sauntered toward the long wooden table on the rock pedestal at the front of the cave, Mentor wondered who he was. At the table, twelve chiefs with huge headdresses sat with stern faces and listened.

"They are outsiders," the nose-feathered man said. His eyes burned. His mouth was a hard, straight line. "You had no right to bring them here. The male stranger must die, but the woman is beautiful; she must live. I wish to claim her." The man put his finger inside of his mouth, sucked on it, and drew an invisible line across Adamis's cheek.

Mentor was enraged, but when other warriors wearing the same black feathers through their noses grabbed him, dragged him to a stone slab already stained with blood, and pressed his face against it, he knew he would never have a chance to do anything about the insult. Above him, the executioner raised his ax, but before he could lower it, Ipec hurled his spear.

When the spear hit the tree behind the stone, Ipec dove at the executioner, knocked him down, and yanked the ax out of his hand. Without taking the gag out of Mentor's mouth or untying him, Ipec carried him to a huge tree carved with elaborate markings and propped him against the trunk. Then he strutted back to the bloodied stone slab and stood on top of it. Mentor had never heard such silence or seen such boldness. While Ipec glared at the nose-feathered man who wanted to kill him and claim Adamis for his own, no one moved.

"I challenge you, Tong," Ipec shouted. "Their lives belong to me. That is our law. I saved them. They are mine and mine alone." From his spot on top of the bloody slab, Ipec turned in a full circle and stared at all of the silent faces before he went on. "They are mine to give or mine to take." When he finished speaking, Tong strutted towards him, but Ipec stayed where he was. Tong circled Ipec for a moment. Then he stopped abruptly, jumped on to the slab, and faced him. While the two glared at each other, they were as close as they could be without touching.

Suddenly the High Chief raised his spear and pointed it at Tong. Tong turned and strutted back to the place where the other men wearing black nose feathers waited for him to join them at the front of the crowd.

Mentor studied Tong. He remembered him. He had been Ipec's companion in the Imperial Courtroom. At that time he had assumed that Tong was Ipec's friend. He had also thought that all savages were too ignorant to speak in civilized tongues. Now that Ipec and Tong had both spoken before the tribal council, he realized how wrong his assumptions were.

Ipec's presumed ignorance and his iron grip had revolted him in the courtroom on the day of his trial, but he could not forget Ipec's unwavering gaze or his strength when Mentor had tried to wrench away. Ipec had held him powerfully in his grasp until the moment that he had decided to release Mentor. He remembered everything about Ipec, and everything else that had happened the day that he had boldly come to take the captives away from their Elweenian captors. Most of all, Mentor remembered shoving his hand away.

In spite of the despicable way in which Mentor had treated Ipec, he understood that Ipec had every intention of keeping him and Adamis alive, at least for now, but he did not know why. Would he have done the same for Ipec if their roles had been reversed? He doubted it. Ipec was a "savage," but Mentor admired him.

When Ipec jumped down from the rock slab, strutted towards Tong, and stood nose to nose with him again, Mentor admired him even more. He had never seen anyone act with such raw confidence. For several long moments, the silent, wordless crowd stared at Ipec and Tong as they glared at each other for the second time. Behind the stone slab, to the right and left of the ceremonial tree, two huge drums started to beat. Ipec and Tong walked towards them. Next to the drums was a large urn. When they reached into the urn, the crowd began to chant "Fight, fight, fight!"

The two challengers whitened themselves with ashes from the urn. The drumbeat continued but the pace was faster. The rhythm dominated the crowd. The chanting became frenzied. Green Feathers carried a large bowl to the open area in front of the drums. Then he reached into the bowl and walked around the challengers. As he did this, he tossed red powder inside the white perimeter of the ring already outlined on the cave floor. When he finished, he pointed to a place just outside of the ring where several of the jeweled chiefs had gathered and waited until Ipec, Tong, and two other men joined them.

"The ring is sacred. The ring is true," the High Chief chanted several times. Then he pointed to the man who stood on Ipec's right.

"Ganta, you are Ipec's father, but you are also an Ayan chief, as is your son." The High Chief paused for a moment before he turned to the man who stood at Tong's left. Then he spoke again.

"Dugor, you are Tong's father, but you are also an Ayan chief, as is your son. I say these words to remind you that we are all Ayans. No matter what our differences are, we must stand together as one tribe. Ipec is the Chief of the Winds and Tong is the Chief of Black Feathers. But you are the elders," he said pointing to the two fathers, "and as the elder chiefs of two of the branches of this tribe, you hold the ruling power." Green Feathers waited until the two fathers bowed to acknowledge his words before he went on.

"In this combat one of you may lose a son, but you must abide by the outcome. You must not make war against each other. If Ipec wins, the strangers will be given a chance to live among us and become members of our tribe. If Tong wins, the male must die and the female will become his wife. I speak for all of the chiefs of every branch of our tribe. Someday one of us will unite all of the tribes in the unknown lands, but the one who does this will not be one who disobeys my ruling here today."

When Green Feathers finished speaking, all of the chiefs bowed again as he passed. Then he stepped into the ring and untied Mentor and Adamis. Putting one hand on each of their heads, he spoke quietly to them. "You are free until the fight is over," he said. Then he stepped out of the ring. Ipec and Tong stepped into the ring where the High Chief had stood and eyed each other.

With his arms raised and muscles bulging, Tong danced around Ipec. Ipec stood in the center of the ring and watched him, but he did not move. Tong darted forward. He tapped Ipec's head with his hand and darted back. When these initial actions had no visible effect on Ipec's calm demeanor, Tong began to flick his tongue in and out of his mouth and danced around again. Then he leapt towards Ipec, spat in his face, and shot out of reach again. Ipec wiped Tong's spit from his cheeks, nose, and eyes, but he stayed in the center of the circle and did not move.

Unable to stand Ipec's undaunted poise any longer, Tong sprang forward and seized Ipec's legs. The two grappled with arms coiled around each other. Ipec lifted his opponent and threw him on the ground. In spite of the throw, Tong was cat-like and landed on his feet, but he was not there for long. He made a fake move to the right and charged Ipec. He tried to choke Ipec, but Ipec rammed his head against Tong's head until Tong let go. Then, in a sudden move, while Tong was still stunned, Ipec wrapped his arms around Tong's waist, lifted him high into the air, and slammed his adversary to the ground.

Tong did not move. Ipec turned to leave the ring. Mentor thought the fight was over, but Tong got up again and charged Ipec from behind. As the two rolled out of the ring, Mentor saw the black tip of a dart in Tong's right hand. It was similar to the poison darts that he had seen the Ayans use against the Zaagotes.

Without thinking, Mentor jumped on Tong's back, and pulled Tong's hand away from Ipec's throat. Instantly, someone grabbed Mentor from behind and put a knife to his throat. Others pulled the combatants apart. A sudden blast from a ceremonial horn ended it all.

After a second horn blast, Green Feathers approached. Mentor saw the question that he expected in the High Chief's eyes. After the chief waved his hand, the knife was removed from Mentor's throat. He told Green Feathers why he had jumped onto Tong's back before he asked.

"He had a weapon. He had a poison dart in his hand," Mentor said.

Green Feathers inspected Tong's hand. There was no dart. Mentor's heart sank until the chief stooped close to the ground, picked up a small object, and sniffed it. After the sniff, he returned to the high platform and sat. There he studied the arrow and sniffed it again. From his chair Green Feathers raised a large stick with a round knob high into the air above him. He held it there until silence reigned once more.

"The sanctity of the ring has been violated. I found this poison dart on the stone floor. That means either one of you could have brought it there to use it against the other. Until the true violator has been punished, neither of you may enter the ring again. However, Tong and Ipec, you remember that we have a common enemy who invades our land. For now you will stay away from each other and fight Zaagotes. On a day to be yet appointed, we will have another contest. On that day we will determine the identity of the defiler."

After the High Chief finished announcing his decision about the violation, he walked toward Mentor, stopped in front of him, and stared into his eyes. Mentor met his gaze unflinchingly until the chief finally turned to look back at Tong and Ipec again.

"On that yet to be appointed day," the chief said, "the two of you will remain outside the ring that has been violated and watch while someone else fights in your place. Tong, you will choose someone from your branch of the tribe, someone who is untrained in a warrior's ways, someone you will train to fight for you." When Green Feathers approached Mentor and put his hand on his shoulder, Mentor's heart was pounding.

"Ipec," he said keeping his hand where it was, "you will train this stranger, the one whose life you saved, to fight for you. The winner and the one he represents will live; the losers will die." Then Green Feathers did something he did not expect. He squeezed his shoulder gently.

Ben Zarek had done this many times when Mentor was facing difficult circumstances. Kor Elion had also done it when Mentor stood in the Imperial Courtroom accused of treason. Now the High Chief from the unknown lands was making the same gesture. Although Mentor thought it was an odd coincidence that both Elion and this Ayan did the same thing that Ben Zarek used to do to encourage him, he knew that his grandfather would have disagreed. Ben Zarek would have said that this gesture was no coincidence because there were no coincidences. For that reason Mentor found the gesture strangely comforting as Green Feathers stared into his eyes and spoke quietly to him.

"You did not ask to be brought here, but you are here. Now you must learn our ways. No matter what happens you will profit from this experience. You may live or you may die, but only one thing really matters; before this is settled you will be one of us—a warrior."

Chapter Fourteen

⌘

The Master

After the chief's pronouncements, a group of warriors surrounded Ipec and Mentor. When Green Feathers held up his hand, all of the warriors stood still and faced him.

"Ipec and Mentor, you are now in the place of isolation," the High Chief said. "You are forbidden to speak to anyone or to approach them, and they are forbidden to speak to you. If you disobey me, you will die. If anyone else disobeys me that one will be severely punished."

At the chief's first nod, the warrior escort handed Ipec his weapons and provisions. At his second nod, Mentor's weapons belt and provisions were handed to him. When the chief held up his hand, the warrior escort withdrew and stood a short distance away.

Near Ipec's father, Ganta, stood his brother, Yola. Adamis was with them. Mentor wanted to run to her. He wanted to throw his arms around her to comfort her. As silent tears fell from her eyes, he saw goodbye in them. Ipec's family shared her pain. Their sadness was visible.

Green Feathers looked as sad as they were when he lifted his spear in the air and pressed the tip against Ipec's chest. He held it there until a steady stream of blood dripped from the wound.

"Ipec, you are accused of violating the sanctity of the ring," the High Chief said. "For this you are outcast. Like Tong and the one he has chosen to train, you and the outsider will live away from your people until the appointed day comes. On that day, the outsider will fight for you and Tong's champion will fight for him. Train this foreigner well. Only victory will make you a true Ayan chief again and save your lives."

As Green Feathers withdrew his spear from Ipec's chest and stepped back, Ipec betrayed no emotion. When the High Chief turned and pointed the same spear at Mentor, he tried to hide his feelings the way Ipec had.

"Young one," he said. "Ipec saved your life. Now you must save his." Mentor did not move when the High Chief pressed the point of the spear into his chest. In spite of the pain, he made no sound. The wound bled profusely before the old man withdrew the spear. Then he turned toward Adamis with the bloody spear in his hand and pointed in her direction.

Addressing Mentor again, he continued. "You must also save your young female companion. Until the next contest your friend will remain a part of Ganta's household and will be under his protection, but only until that day." When Green Feathers pointed the spear at Mentor's chest for the second time and pressed it against his skin in a different spot, he wondered what else the High Chief would say.

"Let this second wound remind you of her," Green Feathers said as he pushed the point of the spear into Mentor's skin once more. Again, in spite of the pain, Mentor made no sound, but this time the old man did not remove the spear. This time he held it where it was.

"Let this continuing pain make you often think of her future," Green Feathers said solemnly. He paused for a moment and pressed harder before he continued. "Tong has already been taken to another place of isolation, so I can speak freely. If you lose the contest, Ipec will die and you will die, but your friend will have a living death. She will become one of Tong's wives. To prevent this from happening, you must become a true member of the tribe. You must learn everything that Ipec can teach you and you must learn it well. If you do, when the appointed day comes and you step into the ring as Ipec's champion, you will win. You will restore Ipec's honor and save your friend."

As soon as Green Feathers withdrew the tip of his spear from Mentor's chest for the second time, Mentor gazed at Adamis. He tried to take a step closer to her, but the warrior next to him stopped him by pointing another spear at his chest. Mentor turned toward Ipec and saw that he had not moved. At that moment he realized that Ipec already understood what it meant to be an outcast in the tribe. He wanted to ask Ipec what would happen to Adamis during the time that he and Ipec would live apart, but when he opened his mouth to speak Ipec had already become an invisible part of the forest.

Only a moment passed before he caught up with Ipec. He tried to think of something to say, but could not so he said nothing. He already understood what it felt like to be an outcast among his own people, accused of something he did not do. And now, for the second time he was robbed of a family. They both were. He ached with the same pain that Ipec had. He boiled with the same anger. Out of respect for Ipec's agony, he did not violate the silence that hung in the air between them.

He followed Ipec through the dark rain forest. He wondered how long they would travel before Ipec would speak. At the end of the day when Ipec threw himself on the ground without a word, he was sure that Ipec would never speak to him again. He could not sleep. He felt guilty about what Ipec had lost because of him, of what she had lost. Wrapped in a blanket of guilt, worry, and pain, he twisted and turned, but he could not escape from the suffocating black cover.

Ipec shook him awake. He recognized the smell of smoke, but this smoke had a sickening odor. He had experienced this odor many times near villages destroyed by Zaagotes. He knew the smell of burning flesh. Before Mentor could stand, Ipec darted into the forest. He was running back the way they had come. He saw the Ayan markings, the same ones he had seen on the path they had taken to get to this place. As he flew over the trail after Ipec, he knew that Ipec was going home because something terrible had happened.

He ran behind the young chief at a furious pace until the smoke became a heavy curtain. Finally they reached the place where the village had been. There, they met an old man sitting in the ashes, staring straight ahead. The man was dazed. He did not seem to see them. Ipec shook the old man, but he did not respond. Bodies and parts of bodies were scattered around him. Ipec dropped to the ground and covered his eyes. He collapsed on the ground next to Ipec and threw up. When he was done, Ipec grabbed him and wrestled him to the ground.

"These Zaagotes followed you here. I've lost everything because of you," he said.

He tried to break free from Ipec, but their confrontation ended as abruptly as it had begun because Ipec let him go. In the distance, somewhere ahead, they heard the sound of screaming. Ipec jumped to his feet and flew in the direction of the shrieking. Scattering smoldering remains as he ran, Mentor followed Ipec to the sounds of the desperate cries. He felt numb, but he forced himself to keep going.

In addition to these cries an animal-like grunt filtered through the trees. Mentor drew his knife from its sheath and crawled behind Ipec. Through the branches he saw a Zaagote half stumble over a girl who had fallen on the path. The Zaagote had been pushing her along. Ipec turned to Mentor, pointed to the knife in his hand, and whispered. "Not yet. This maggot will lead us to other captives." Following Ipec's lead, Mentor inched along behind the Zaagote and his prisoner.

When night fell, he and Ipec peered through the trees at additional prisoners who sat around the Zaagote fire. They were bound with heavy ropes and gagged. Ipec's father, Chief Ganta, his brother, Yola, and Adamis were not among them. A wave of despair swept over him until he remembered what happened to important captives. Because Ipec's father was a chief, and Ipec's brother and Adamis were with him, they would be regarded as the family of the chief and would probably be taken back to Zaeg, alive, to be sacrificed. Ipec nudged Mentor.

"Do you understand the Zaagote tongue?" Ipec said in a whisper.

"Yes," Mentor replied without looking at him.

"Listen carefully then," Ipec answered. "Many lives may hinge on how accurately you hear."

Nodding, Mentor crawled behind Ipec until they were stretched flat on the ground under some low bushes closer to the Zaagote fires.

"Tell me what they are saying," Ipec said nudging him again.

Mentor focused on every word and syllable. He listened for a long time before he trusted himself to provide Ipec with an accurate translation. "Fade is looking for me because he has captured my grandfather and wants information from him. They say that if I am captured, my grandfather will tell them everything they want to know."

"What else?" Ipec said quietly.

"They think they were fortunate because I led them to you. They say Fade wanted to capture you and your family because he feared your father would unite the tribes against them. The Zaagotes are still looking for you. Your father, your brother, and Adamis are heavily guarded. They are already on their way to Zaeg, but they are traveling there on another path. Even these guards do not know which way they were taken. They are to be held prisoner at Keldac where they will be kept until the Zaagote high day of sacrifice."

Ipec took a deep breath before he spoke. "At least you are useful in one way." Saying nothing more Ipec wove his way in and out of the low bushes. Beyond the light of Zaagote campfires, when they were far enough away to speak without being heard, Ipec finally spoke again.

"We cannot follow our loved ones if we do not know which way the Zaagotes have taken them. There are too many ways to Zaeg."

"What about later?" Mentor replied. "The next day of high sacrifice at the citadel in Keldac is almost a year away." From the stunned expression on Ipec's face, Mentor could tell how surprised Ipec was at his knowledge.

"You know their language. You know their customs," Ipec said. "How is it that someone so learned was ignorant enough to trespass into the unknown territories?"

Mentor closed his angry fists, but did not hit Ipec. He did not tell him that he had gone there deliberately, not ignorantly, to escape his hunters. He knew that Ipec had paid a high price to save Adamis and him. Ipec had many good reasons to hate him; nevertheless, it was insulting to be called ignorant and stupid. His anger subsided when he reminded himself that he did understand the Zaagote language and their customs, things that Ipec did not know. Also, thanks to Takal, he could show Ipec the best way to get to the citadel. Perhaps his knowledge of Zaagotes had finally put him in a superior position. He could not wait to show Ipec what he knew. Soon Ipec might ask him to direct their two man rescue plan. Maybe then he would gain a small measure of the Ayan's respect.

"I have a friend who is wise and who can change one thing into another," Mentor said, but he decided to keep his idea for gaining Ipec's respect to himself. "He knows all about Zaagotes and all about Zaeg. He even collects and preserves parts of them and their trackers whenever he can. We have been dissecting them for years to study them. His maps have guided me many times. He has many maps. He can help us to decide how to get to Zaeg and advise us about the best way to disguise ourselves. If you follow me, I will take you to him." Certain that he had convinced Ipec to let him take the lead without really saying it, he could not suppress a satisfied expression while he waited for Ipec to respond.

"No," Ipec said firmly. "My village has been discovered. There are too many Zaagotes around. If we were to go to your friend now, there is a good chance they would follow us. If we are to survive and keep your friend alive so that he can help us, we must travel deeper into the unknown lands to mislead them before we go to him."

"How can we be sure that no one will follow us wherever we go?" Mentor said. His voice betrayed his disappointment.

"With Zaagotes and trackers you can never be sure," Ipec said.

"We can fight if we have to," Mentor said touching his sword.

"I can fight if I have to," Ipec said confidently. "You are not ready."

He knew that Ipec's words were accurate, but they angered him. He refused to admit that Ipec was right.

“I can be ready if I have to be,” Mentor replied. Ipec ignored him, but he went on. “We are wasting time by going further into the unknown lands. I am going to my friend now.”

“How unlike your grandfather you are,” Ipec said angrily. “When Ben Zarek came here to see us in secret, he respected us by doing what we asked. He wanted to explore the possibility of forming an alliance between the tribes, New Earth, and Tire Elween. We asked him to wait until a leader was chosen who would unite all of the tribes. Your grandfather agreed. He always valued my opinions when I spoke with him.

It was out of respect for your grandfather that I rescued you. Now you *will listen* to what I say. You are not ready for the journey into enemy territory and neither am I. To get in and out of Zaeg alive, we need time to prepare. We also need powerful weapons. I saved you; your life belongs to me. You will do as I say.”

When Ipec finished speaking, Mentor was speechless. He was astonished that Ben Zarek had gone to the tribes and spoken with Ipec. He felt embarrassed and small for acting so immaturely. He wanted to apologize, but before he could think of the words to say, Ipec was gone.

He took the direction that he thought Ipec had taken. He felt humbled. Ipec was right about everything. He had no real combat experience, only practice experience, and he had not practiced with all of the weapons that he was supposed to learn how to use. He also knew how powerful some Zaagotes and trackers were, and how ineffective many weapons were against them. When he recalled how effective Ipec’s arrows had been against the Zaagotes, he realized how much he could learn from the Ayan’s experience.

As the boar-like creature charged, he had a chance to see just how valuable experience was. While it pounded through the thicket just missing Mentor with its massive hooves, he realized that it was some type of tracker. He had never seen this breed before. It was faster on its second assault, but Ipec shoved him out of the way and rolled away from it.

Furious about missing its targets, the animal stabbed its large horn repeatedly into a massive tree trunk. Ipec positioned his arrow and aimed, but before he could fire, he could hear other trackers coming in their direction. Jumping into a nearby ditch, they covered themselves with leaves and watched. "There are too many in the area," he whispered. "We have to wait. Where there are trackers, there are Zaagotes who summon other Zaagotes and more trackers."

From their hidden position in the ditch they could see everything. After the first tracker stopped stabbing the trunk, pulled its horn out of the tree, and looked back in their direction, Mentor saw a seldac impaled on the horn protruding from the beast's head.

He knew the dead seldac had done nothing to provoke the horned tracker. Seldacs were the most peaceful of all of the animals in the forest.

He hated the seldac killer like he hated the stag killer. No matter what size or shape trackers came in, they had one thing in common, like their Zaagote masters, they were merciless. They hunted everything and they killed everything they hunted. When the Zaagote removed the impaled seldac from the tracker's horn and fed it to the beast, Ipec nudged Mentor, pointed to the killers, and whispered.

"Trackers come in all shapes and sizes. Some are large; some are smaller like you. You are a little smaller than the first tracker that charged us. If I could manage to look like the Zaagote and you could look like the tracker, we would be able to get in and out of Zaeg and rescue our families before any of the Zaagotes realized who we were."

"Exactly," Mentor said, but he knew what Ipec was thinking and he did not like it. He swallowed hard.

"So when the time comes for us to go to Zaeg," Ipec said, "can your friend help us to look like a Zaagote and his tracker?"

"If anyone can, he can," Mentor replied, but he hated the thought that Ipec would be the Zaagote and that he would be the tracker.

"Good," Ipec said. He was already moving away from Mentor. "Now let's go while they are moving away from us. This place is full of Zaagotes and trackers. Soon more will come."

Ipec started to crawl toward the opposite side of the ditch where they had been hiding from the Zaagote and his boar-like tracker. As he made his way through a thicket of heavy bushes, he turned, looked over his shoulder, and whispered again. "It pleases me that my size, my looks, and my experience as a fighter qualify me to be the Zaagote and you to be the tracker. It pleases me because nothing will change. Our relationship will be the same." He smiled broadly before he went on. "You will always be the slave, and I will always be the master."

Chapter Fifteen

⌘

No Choice

Ipec and Mentor fled from the Zaagote, his boar-like tracker, and the other trackers still roaming the area where the seldac had been impaled. They avoided other Zaagotes and trackers who passed them and those who were still combing the area to search for anyone who might have escaped the raid on Ipec's village. When they were on their feet, they stayed close to the ground, but in places where they could be more easily observed, they crawled for a long time. In spite of the distance that they put between themselves and their pursuers, Mentor knew that some Zaagotes and their trackers would eventually find them. After Ipec finally stood up and started to walk like a man again, he did the same. He felt better walking, but he was jumpy.

There were reasons for his jumpiness. They were finally far enough away from the search area to walk or run, and he really did want to avoid the crawling stretches that they both hated, but now they were going to places where no Zaagote or tracker had ever been seen, to the deepest parts of the unknown lands, where other shocking things waited for them. In addition to these new threats, he was sure that the Zaagotes and their trackers would attack in greater numbers as soon as they picked up their scent. They were relentless hunters. The only thing he did not know about their Zaagote pursuers was what type of tracker they would use in the hunt.

On their journey Mentor shared what he knew about Zaagotes and trackers. Ipec did the same, but apart from the sharing of this necessary knowledge, he said nothing. Mentor could think of many reasons why the Ayan loathed him, but he was sure about the biggest one---Ipec had no respect for him.

When they came to an overgrown area he forced these reasons from his mind. While Ipec pulled two pieces of catia wood from his pouch and started a fire, he began to break off pieces of brush and added them to it. It was only after Ipec made a torch with the surrounding brush and ignited the undergrowth that he saw the enormous burrow openings underneath. In all of his travels as a runner he had never seen any holes like these. While he was wondering about the burrows, Ipec lit a second torch and held it in front of him. Sparks flew from his eyes.

"What are you thinking about?" Ipec said. "Keep your mind on what you are doing now. Remember, I saved your life. I lost my family and friends because of it, so I have earned the right to tell you what to do with yours. I am the master. You are the slave. You must do what I say. Take this torch. Do what I just did and do it quickly or we will die before we leave this place."

Mentor took the torch and stared into Ipec's eyes. He held the torch away from his body and did not move. "I refuse to take another order from you until you tell me why we are doing this." The heat from the two torches did not bother him, but the fire in Ipec's eyes burned his pride.

"We are hunting snakes!" Ipec said. "Big snakes----snakes with venom powerful enough to kill any Zaagote, any tracker, or five of someone your size, so do as I do before one of these snakes pops out of its burrow and I have one less person to take care of."

Following Ipec's example, Mentor raced from one burrow to the next until they were done. Then he followed Ipec to a hillside a short distance away. When Ipec sat down on the hill and pointed to the burning burrows, Mentor sat down beside him.

He wished that he had kept his mouth shut and just done what Ipec had told him to do. Ipec was older than he was. How much older he did not know. Mentor hated being fifteen. Ipec was clearly more experienced than he was in every way. There was nothing he could say to make Ipec regard him with less disdain. He decided that the best way to make up for his big mouth was to obey Ipec without protest.

Not protesting, keeping his mouth shut, was the least he could do for someone to whom he owed his life. He made up his mind to swallow his pride in the future. He was determined to stop being angry each time Ipec tried to teach him something. For now he had to accept his status as Ipec's slave. As they sat there on the hill, he was prepared to follow Ipec's next order without questioning him, but no order came. Instead of giving him an order, Ipec pulled some roots from the ground near them and handed them to him.

"Even slaves have to eat," Ipec said as if he could hear what Mentor had been thinking, "but a good slave knows that roots taste better when you rinse them off." Ready to obey Ipec's hint, Mentor stood up, but Ipec pushed him back down to the grassy spot where he had been sitting.

"Do you know which way to go to find water for rinsing? Have you been listening to the sounds around you?" Ipec gave him a piercing look.

"No," Mentor said. He hated to admit that he had been so full of his own thoughts that he had paid no attention to anything that was around them, but it was true. The night air was cooler away from the fires burning over the burrows, but his face was hot again. He was embarrassed because Ipec did know which way to go, not just from his experience, but because he had been listening. He had been paying attention to their surroundings. Ipec *did* know what to do and *he* should have known too. He was furious, but not with Ipec. He was furious with himself.

"Warriors do not let their emotions distract them," Ipec said. "Warriors always concentrate on their surroundings so they can use them to their own advantage. For example, I am thirsty and hungry, but I already know where the water is and I knew where the roots were because I noticed the plants that were growing here. You will learn, but it will take time." Mentor expected Ipec to remain angry. He was surprised when he did not, and even more surprised that Ipec had already begun teaching him a warrior's ways.

As they sat in the moonlight and chewed on the clean roots, Mentor considered his relationship with Ipec. He wanted to ask why Ipec had rinsed off the roots himself instead of ordering Mentor to do it, but he knew that Ipec would not tell him. Although he was sure that Ipec still despised him, at this moment, in this place, he began to wonder. His relationship with Ipec went beyond that of a slave's relationship to his master, but he did not understand how or why.

The next morning when Ipec shook him, pointed to the burrows where they had lit the fires the night before, and raced towards them, he understood their relationship no better, but he raced after him. If there was one thing he was beginning to comprehend about Ipec, it was this—he preferred action to words.

Ipec pointed to the trails left by the snakes and spoke confidently. "Fighting serpents is good training for those who must face Zaagotes and trackers. These serpents are like them. They are aggressive. They are even more aggressive when their burrows are invaded. After you go into this burrow and get this snake, you will be ready for anything."

Go into this burrow and get a snake? He can't be serious! were Mentor's thoughts, but he could tell by the way that Ipec was looking at him that he was serious. His body felt numb. He was standing but he could not feel his legs under him. His stomach turned inside out. The last thing he wanted Ipec to see on his face was fear, but it was there. He knew that the Ayan saw it, but Ipec acted as if the fear was not there and went on.

"I will teach you how to be ready for anything," Ipec said ignoring his terror. "A master always tells his slave what to do, but a great master shows him. First, we prepare for the hunt. We make an offering to our gods." Ipec pointed to what looked like a small black animal climbing a distant tree. The animal was so far away that he did not know what it was or how Ipec would shoot it from this distance, but when the Ayan fired the animal fell to the ground.

"Bring it to me," Ipec said. When Mentor reached the tree he recognized the snorka by its long pointed snout and the gray bristles around its neck. Picking it up, he brought it to him and watched him pull the arrow from its body. He waited for him to say something, but Ipec did not speak. He held the snorka reverently and bowed his head in a silent prayer. When the Ayan finally looked up, Mentor could tell from his serious expression that he was about to say something important.

"The first time I came to watch the men of my tribe hunt snakes, I was too young to hunt myself, but my friend, Anda, was older so he had to go into the snake hole. The night before the hunt Anda told me about his fear. I remember that his father made no sacrifice before the hunt that day. He also made no prayers. This is what Anda's father said to him when he forced his son to enter the burrow.

'Go in and do not come back until you bring a snake with you.' Then, you know what his father did? After Anda went in, his father blocked the exit by sitting in front of the hole. There, Anda's father sat and waited for Anda to bring back the snake, but Anda did not return. What do you think about this story? Kneel beside me and tell me while I prepare. I will listen."

Ipec waited for him to respond but he did not know what to say. Anda's story grieved him. Although Mentor's father had never forced him into a snakehole, the story reminded him of his own father's style of parenting. In addition to his sadness, he felt shocked. It was the first time that Ipec had ever asked him what he thought about anything. He decided to honor his question by answering honestly.

"My father never prayed," he said. "He never really helped me with anything. My grandfather always prayed and he was always there to advise me. He used to say that he knew God and that God knew him, that they talked together every day. He always looked peaceful after he prayed.

According to my grandfather, God sacrificed His only son to pay for the sins of the people, and because of that no further sacrifices ever need to be made. His religion was one of Old Earth.

I do not know what I believe about the Old Earth religion that my grandfather believed," Mentor went on to say, "but I do know that Ben Zarek's faith in this God always empowered him." He was surprised that he was sharing the beliefs of his father and his grandfather. It felt strange to be talking about his family and God with an Ayan. When Ipec just nodded, he kept on talking.

"If there really is a God," Mentor went on, "I do not think you can get to know him just by listening to what someone else tells you about him, even if that person is someone you love and respect, like my grandfather."

"How do you think you can know him then?" Ipec stared at him intently and waited for his response.

"Only by experiencing him, but I do not think this can happen for me." He could not believe that he was telling Ipec how he really felt and that Ipec was still actually listening to him. "If the God that my grandfather believes in is real, why would he listen to me? I have never talked to him before."

When Ipec finished smearing the blood from his sacrifice on his knife, he said a final prayer. In this prayer he asked his god for victory. Then he stood up.

"My god demands blood sacrifices before I can speak to him. It sounds like your grandfather's God is far more merciful. I would talk to him. If he's not real, he won't answer. If he is…" Ipec paused to think before he went on. "What better way can there be to experience God than to get His help when you really need it? What have you got to lose? Only your fears, and you are riddled with them. If you could get rid of fears on your own, you would, would you not?"

"I would," answered Mentor.

"Can you?"

Ipec stared into his eyes and waited for his reply. Mentor wanted to say yes, but he could not.

"No," he said finally. "I can't".

"Then pray to the god of your grandfather. A real prayer to a real God gets results. You cannot win any battle until you overcome your fear."

"I know you are right," Mentor said. He hated himself because he was afraid.

"Before we face the snakes, you must admit that your fear is there."

Mentor's heart sank. "I admit it. I am afraid," he said.

"You should be," Ipec replied. "There are many things that you should fear, and there is nothing wrong with being afraid. What is wrong is allowing fear to control you. Ask your grandfather's God to protect you now and to give you courage to go into the snake hole. If He answers this prayer, He will protect you from Zaagotes and trackers too." When Mentor did not reply, Ipec stood up.

"I will be just over there, beyond that tree, talking to *my* god," he said. "When I am done, I will go to the snake burrows. If you come I will know you are hunting with me. If you do not, I will know that I am hunting alone. If we conquer the snakes, we will collect one of the strongest poisons in our world. We can use it against the Zaagotes and their trackers and go on to rescue the ones we love."

After Ipec left, Mentor knelt behind the trees the way that he had seen Ben Zarek kneel so many times. He did not know what to say, but he remembered what Ben Zarek had told him: "*When you talk to God, use simple words. Talk to him as you would talk to me.*"

His heart was pounding. He opened his mouth and said the only thing he could think of. "God of my grandfather, if you are there, please send help." Then he got up. On his way to the snake holes he wanted to turn around and run the other way, but he kept walking forward. When he reached the holes, Ipec pointed to the biggest, deepest trail left in the ashes. Mentor took a quick step back. He followed the first step with another. He considered bolting, but he stayed where he was and resisted the impulse to flee.

"We're going after the biggest one first," Ipec said. "Remember—a master always tells his slave where to go, but a good master shows him the way. I cannot stand by the hole and wait for you. I must go into the snake hole with you."

Ipec's words astonished him. The part of him that did not believe in God thought that Ipec's announcement was a coincidence. The part of him that did believe was sure that his prayer had been answered. Before he could think any more about whether it was a coincidence or not, Ipec's voice interrupted his thoughts.

"Now listen carefully. When we are in the holes we are soldiers going after an enemy, but we are always in control. Follow me."

Ipec crawled into the snake's burrow with his torch out in front. Mentor worked his way along the narrow corridor after him. Greasy with sweat, he tried to gauge whether or not they could move forward without being stuck. If the tunnel allowed no space to turn and they had to back out quickly, he wanted to be sure they could. Suddenly there was no time to think. In front of Ipec, he saw a large black snake. With a blue-black fan around its head, it rose from its coiled position on the dirt floor and bared its fangs. Ipec was face to face with a serpent.

Ipec held the torch with his right hand to keep the snake back. He protected his left hand with a piece of animal skin, but before the snake could strike, Ipec covered its eyes with the skin, threw down the torch, and grabbed the back of the snake's head.

Mentor backed out of the cave. Ipec did the same, dragging the snake out of its hole after him. Mentor tried to breathe normally, but he was gasping for air. When Ipec finally extracted the writhing serpent from its burrow, he ended the struggle by stabbing the snake with his knife. Then he turned to look at Mentor and laughed.

"Now I will repeat what I told you before. Fighting serpents is very good training for those who must face Zaagotes and trackers. That is why we are going into another burrow. Today you will learn what every true warrior must learn before he can be truly great in battle —how to control your fear."

When Ipec handed him a forked stick, Mentor wanted to hand it back and say that he had changed his mind, but he didn't.

"Keep this handy," Ipec said. "You may want to pin the snake's head against the burrow wall and kill him there instead of covering his eyes and grabbing the back of his head before you drag him out and stab him. This time you will go first, but I will be there to help if you need me."

In the burrow, Mentor hitched himself forward on his belly with one hand and used the other hand to light his way with the burning torch. When he looked over his shoulder, he saw Ipec right behind him. When a snake hissed and wriggled in front of him, he jumped but he did not back away. The snake coiled into a tightly knotted pile of rope and lunged at him. With a swift movement, almost a reflex, Mentor pinned its head against the burrow wall with the forked stick. Then he threw the torch down beside him, slit its throat, and dragged it out by its tail.

Outside the burrow, Ipec stood with his arms crossed over the front of his chest and grinned. Mentor was still shaking, but he knew he was smiling back.

"Now come," Ipec said. "I will show you how to collect the poison. My people have been taking the boys of my village to this place for many years to teach them. There are many collecting pots buried under the ground here."

Ipec led Mentor to a tree. There, he threw the body of the first snake over a large branch so that its head hung down. Then he uncovered a pot buried in the ground nearby. Placing the pot under the snake's head to catch the dripping poison, he slit the snake's venom sac.

"Did you use this poison to kill the Zaagotes who were chasing us when you pulled me from the river?"

"Not this poison. Another poison from weeds. Sometimes poison arrows work on Zaagotes and trackers, and sometimes they do not. The Zaagotes who were chasing us were only unconscious for a short time. They did not die. The poison from the weeds was not strong enough to kill them. That is why they followed us later and destroyed my village. The virus that is affecting the Zaagotes seems to be making them immune to some of our poisons. That is why we have to collect stronger poisons or mix the poisons that we have into more potent combinations.

"How does this poison work?" Now that the snake was dead, he felt more curious than ever.

"For this type of snake, you must wait until the poison congeals and sets into a thick, red colored gum," Ipec said as he paused to dig up another pot. "After that, you take another pot and collect the watery serum that flows from the carcass. The two poisons of this snake must be kept separate. When they work, they do so in different ways. At times we may want to mix them, but don't think about mixing today. Just pay attention to today's lesson."

"I will," he replied.

After Ipec had finished the poison-collecting procedure, Mentor knew it was his turn, but he waited for Ipec to give the order before he got up.

"Now you do it," Ipec said.

When he had thrown his snake over the same branch a short distance away from Ipec's snake, Mentor stared at its blue-black body. It was hard to believe that he had killed such a deadly serpent. After he placed the two pots under his snake to collect its poisons, Ipec dragged him toward another burrow.

"Now we do it again and again, until all the burrows are empty," Ipec said. He started to turn from the tree where the two snakes hung suspended over the collecting pots when a beast charged out of the brush and thudded toward them.

Ipec jumped out of the way to its right side. Mentor leapt to the left, but when he stood up he saw Ipec lying motionless in the field. He knew the Ayan would die unless he did something. He ran to the pots where they had collected the poisons, pulled several arrows from his quiver, and dipped them into the toxins. Then he knelt in a firing position that put him between Ipec and the tracker.

The beast charged again. His first arrow hit its shoulder, but the beast kept coming. It was almost on him. When the second arrow hit, the tracker rolled on its side away from him and groaned. Before it could get up again, Mentor fired the third arrow into its huge horny head. It did not move. It was dead. Turning away from the beast, Mentor started to run back to Ipec, but Ipec was already sitting up and smiling at him.

"You killed your tracker before your tracker killed you," Ipec said still grinning. "That is good for a novice. However, your aim needs to improve if you are to serve your master well."

When Mentor helped Ipec up, his heart was still thudding, but it was the first time in days that he did not feel afraid or bitter about the terrible things that had happened to him. As Ipec leaned on him and limped, Mentor wondered if the chief was pretending to be hurt in order to help him overcome his fear of trackers or if he really was injured. Either way what had happened was a good thing. Mentor kept his shoulder under Ipec's arm, sat him down in a shady spot, and waited for his next order.

"Get everything together," Ipec said massaging his leg. "We are leaving this place. Other trackers will be coming here with their masters," he added rubbing a deep gash on his ankle with some salve he carried. "If we use all the poison that we have collected on them, we will not have enough for our trip in and out of Zaeg. There are other places we must go to collect toxins. We must get them before the Zaagotes get us. We have to stay ahead of them! We must hurry!"

As they left the place of the snakes, Mentor wondered if collecting new poisons in those other places would be as dangerous as it had been in the snake burrows. Before he started to worry he decided to take Ipec's advice. He forced himself to think about what he was doing now instead of thinking about the future. He finally understood how useless it was to worry over things that were not in his power to control. He had to focus on the present to achieve his goals. If he wanted to rescue Ben Zarek and Adamis and help Ipec save his family, he had to go to these dangerous places and get these deadly poisons. He had no choice.

Chapter Sixteen

⌘

Meant to Be

They had traveled a great distance from the land of the snakes and from the strange tracker Mentor had killed with the poison arrows, but it would not be long before they would face other hunters. Although he had not seen any signs of Zaagotes or their trackers, he knew they would never give up searching for them. He hoped they would not encounter any new adversaries before they reached the place where they would collect the next poison.

As he and Ipec trudged through the steamy heat, many questions passed through his mind. Would the next collection spot be more dangerous than the first one? Where were they going? What would they have to do when they arrived? How much farther would they have to travel before he could rest?

"Where's the next camp?" he finally said. He could stand the suspense no longer, but Ipec kept on walking and did not answer. He decided to repeat the question.

"Where's the next camp?" he said again.

"Where the flowers are," Ipec replied.

"And where is that exactly?" When Ipec stopped, turned around, and tossed a penetrating stare in his direction, he wished he had not asked. Swallowing hard he tried to look stoic and prepared for the worst.

"Where the bees are, big bees, and volcanoes," Ipec said. "We are not just going there to collect what we need. We are going there because it is a more dangerous place than the ones we have already been to; many will be afraid to follow. Now, aren't you glad you know? If you could see your face you would understand why I don't tell you more ahead of time."

Before Mentor could reply Ipec touched his ear and dropped to the ground in a crouch. Then he pointed to a tree where an excited monkey jumped up and down and rustled the leaves.

"How many times do I have to tell you to think about the present? The bees and volcanoes are in our future; the monkey is here now. If you were listening to the trees around you, as you should be, you would have heard the rustling above us. For small game like this monkey you can use a dart or an arrow. Aim carefully like I do before you fire."

With Ipec's perfect aim the monkey dropped to the ground. Mentor wanted to impress Ipec by hitting his own target, but when he heard more rustling in a nearby tree, he aimed too quickly. When he fired at a second monkey screeching there, he missed.

"You have to be accurate all of the time. Someday my life may depend upon it," Ipec said shaking his head. "I can see that it will take more time." When the chief pointed to the knife in Mentor's belt, he knew that his next order would be to skin the monkey so they could eat it, but before Ipec said another word, he pointed to his ear again.

"Listen! Hear the whistling." Ipec pointed to a bird scampering towards them. "Oma searching for his mate. Two birds—lots of good meat; better than monkeys." Ipec pursed his lips and sent out a delicate fluting sound that gradually faded away. They heard more rustling. Another bird approached the first one.

In an awkward attempt to draw closer, Mentor tripped over a root sticking out of the ground. The birds flew away before Ipec could fire.

With an arrow still poised in his bow, Ipec turned away from the place where the birds had been and gave Mentor a stony look. "You are clumsy. A true warrior is an artist—precise, graceful. I can see that it will take time." Mentor did not utter any response. The Ayan would not listen to anything he had to say. Until actions made the slave's reply very clear, he answered only in his thoughts.

It will take time. It will take time. Today I will show you, Ayan, just how little time it will take. It's time for the slave to put the master in his place. That's what it's time for. He had to attract another bird and kill it. He concentrated on the boundless greenery and on the molding leaves covering the ground. He listened to the sounds around him. He tried to imitate the mating call that Ipec had used to attract the first two birds. When he heard what sounded like another oma coming toward them, he tapped Ipec's shoulder and whispered with smug satisfaction.

"How much time did that take?" He gloated while he waited for Ipec to reply. When Ipec gave him a nasty glare, Mentor whistled the mating call again. This time several birds twittered and shot past him.

Again he imitated the mating cry, but this time birds flew by cawing loudly. Ipec pulled him down. As they crouched on the ground and listened to other birds sounding their alarm, he heard a rustling noise followed by a heavy thud. Something large had leapt to the ground. Ipec crawled into a dense thicket. Mentor followed him.

For the next few moments the silence was unbroken by the sound of any living creature. Then there were more heavy thuds followed by the sound of feet pounding through the jungle. They were being hunted again.

Keeping out of their enemies' eyes, they crept away from their hunters. In the thicket that meandered endlessly through this part of the jungle, they squatted and listened for further signs of their pursuers. They stayed where they were until it grew dark, but they did not hear anything else. Then the crackling of wild thunderbolts came. Lightning shot through the sky and rain pounded the ground. Now the sounds of the wild storm drowned out every other noise there might have been.

The heavy rain gushed down. It transformed the barely discernible path on the other side of the thicket into a brook. They kept moving until they reached the shelter of a small cave. Resting against the wall of their stony refuge, Mentor closed his eyes and listened to the deluge and to the crackling and crashing in the furious weather all around them.

"The storm saved us," Ipec said. "They could not hear us and we could not hear them. They could not follow our tracks in water. Since we do not know how many hunters there are or who they are, we will avoid a fight. We are close to our destination, but we do not want to lead our enemies to the place of the bees. Tomorrow we stay here and watch. If there are no further signs of trackers or Zaagotes, we will leave at nightfall."

Mentor hated the idea of waiting and watching. He did not want to wait. He wanted to press on, to stay ahead of the Zaagotes no matter how risky it was. Ipec's decision angered him, but he swallowed his objections. He remembered what he had promised himself. He recalled his intention to apologize to Ipec for all the pain he had caused him by not arguing. He also thought about the way Ipec had treated him in the land of the snakes, especially about the moment when he asked him what he thought and listened to him. Because of these things, he said nothing.

The next night Mentor followed Ipec until they reached the land of the bees. Here the odor of fumes filled the air. It came from the ring of volcanoes in the mountainous spine nearby. In the bright light of the full moons, hordes of large white flowers glowed eerily. Their sweet, heavy fragrance mixed with the volcanic fumes to form a unique heady smell, but the strangely scented night was not silent. The low steady rumbling of the volcanoes mixing with the loud buzzing sound of bees was unnerving.

He did not see any bees, but he heard them. As he watched several streams of red lava wiggle downwards from the high volcanic peaks that rose in a ring around them, he was mesmerized. The fiery crimson streaks held his attention until Ipec tapped him on the shoulder and pointed to three round hives. They hung from branches high above them. Silhouetted against the bright moonlight, the hives looked like black melons on a shimmering blue cloth of stars.

"Hives! Honey!" Ipec said still pointing.

As Mentor stared at the hives on the moonlit branches of the trees, he sank to the ground. He had never imagined being in such a breathtakingly beautiful place, but the thought of bees anywhere near made him sick. Before he had a chance to think about the bees anymore, a tall man in a yellow feathered crown appeared in the distance and raised his hand in greeting.

"Ipec," he said. "It's good to see you." The man smiled as he approached them. Then he extended his hand and placed it on Ipec's head. "You are welcome here."

"Thank you, Chief Ora." Ipec bowed deeply and remained in the bowed position until the chief touched his shoulder. The chief waited until Ipec stood before he spoke again.

"The drums told us about the burning of your village and about the captives taken," Chief Ora said. "I am sorry." Then he turned his gaze on Mentor. Once more he chose to remain silent, but a critical question went through his mind: *Would this man feel the same way Tong felt about his arrival without an invitation?* Before he could ask himself this question again, Chief Ora addressed him.

"The drums also spoke of you, the hunted young man from the civilized lands," he said extending his hand in Mentor's direction. He bowed deeply the way Ipec had and stayed that way until the chief touched his shoulder in a similar fashion. "Ipec is now the second hunted one, but you are both welcome here. They say the Zaagotes hunt you because your grandfather, the great war chief of New Earth, will tell his captors whatever they want to know to save his grandson's life. They hunt Ipec because he is his father's oldest son—the oldest son of the oldest branch of the Ayan tribe. Because he is who he is, the Zaagotes fear that he will take his father's place as chief and unite the tribes against them."

Ipec smiled proudly and bowed again before he spoke. "Thank you for the faith you have in me. You have been a family friend for a long time. Please forgive our intrusion. Our presence here brings danger to you and your people. We are sorry, but we need your help."

"Do not be sorry," Chief Ora said. "Sooner or later trackers and Zaagotes will come here and we will have to fight them. Tell me how we can help you."

"We need the poison honey," Ipec said. "We are going to Zaeg to rescue my father, my brother, Mentor's grandfather, and his friend, Adamis."

The chief nodded thoughtfully. "Follow me," he said as he led them to the base of one of the trees.

In all of his travels Mentor had never seen such trees—ancient trees so wide that ten big men joining hands would not have been able to make a connecting circle around them.

Around one of these trees three figures huddled together and fed leaves into smoldering fires. As the chief pointed up at several large hives suspended high above them in the branches, Mentor studied them until he was so dizzy that he had to stop looking up. Suddenly nauseous he sat down on the ground and took a deep breath, but he felt no better. As he sniffed the light breeze that blew around him he realized what was happening and why. The air had thickened considerably with fumes from the smoking volcanoes rumbling around them.

"My people and I are leaving this place so you must collect the honey yourselves," the chief said, "but you can tell from the smoke in the air and from the rumbling of the volcanoes that time is short. The mountain gods are angry. The Zaagotes have invaded our lands. They have burned Ipec's village. They have killed many people of his tribe and taken others as prisoners. It is not safe to stay here any longer. Soon Zaagotes and trackers will find this place. If we are here when the mountains come down upon them, we will die too."

Before the chief withdrew he took out his knife with his left hand and stretched his right arm toward Ipec. Then he made a deep cut on the inside of his forearm. He waited until Ipec imitated his gesture.

"If anyone can unite the tribes, I know you can," Ora said as Ipec pressed his bleeding arm against the chief's arm. When the chief turned toward Mentor, he started to take out his own knife to do what Ipec and the chief had just done, but the chief stopped him before he cut himself.

"No," the chief said. "You are not one of us yet. If, and only if you become one of us, will your blood mix with ours, but I do have this to say to you. Unlike many others who live in New Earth and Tire Elween, your grandfather demonstrated respect for the people of the tribes. Against the will of many, and at great personal risk to himself, he urged the emperor to free those of us kept as slaves in Tire Elween. He wanted the tribes to be part of the alliance between Tire Elween and New Earth against the Zaagote invaders. Ben Zarek was on his way here with the agreement for this alliance when he was captured. After the emperor had gained enough support from his lords, he was going to recognize the unknown lands as the lands of the tribes, not claim them as part of his empire. Because of the way your grandfather has respected us and tried to help us, I respect your grandfather and I wish you well."

He was stunned by the chief's startling revelations, but he did not move or say a word until Ipec bowed deeply before the chief in a final farewell.

"Thank you," Mentor said, also bowing politely, but before he could say anything else the chief put his hand on his head, turned, and left.

Dense columns of white smoke filtered upward through the massive limbs of the giant trees from huge fires below them. As the smoke from these fires and the toxic fumes of the active volcanoes surrounded them, Mentor found it hard to breathe. He tried to stop coughing, but couldn't. Ignoring his hacking, and the hacking of other people all around them, Ipec opened a pouch that one of the departing honey hunters had given to him and pointed to the fungus-like gray paste inside. "Think the air is bad now?" Ipec said. "Wait til the volcanoes explode. Hurry! Smear this over your body; we don't want to be here when the tops of the mountains come off." Imitating Ipec, Mentor spread the paste on his arms, legs, and face.

"We will use the ax, ropes, and torches the honey hunters have left for us. Now I will climb. You will climb with me and do what I do." Ipec stopped and stared into Mentor's eyes before he moved. "Remember this," he said solemnly. "You only fall and die when your life is over. If your life is not over, you will not die because you still have things left to do. Now give me some of that bark you shared with me the other day and eat these ferns; we need power and speed to do what we have to do today." Ipec swallowed the bark that Mentor was already chewing, handed two green leaves to Mentor, and ate two leaves himself.

"The bark and the ferns will help to protect us from the poison in the honey and from the venom in the bees. These bees are different. They plant stingers into deeper layers of skin. The stingers are excruciatingly painful, but they won't be lethal. The fall may kill you but the bees won't, even if they are the most painful things you have ever experienced."

Mentor finished smearing the paste over himself, swallowed the final traces of ferns and bark, and asked himself why Ipec was always so encouraging. He watched a few of the last collectors spiral down their ropes and land on the ground. He tried to convince himself that the task ahead would be less daunting than it was. After one of the honey gatherers collapsed with a dazed expression, he stopped trying. He cringed when he saw the man's swollen face and heard him moan. In spite of the palliative effect of any leaves he might have eaten, the protection of the paste, and the net over the honey-hunter's head, the bees had stung him severely.

While another climber sat down next to his dazed, suffering friend and pulled the stingers in his skin out, Mentor's heart dropped into the soles of his feet, but Ipec was already pulling a net over his head and fastening a belt with the things that he would need around his waist. When Ipec started climbing, he did not move. He was still staring at the honey-hunter's swollen body. The chief shouted at him from above.

"Remember Ben Zarek! Remember Adamis! Now climb to me. I will wait until you catch up."

Mentor jumped on to the tree and climbed until he reached Ipec. Side by side they hurried toward the hives that were hidden in the towering canopy of branches and leaves. With nothing to protect him from the bees except the sticky fungus that he had spread over himself and the net over his head, he realized that honey collecting was going to be a terrifying experience; he hoped that the bark and the leaves they had ingested would counteract the poison and the pain.

When the volcano rumbling turned to thunder, he knew the terrifying experience would become lethal if one or more of the volcanoes exploded. Next to him Ipec chiseled stepping notches into the bark with an ax. He did the same. In the sweltering heat and choking fumes his progress was slow. Every muscle ached and begged him to quit. Wood chips flew from their axes. Sometimes the chips bounced off him before they fell to the ground, but he kept climbing. He wanted to go back down, but they had almost reached the hives. Finally, they were just above the first. He balanced himself on twisted branches to reach it where it hung, but a bee burrowed through the net and buried itself in his hair.When he tried to dig it out, it stung his scalp and planted a stinger there.

Another bee worked its way through the netting. Mentor told himself not to panic. Angrily squishing the bee against his cheek, he held on to the branch where he was and tried to focus. The pain from the second stinger raced towards his eye like fire. By the time Ipec eased his way on to a narrow branch next to him, Mentor's head and face were throbbing.

While Ipec tied his rope to the branch, Mentor lit the prepared torch that he had tucked inside his belt. Ipec held the smoking torch close to the hive to subdue the bees with one hand and grabbed a honeycomb with the other. He placed it in the empty sac that Mentor held out to him. The chief hurriedly added more honeycombs to the sac, but Mentor didn't know if he would be able to hold on. He felt like he was suffocating as the pain from the stings worsened.

Drugged by heat, smoke, bee toxins, and volcanic fumes, he felt very weak. Was he going to fall? Another cloud of bees came toward him but buzzed by. Some clung to his face net and stung him through it.

He thought the stingers were making him see things when an arrow flew past his nose. Below he heard the remaining honey hunters screaming. As more arrows flew upwards towards them, he and Ipec climbed higher in the trees to hide themselves from Zaagote archers. Ipec yelled over the noise coming from below.

"Up here the vines and branches connect the trees like bridges. Go from branch to branch, from tree to tree, until we can climb down in a safe place."

Before he could answer something shook the tree fiercely from below. He looked down and saw an enormous, panther-like creature crawling up the tree towards him. Was there time to get away? As the tracker ascended, Mentor asked himself if he was meant to die this way. When he recalled the sac full of toxic honeycombs on his back, he knew that he was not. He was thankful for this secret weapon.

Slowed to a stop by bees that tormented its climb, the tracker stopped long enough for Mentor to pull a honeycomb from the sac and throw it at the cat's eyes. Blinded, the huge beast shrieked and fell from the tree. He climbed higher. In a moment another tracker would take its place and crawl towards him once more. He scrambled over the heavy branches and vines in the endless jungle canopy at the very top until he reached Ipec.

They were inching forward over the heaviest vines when a powerful explosion ripped the smoky air. White ash began to fall like snow, but they wriggled from tree to tree until they finally found one covered with thick vines reaching the ground.

With the sacs of toxic honeycombs around their necks, they hit the ground running and flew through the forest. More explosions ripped through the air. More ash rained down. Behind them Mentor heard animals growling and Zaagotes shouting commands. In front of them a narrow stream of lava widened, but they could not go back. When he managed to jump over the stream after Ipec and land next to him, the growling he had heard turned to fiendish shrieking. He did not look back. They hurried forward up a hill.

Halfway to the top, they stopped to look back down. What had only been a stream of lava moments ago had become a fiery river that two more of the cat-like creatures and their Zaagote masters could not cross.

As the trackers shrieked and their Zaagote masters shouted curses from the other side of the flaming barrier, Mentor and Ipec disappeared inside the ash covered forest ahead of them. Although Mentor hoped that the Zaagote hunters and their trackers would not find a way to follow, he was sure they would try.

While he trudged forward behind Ipec, ashes poured down on them; it was almost impossible to see. He thought about the storm that had saved them earlier and about the volcanic eruption and lava which had saved them moments ago. Though he knew many who would have said that he and Ipec had been saved by coincidence, he was starting to think that everything that Ben Zarek had told him was true—-that there really was a God, and that in His plan even terrible things were used for a good purpose. For the first time in his life, he was really starting to believe that some things were just meant to be.

Chapter Seventeen

⌘

Spiders

As they traveled away from the lava, Mentor and Ipec heard the shrieks of the panther-like trackers and the curses of their Zaagote masters for a long time. Finally their hellish cries diminished. Around them the lava flows prevented movement in every direction but one—up the strange looking, vine covered hill.

Mentor watched Ipec try to pick his way up the hill on top of the strange vines, but each time he made a little progress he had to stop to untangle a foot. He studied Ipec's painfully slow ascent; he knew their pursuers would catch up as soon as they found a way around the lava.

Mentor inched along behind Ipec. They both took careful steps, but he avoided putting his feet on the places where Ipec had broken through the vines and become tangled. In spite of his careful footwork, he broke through the vines as often as Ipec did until he was caught. He tried to pull his foot out of the tangled web, but could not. Ipec had to stop and help him.

To free him, Ipec twisted his foot to the left. Then he twisted it to the right. When he repeated the process and still failed to pull Mentor's foot out of the tangle, the Ayan rolled his eyes and sat down next to the webbed trap that held his slave prisoner. Mentor sat down next to him. He did not think anything could make Ipec more disgusted than he already was. Their painfully slow progress and his viny predicament enfuriated the chief, but he decided some payback would be fun. Ipec's previous jibes and his *This is your fault for not paying close enough attention* stare egged him on.

"I know you will get me out," Mentor said, "but I can see that it will take time." Repeating Ipec's familiar taunt with a grin made him want to laugh in spite of their dangerous situation. An angry glare in Ipec's eyes confirmed that his jibe had worked, but his satisfied feeling did not last. When Ipec jumped up, pulled him to his feet, and pointed to the bottom of the hill, he knew they were in serious trouble.

"Those trackers are huge," Ipec said in a low voice. "If it takes longer to get you out of this hole than it does for them to get up here, we will have to use some of our venom to kill them." Ipec drew his knife, bent down, and tried to saw through the thickest of the vines. "We won't use the venom unless we have to," he added. "The cats may get stuck in the vines the way you did and never reach us."

"Don't worry," he said reminding Ipec how he had saved his life when the boar-like tracker had attacked them. "I will shoot the way I did the last time your life depended on my skill." He wanted to lighten the heavy situation with a joke, but neither of them laughed. The huge cats were pawing their way up the hill towards them.

"Forget the last time," Ipec replied. "Just tell me when I need to stop sawing and shoot with you," he said as he hacked away at the vines. "Cats jump, remember?"

While Ipec kept trying to break through the vines to free Mentor's foot, he dipped arrows into the venom and eyed the cats. The beasts were climbing fast. They were already halfway to the spot where he was trapped. Though he did not know how far these enormous cat-like beasts could leap, their huge black bodies and their long, heavily muscled legs made him certain that they could jump great distances. Soon they would pounce.

"It's time to stand up," Mentor said as he handed several of the venom dipped arrows to Ipec. The Ayan put his knife away and took aim. "Wait," he said. "Let them get a little closer." They stood side by side and eyed the monstrous cats. The extraordinary stalkers crept towards them. Ipec pointed to the one on the left.

"He is the size of a bull," Ipec said as the strange animal clawed his way forward.

"The other one is just as heavy," Mentor added. "I will take the one on the right."

"Rapid fire," Ipec replied. "When I say shoot, fire one arrow after the other until they go down. The venom is powerful but the beasts are huge. We do not know what it will take to kill them."

Closer and closer the hunters came, carefully pawing their way over the tangled web of vines that held him captive. They did not get caught in the small spaces between the vines that had so perfectly snared Mentor's foot. Their paws were too big; their weight was distributed over four feet. He eyed the killers and waited for Ipec's command.

"Shoot!"

His arrow penetrated his target's left shoulder, but the tracker kept coming. He fired again. The cat was still on its feet padding toward him over the vines when the second arrow penetrated its massive neck. The hunter paused in a moment of pain; then it leapt at him, but Mentor fired a third arrow into its chest. The huge beast fell and landed in front of him. Its enormous weight broke the tangled web that had kept him from escaping and pulled him down. He fell into a deep hole and landed on top of the dead tracker.

When he opened his eyes, he saw Ipec sitting on top of the other dead tracker right beside him.

"We killed them," Mentor said, but as he studied their dark surroundings and looked up at the sky far above, he did not like what he saw.

"I can see that they are dead," Ipec replied.

"Are we where I think we are?" He looked around in the dark hole. He waited for Ipec to make his usual critical comment and enjoy whatever pleasure he might get from it, but he really didn't want to hear the familiar criticism.

"Since you have to ask I can see that my lessons about a warrior paying attention to his surroundings still haven't penetrated that thick head of yours." Ipec shook his head before he continued. "Eventually you may obey me. A good slave would, but I can see that with you it will take time." He wanted to say sorry master and laugh at the ridiculous idea of being Ipec's slave, but he was too agitated to laugh. That they were far below the surface of the hill and that it would be hard to get out were things that the "inattentive" slave had already surmised, but he didn't want to rob "his master" of a chance to provide his own assessment of their situation, so he kept quiet and listened.

"Now to answer your senseless question about where we are—if you carefully observe our below the surface location, you will see that we are in a pit below the vines," Ipec replied. As he pointed up at the only piece of orange sky that they could still see from their deep hole under the ground, Mentor dreaded the climb.

"And if you look under us, if you carefully observe our surroundings, you will notice that we are on top of two huge cats that were very hard to kill," Mentor added proudly. He refused to let Ipec talk down to him any longer. He had fired his arrows rapidly and accurately. In spite of their terrible plunge into the pit below the vines, he could not keep the note of accomplishment out of his voice.

"It *was* good shooting," Ipec said as he stared at the arrows embedded in the bodies of the cats. "Now aren't you glad I made you practice on smaller game every day? I knew that if you could hit smaller things, you wouldn't miss the bigger killers when they came our way. There's no doubt about it. You might be on your way to becoming half as good as I am."

Pleased at Ipec's compliment, he readily agreed. He did not mind giving Ipec the pat on the back that his "master" sometimes liked to give himself. He thought about thanking Ipec for teaching him so much about shooting. Now he could shoot anything and hit it, but before he could express his gratitude, Ipec spoke again.

"Still, it is too bad you had to use three arrows. If they'd been better placed, your cat would have gone down faster. I needed only two. However, your aim is definitely improving, but I can see that it will take time."

It will take time! It will take time! Again, he thought to himself; *well let's see how little time I take getting out of here or if you can keep up with me.* He was barely controlling his anger as he began to climb up one of the vines to the surface. After the slippery vine broke under his weight and he slid back down, he realized that he had something more important to think about than Ipec's needling.

"Getting out is going to be a challenge," Ipec said. "I tried to climb out quite a few times while I waited for you to wake up, and as you can see I'm still here."

Ignoring Ipec, Mentor clawed his way up another vine but failed once more. He thought for a moment before he spoke. "We were on a hill when we fell through. If we dig a tunnel in the right direction we can get out." He was pleased with himself for what Takal would have called brilliant reasoning, but there was no compliment on Ipec's face. There was only a penetrating look.

"Good to know there is a way out, but no good if you don't know which way to go," Ipec said.

He readied himself for another jibe about how, if he'd paid better attention to the hill before they fell through, he would have known what direction to dig in. When the comment never came, he was relieved.

"I am not sure either," Ipec said. "Let's try this way," he pointed. "We only have a little daylight left. Let's dig until it gets dark and see what happens."

They dug at a furious pace, but he stopped digging when the vines above came alive. Nudging Ipec, he pointed to them. "Tell me I am wrong," Mentor said. "Tell me that there is nothing moving on those vines."

Ipec stared at the vines above them for several long moments before he spoke. "I wish I could," he replied as he stared up at them.

"What is it?" He asked, but he did not want to know.

"What are *they* is what you mean," Ipec answered.

"All right, what are they?" He braced himself.

"Pit spiders," Ipec said with his usual stony face.

"What are pit spiders?"

"They are venomous creatures and they are day feeders. That means they are coming down here to spend the night in the pit with us. We have to hurry if we want to stay alive."

"Tell me what to do," he said trying to stay calm.

"These spiders are killers, but the skin on these dead beasts is thick. If we skin the cats and wrap ourselves inside their thick hides, we should be safe until morning. It will take the spiders more than one night to eat through the thick hides and get to us. As soon as daylight comes, they will crawl up the vines and leave us alone here. Then we can dig our way out."

Grateful that he had learned to skin an animal on hunting trips with his grandfather, Mentor plunged his knife into the cat that he had landed on. He removed the heavy hide in one unbroken blanket. Making sure that he had wrapped the heavy hide around his body, he stared at the steady stream of spiders jostling down the vines towards them.

"Why are you looking at them?" Ipec was furious. "How many times do I have to tell you not to waste time on something that you can do nothing about? Here," he said. He cut two small squares from a leftover piece of hide and handed them to Mentor. "Cover your face. Cut slits for your nostrils and for your eyes. You have to breathe and you have to take a peek later to make sure they are gone."

"Anything else?" he asked apprehensively. Dreading the ordeal that they were about to endure, he could not think of anything else that they could do before the spiders came down on them, but he was hoping the Ayan would.

"Yes," Ipec said. He dipped his finger into the honey they had collected. A sticky glob of it sat on his fingertip. "Rub the honey around the slits for your eyes and nose. It will keep the spiders away. They do not like the smell." When Ipec put his finger closer to Mentor's mouth he knew what Ipec expected him to do.

"Why would I want to lick *your* finger?" Mentor said sarcastically. "If I have to lick a finger, I would rather lick my own."

"And I would rather have you lick the honey from your finger than mine, so wipe it off mine with yours, swallow it, and be glad I measured it this way. Too much honey will permanently disable or kill you. Only the right amount will put you to sleep and paralyze you for the night. Believe me! You want to sleep and you want to be paralyzed. If even one spider broke through the skin, you would suffer horribly. If you sleep, you will not know the spiders are there and they will not know that you are there. If you do not move, the spiders will not stab you or eat their way through the animal skin. If everything goes well, they will not bother us at all."

"They bother me already," Mentor said. "They are almost all the way down." He tried to sound stoic, but he did not feel that way.

"Swallow the honey now," the chief said. "It takes a little time to work."

He swallowed the honey and propped himself against the wall of the pit. He watched while Ipec dipped his finger into the honey again and swallowed some of it himself. As they saw the spider horde descend, he willed himself to remain still until sleep and paralysis could set in.

On top of the hide that Mentor had wrapped around himself, a mass of enormous, round, hairy bodies swept toward him. Some crept toward his face.

He had never seen anything as grotesque as these spiders, not even in his worst nightmares. Their thick strong legs were covered with black and white stripes on top. Underneath they were red. At the end of the spider legs, sharp claws protruded from the tips in thick brushes of hair.

On top of these legs were the black spider bodies. Each spider body had a thick white dorsal stripe that extended down the middle of its back. In the center forward part of each attacker was a huge eye framed by a white ring. Around this ring were several pairs of fiery red eyes. These smaller pairs of eyes burned brightly in the darkness of the pit. They moved side to side and up and down in a search and destroy kind of motion. The spiders were altogether horrifying.

But the most disturbing things were their behaviors and the sounds they made. Each time the spiders stopped and reared up on their back legs, they made a low hum. This hum became a buzz. That buzz became a whistling shriek. As frightening as their aggressive posturings and their hunting sounds were, there was one more thing about them that filled him with dread—their long yellow fangs. Some of these fangs pointed sideways, but others pointed down like a snake's, and though he tried to believe that the spider army would not sense his body under the thick hide, he imagined the terror he would experience if any soldiers did.

If they did sense his presence, they would stab their way through his protective covering. They would sink their fangs into his body. They would shoot enough venom into him to render him powerless and devour him while he was still alive to witness his own agony. They were fierce.

As these fierce, hand-sized bodies clawed over every part of the animal hide that protected him, he closed his eyes. He did not want to see any more of the wriggling spidery mass. He did not want to feel the painful, fatal fangs of the spiders if they pierced the hide. He thought of his grandfather and of the One his grandfather believed in and to whom he prayed. He also prayed—for the sleep that would make him unconscious of the spider's presence and for the paralysis that would keep him still so they would fail to detect him.

He woke up in time to see the last few spiders moving back up the vines. They were on their way to another day of feeding in the bright morning light. Through slits in the heavy hide he watched and waited for the last one to go. Then he recalled the dream he had had. He wondered if his grandfather's God had given it to him. He threw off the hide and shook Ipec awake.

"I had a vision last night. In it, I saw myself touching some hot surfaces where we were digging."

"My people believe that dreams can be important," Ipec said. "What do you think your dream means?" He rubbed his eyes and waited for an answer.

"Hot rocks might mean we are digging toward interior lava flows—that we are digging deeper into the hill instead of towards the outside of it."

"Let us see," Ipec said. He started digging next to Mentor again in the spot where they had been tunneling and found two very hot rocks. When the Ayan gave them to him, he grinned with satisfaction. They threw themselves against the opposite wall from where they had been digging and started another tunnel.

They dug for hours. Mentor did not know how close they were to the outside of the hill when the sun started to set. Above the sky darkened. Thunder crashed and lightning crackled. In the middle of a furious torrential downpour, the pit began to fill with water. The spiders started to come down.

When the water reached his knees, Mentor knew that hides would not keep them alive any longer. As the first few spiders floated toward him, he knew that he and Ipec would drown painfully in this terrible hole under the ground. Then, unexpectedly, as thunder rumbled and lightning sparked the air right above them, he heard another sound—a roar and a whoosh.

In the roar, the wall they had been digging through gave way against the pressure of the water and Mentor found himself drenched on the ground outside of the vine covered hill.

He jumped up and scrambled away from the opening that the flood had made. Ipec was by his side. Together they inspected the ground around them. It was covered with a mass of dead, drowned spiders. Taking no chances that any spiders might still be alive even though they appeared to be dead, Ipec stabbed each spider body with his knife, slit each venom sac, and collected the poison. Mentor did the same.

When they had collected as much venom as they could carry, he pointed to a mountain in the distance and smiled. "I have paid attention to our surroundings," he said. "I recognize that lake. Across it and just a short distance away is Takal's mountain. Are we ready to go there to meet my old friend?"

"We are ready," Ipec replied. "We have collected enough to make any weapon more powerful. We will use these poisons against any Zaagote or tracker who attacks us or tries to keep us from rescuing our loved ones. It is time to go and see your wonder-working teacher."

Mentor's smile became a wide grin. "This time the master must follow the slave. We are leaving the land of the spiders."

Chapter Eighteen

⌘

Bridge of Flames

Clouds clung to the mountain and floated past Mentor. In spite of the heavy cloud cover, he was grateful for the horses that the villagers at the bottom of the mountain had lent to them. As he climbed through the dense cloud curtain on horseback, he looked over his shoulder from time to time and stared into the mist until he saw Ipec climbing up behind him.

As they trekked higher, the clouds thickened. At this dangerous altitude, he stopped many times to make sure that he could still see Ipec and that Ipec could still see him. In the dense atmosphere, he had to search for his companion through the clouds that kept wrapping themselves around the dark mountain peak.

Patting his horse to calm him, Mentor spoke to the animal often during the difficult climb. He and Ipec did not stop. They inched upwards another thousand feet toward the Jalca Ledge. That was where Takal lived whenever Zaagotes and trackers made it too dangerous for him to live anywhere else. There, in a stone complex of twelve tombs built into the high rock cleft of the northern cloud rain forest, Mentor would find his teacher and his friend safely hidden.

The perpetual humidity of the clouds created a ghostly, dimly lit world. The clouds usually set in by the afternoon. The visibility was practically zero. The Jalca Ledge remained invisible to eyes not trained to look for it.

As even heavier clouds slid down over the mountain and curled around it, he could still hear the sounds of trackers following them. In spite of the proximity of these hunters, the trackers could not see them. However, because this part of the path was where the thick brush and mist camouflaged sheer drop-offs, the danger of falling had greatly increased.

The wet mist shrouded the ancient trail until it was nearly invisible. Mentor searched for the landmarks that Takal had made him memorize. He could not find them. Though he knew the way to the tombs without these landmarks to guide him, the deep chasms between the peaks were as dangerous to him and to Ipec as they were to Zaagotes or trackers.

The heavy air absorbed the sound of their horses' hooves as they plodded upward, but it did not muffle the periodic howling noises from the hunters below them. He listened and wondered what type of trackers were coming after them, until the sickening sound of a wild tumble, the clatter of hooves, and a terrified wail from his horse pierced the air.

In that same instant, he found himself dangling over the empty space into which his horse had disappeared. All he could hear was the pounding of his own heart. With his arms around tree branches that he had grabbed when his horse plummeted through the impenetrable cloud cover, he tightened his grip on the limbs above his head.

He did not know how deep the abyss was. He did not want to know. His horse had landed so far below him that he did not hear the animal's life end. The dense, murky cloud cover was not his fault, but he blamed himself for the animal's death. He knew that he should have been more focused on the climb than on the trackers howling below them.

While he was still hanging in the branches of the tree, he knew what Ipec would have said about listening to the trackers below instead of concentrating on what he was doing. He wondered where Ipec was. He stopped wondering when other howls, wails, and shrieks from the persistent trackers told him that they were approaching. He had to stop thinking about his mistake with the horse, and about Ipec, and decide what he should do next.

He wanted to call out to Ipec but he knew that his voice would alert the trackers to their exact positions. He quickly managed to climb the tree which held him. Soon he saw the almost invisible trail in front of Ipec's horse from his perch above. The horse snorted below him, but he could not see Ipec. The intermittent howling, wailing, and shrieking that had been somewhat distant, sporadic, and muffled, was now piercing.

As the trackers approached, Mentor stared at the thicket to which Ipec's horse was tied. He dropped down, untied the horse from the hedge, and re-tied it to the tree where he had been hiding. He wanted to push his way through the forest wall without disturbing the animal. The path was overgrown, but it was still there. He remembered how narrow it was and how lethal the fall would be if he stepped too far to the right or left.

Had Ipec fallen? It was a possibility. There was still no sign of the Ayan. Pushing his way a little deeper, he finally bumped into the chief. He was relieved to hear his voice.

"If the tracker goes for the horse, I'll shoot from here," Ipec whispered. As the howling grew louder, the chief held a venom-tipped arrow in place and knelt in a firing position. He stiffened at Ipec's sudden move.

"Don't budge too far to the right or left," he said. "The path is narrow; you will fall off."

"Thank you," Ipec replied. "A slave should remind his master of important things. And where will you be?"

"In the tree. When the first tracker goes for the horse, you will be able to shoot without being seen from where you are. I will stay hidden in the tree above; that will allow us to attack from two directions." Mentor did not wait for Ipec's approval; he climbed into the branches above the horse, aimed his own poison arrow, and waited.

While he waited, he stared into the mist and listened intently, but all was silent. Why had the howling stopped? He would have liked to believe that the trackers had gone away, but he knew better. He had a different theory. These hunters were higher ranking Zaagote predators, trackers more intimidating than those they had met before, and different—another breed entirely.

He was not sure how intelligent these trackers were, but he was sure that they knew how to frighten the hunted upon approach. One of their strategies involved creating a debilitating form of fear, a paralysis of terror that made victims powerless to fight or to run away.

It was an effective strategy. The constant howling of the trackers was unnerving, but their silence now was not evidence of their withdrawal; it was the next step in their process of intimidation.

Finally, he saw a vague form slithering along the ground towards the horse. While it approached, he wondered if it was a snake or an animal. Heavy mist swirled around the tracker and around him where he sat in the topmost part of the tree. He caught only fleeting glimpses of the strange creature through the leaves. This quick look revealed a large muscular creature covered with gray fur.

Though he thought there were at least two trackers, he only saw one as it crouched a short distance away from the horse. When the creature started howling again, this time in a low wail, the cloud cover lifted a little. The horse neighed frantically and pulled at the rope to escape from the spot where it was tied. The tracker remained out of the horse's sight and grew quiet again. Now it crouched in silence under a low growing leafy cover and stared at the horse again. By the time it emerged from its hiding place, the result of its invisible intimidation had brought about the desired hysteria.

While the silver tracker stared at the crazed horse, a sadistic grin spread slowly across its broad face. It clearly relished the horse's frenzy, but the enormous cat was in no hurry to complete the kill. It had some form of evil intelligence, a nefarious mind that allowed it to enjoy the terror that its presence inspired. This tracker enjoyed the pre-kill terror as much if not more than its victim's death. The hunter had a broad body with red eyes shaped like vertical slits, but it was different than the other cat-like trackers that he had seen. It was bulkier and its tail captured Mentor's attention. Long and spiked, ending in a hard, round, heavy knob, the tail was a formidable weapon. When the cat lifted the knob, he knew that the moment of attack had come.

From its crouched position the cat sprang at the horse, but before it could do any harm, Ipec's arrow flew out of the thicket and penetrated the cat's face in a spot between its eyes.

After the unusual, feline tracker dropped to the ground at the horse's feet, the horse calmed a bit and his own breathing slowed, but before he could reach normal respiration, another cat, slightly bigger than the first, took the first tracker's place. He expected Ipec to kill this one too, but when Ipec did not fire, he knew that something was terribly wrong. Before he could figure out what, the horse rose into the air on its hind legs and came down on the creature with striking blows until it was lifeless on the ground.

Where was Ipec? What had happened to him? Mentor felt panic rising inside of him. He thought about climbing out of the tree. He wanted to go into the thicket to look, but he did not want to expose his hidden position in the tree, or lead another tracker to the place where he had last seen the chief.

As a third and even larger cat appeared, Mentor felt that he had made the right decision, but when the horse yanked free from the tree in a fit of hysteria, the tree split in half before he could fire.

His half of the tree broke free from the other half and crashed against the side of the cliff; before it snapped away and plunged into the bottomless gorge below, Mentor grabbed the thick vines that grew along and over the edge and pulled himself toward them.

In the part of the tree that was still standing, the enormous tracker hovered above the place where he held on and howled at him. It wanted to climb down and snap his neck in its powerful jaws, but when it saw no way to descend without plummeting into the abyss below, the cat's eyes narrowed. After it finally disappeared inside the thick brush that surrounded the tree on the cliff's edge, he knew the cat was still there, but Ipec's words kept passing through his mind: *Keep your mind on what you are doing now. Then figure out what to do next.*

These were his thoughts, but there was still no sign of Ipec. He had to find the Ayan. He hoped that Ipec was somewhere nearby and still alive. He could not see anything but clouds. He hung on to the vines that grew from the cliffside in a death defying grasp. Sensing that Ipec needed his help, he stretched his hand out to the right and felt a stronger vine there.

He decided to stretch his foot out too. Under it he felt a very narrow ledge. He pushed on it a little to see if it was solid. After he was sure it was, a plan began to form in his mind. If he could pull himself far enough around the side of the cliff, he might be able to climb back up on the other side, surprise the cat by attacking it from behind, and kill it.

In a steady, sideward pulling motion, Mentor dragged himself along until he could execute his surprising back side offensive. How long it took him to pull himself all the way around the ledge to the far side of the cliff, he did not know. It took him almost as long to find a way back up the cliff without being seen. When he finally reached the top, he took a breathless peek over the edge.

While he stared at the back of the huge cat now sitting in the tree, waiting to see if he would try to climb back up from the place where he had disappeared, he understood why the horse was still alive. His theory about some trackers having an evil intelligence that directed their hunt was correct. This cat was not interested in the horse any more than the other had been.

These trackers had made it appear as if they were ready to kill the horse in an attempt to draw Ipec and Mentor into the open. The more he thought about this, the more certain he became that he had made the right decision by moving around to the other side of the cliff to attack the cat. When Ipec's arrow flew out of the thicket to protect his horse earlier, the cats had succeeded in discovering where he was. Mentor knew he had to keep his location hidden from the tracker until the last moment.

He had just reached this conclusion when he spotted yet another giant cat with its teeth fastened around Ipec's leg. It was dragging Ipec's motionless body behind it. Suddenly the evil intelligence of the cat and its strategy meant nothing. Was Ipec still alive? Could he save him?

Aiming one of the venom dipped arrows at the cat, Mentor fired and struck it between the eyes. Still holding Ipec's leg in its teeth, it dropped to the ground and did not move. Then Mentor fired at the cat in the tree. Before it could turn to see who had fired at it from behind, it fell out of the tree and disappeared through the mist into the abyss below.

He pried the cat's jaws from Ipec's leg. As Ipec lay bleeding in his arms, the chief's breathing was shallow. His blood was everywhere. Takal's hideaway was not far, but he had to make a tourniquet to stop the bleeding before he could move him. He could hear the sounds of other cats coming closer.

While the purring noises vibrated louder and the terrible mewling assaulted his ears, he put the tourniquet in place, but Ipec was still unconscious. They would die here unless he could find a way out. As he started to lift Ipec on to the horse, he remembered the advice that the Ayan had given to him when he'd faced the snakes. With nothing to lose and everything to gain, he decided to pray.

Suddenly Takal appeared in the mist. The sage had always been an imposing figure, but he had never looked more impressive than he did now. In his dark gray robe, he came toward them in long silent strides. When he reached them he put his towering staff down, helped position Ipec onto the horse's back, and stared into the animal's face with his dark gray eyes. He quieted the frightened steed with a few words spoken in an ancient language that Mentor did not understand. Then he turned toward Mentor, put his hand on his shoulder, and whispered in his ear. "The path we will follow is even narrower than the one I taught you to use. Stay right behind me."

As Takal led Ipec's horse back into the dense cloud cover from which he had appeared, Mentor kept his eyes on a small piece of white rope that secured the waist-long braid dangling in the middle of Takal's back. Because Takal wore gray and even rode a gray horse to better blend in with the fog and mist around him, it was hard to keep him in sight when he was riding or when he was walking like he was today.

Although Takal completely matched his murky surroundings, Mentor realized that he had not come to them out of thin air. He had arrived on another path. Mentor was unfamiliar with this approach to Takal's hideaway.

Nothing but thin air bordered the rocky path on both sides. On either side all Mentor could see were clouds and mist, but he knew that under the clouds and mist was the bottomless, rocky gorge. They finally reached a bridge made of ropes and wooden planks. The swinging planks rattled in an increasing wind, but Takal turned and spoke to him above the rattling.

"Trade places with me. Lead the horse over the bridge before the storm is upon us. Go quickly. I will follow, but first I have to be sure that no tracker will live long enough to lead anyone back to this place."

Before he handed the lead to Mentor, Takal placed a hand on the horse's heart and whispered one word—"Courage." After this spoken word, the horse calmed down.

The bridge swayed in the wind. The sound of thunder rumbled through the gorge. Lightning flashed around them, but Mentor kept talking to the horse the way his grandfather had taught him to do during storms. He didn't know how the one word Takal had spoken had calmed the horse enough to make him move, or if his own words were adding to the animal's calmness, but he was able to keep the horse moving forward until their destination was in sight.

As soon as they reached the other side safely, he led the horse into a small cave that appeared in front of him and tied him securely to a rocky post. Then he raced back to the bridge. When he was on it again, already half way to the middle, he saw Takal standing at the midpoint. Running toward his old teacher, Mentor drew an arrow from his quiver and prepared to defend him. Without turning around to look at him, Takal stretched his arms straight out in opposite directions. Then he lowered them until they were flat against his sides and yelled "Stop!"

"You must not use an ordinary weapon today, my young friend." When Takal shouted above the wind, his back was still toward Mentor. He was still facing the direction from which they had just fled, but Mentor knew his teacher was directing him. He strained to hear every word the wise man said. "Using a familiar weapon is not the way we will fight evil today." After he finished speaking, the first cat-like beast came onto the first wooden plank of the bridge. The tracker was still a distance from where Takal stood, but close enough for Mentor to see him glaring at the challenge that Takal had just made.

Like the other cats, this leader was tremendous in size, evil eyed, and muscular. Its large yellow and red eyes, its sharper and longer fangs, and the thick black stripe that ran from its brown nose all the way down its broad gold back distinguished it from the rest. Once more Mentor reached for his quiver to pull an arrow out. Again Takal spoke to him as if he could see the defensive move that Mentor was making behind him.

"Oh, my dear apprentice, I already told you that no common weapon will do what needs to be done today. If you act now, many of the beasts will survive. We must make sure that none do. We must preserve the sanctity and the secrecy of this place. Just do what I do and all will be well."

With the arrival of the second tracker on the bridge, Takal took another step back. Mentor did the same. This continued until the bridge was filled with too many cats to count. Then Takal spoke once more. "The number is complete. There are thirty-seven cats on this bridge."

"How do you know?" Mentor asked. "We can't see all the way to the other side. The cloud cover is too heavy." Staring into the thick black fog that kept rolling on to the bridge with the cats, Mentor saw only those closest to them.

"Trust me. I am certain," Takal replied calmly. "Now listen very carefully. I am much older than you are. I cannot run as fast, but you were created to be a runner by someone who knew this moment would come. I am going to walk all the way to the safe side of this very long bridge and leave you here. As soon as I am safely there, on the other side, I will whistle. When I do, run toward me with your knife in your hand. When you reach me, I will be holding my knife. I will cut the rope on my side. You will cut the rope on yours, and these cats will disappear forever."

Mentor pulled his knife from its sheath, faced the cats bravely, and held his weapon in readiness while Takal walked to the other side. On the swaying bridge, the cats crept cautiously closer.

The storm pounded the shaking bridge. The cats shrieked as they inched closer, but he listened for Takal's whistle. In the blowing wind he found it hard to stand up, but he was determined to run as fast as he could when Takal's signal came. Then, finally, he heard it, a distinct and unmistakable, high-pitched note in one of the brief pauses between the noisy sounds of the storm.

While the unusual high note continued, he pivoted and ran, but he fell. He sprang to his feet but when he stood up, the cat closest to him on the bridge leapt through the air and landed right behind him. As the cat's huge paws stretched toward him, a bolt of lightning hit the small space between the cat and him.

With that bolt came momentary blackness, but when he opened his eyes the bridge behind him was on fire. Behind the fire, the cats shrieked and pawed the air to get to him. Jumping up, Mentor pulled out his knife and ran from the furious trackers to the other side. As soon as he was there, he joined Takal in cutting the ropes that held the sides of the bridge until only a sliver of rope on each side remained.

While he was still slicing the rope on his side, Mentor looked up in time to see two huge cats jump through the fire, but before the cats could reach him or Takal, they severed the last threads. Thirty-seven cats perished. They fell into the bottomless gorge on the bridge of flames.

Chapter Nineteen

⌘

Terrible Transformations

They hurried away from the bridge of flames. Takal guided the horse through the narrow opening in the rocks that led to his hiding place. Mentor followed.

Inside the outer entrance to the tombs, Takal pointed to the litter that leaned against the rock wall. As they slid Ipec gently off the horse's back, Mentor supported his arms and Takal supported his legs. Gently they placed him on the litter and carried him deep inside. When they reached the innermost chamber of the tomb complex, Takal pointed to a flat stone slab in the center of the room. This slab served as a treatment table and an altar where Mentor had often seen Takal work and pray.

Ipec's blood soaked the gray stone slab and dripped over the side. Mentor believed in Takal's abilities, but he did not know if Takal could bring someone who appeared to be dead back to life. Takal had many extraordinary talents, but he did not think resurrection power was one of them.

"The healing arts have very little to do with someone's recovery when the wound is this serious," Takal said. "Faith has everything to do with it. If you don't believe in divine intervention, step away. Your unbelief will hinder my efforts." Mentor wanted to believe that a positive outcome would occur, but he had never seen anyone lose so much blood. He wanted to believe that Ipec would live, but he did not see how anyone, even a gifted healer like Takal, could save Ipec's life. He hated feeling the way he did, but he had no faith for Ipec's recovery. When Takal gave him a penetrating look, he acknowledged his faithlessness by stepping into an adjacent chamber. There he sat down on another stone slab. He was close enough to see Takal's back as he bent over Ipec's body, but far enough away to keep unbelief from poisoning the atmosphere of faith so vital to healing.

Takal stood between him and Ipec, but he could see the healer's hands flying over boxes, jars, and vials until he found the one he was looking for. He brought this vial close to Ipec's lips, gently parted them, and poured a few drops in. After that Mentor watched in awe as Takal's steady fingers threaded the long needles that he would use to sew Ipec's leg back together again.

While Takal closed the wound, Mentor heard him pray out loud. It was the way he always prayed when he worked on someone so seriously wounded. In the soft glow of the candles that lit the inner room, his old friend bent over Ipec's leg for a long time and repeated the words he said each time death was about to raise its voice in a victorious roar.

"Oh Thou who art plenteous in mercy to all those who call upon You, have mercy on Ipec," Takal said quietly. As his teacher kept saying these words, Mentor wanted to believe that there was a God and that he was merciful, but when he thought about what had happened to his father, to his mother, to Adamis, and to Ben Zarek, these heart-breaking things always got in his way.

Sometime during the mercy prayer he fell asleep. When he woke up Ipec was alert, sitting by the fire. While Takal was telling Ipec that he would soon be completely well, Ipec responded by nodding. With a gleam in his eye Takal turned towards Mentor, nodded, and spooned a thick, creamy soup into a bowl that he handed to him. Then he poured more of the same soup into a bowl that he held in front of Ipec and gently spoon-fed him.

"You are weak," Takal said to Ipec, "but after you drink this soup, you will be strong. Mentor will be too. Now both of you listen! I know what you are thinking about. I saw it in a dream, just like I saw those thirty-seven cats. If you and Ipec leave soon, you will reach Keldac before the Zaagote day of high sacrifice, but we must make a plan to get you two safely into and out of Zaeg. I have been making crazy plans all of my life, and for that some call me a lunatic, but that is how Mentor and I became close, isn't it my fine friend?" he said as he turned toward Mentor and gave him a proud nod of approval. Takal waited for Mentor's nod of agreement before he went on. With this nod, Mentor's heart beat a little faster. He considered what kind of risks the crazy plan might involve.

"By taking some risks and making some bold moves, Mentor and I have succeeded in achieving what only few in life have ever achieved—a deep and lasting friendship and successful results from our experiments." He put his hand on Ipec's shoulder, paused, and smiled before he went on. "Now three of us have a chance to do what the two of us have done before, if you are willing, if we work together." While he watched the Ayan nod his own agreement with what they were about to do, he swallowed his soup as fast as he could. He couldn't wait to ask the next questions.

"What kind of crazy plan will it be this time, and what bold moves will it require us to make?"

"A plan that first involves the study of a map," Takal said excitedly. "Not an ordinary map, but an ancient map that will get you and Ipec into and out of Zaeg alive." As Takal turned toward Ipec, he placed his hand on one side of a very large scroll which he began to unroll.

"You, Ipec, my brave Ayan patient, will hold this side of the map," Takal said, "and you, Mentor, my reluctant geography student, will hold the other." Takal traced his finger along a dark black line as he spoke. "This path will lead you to the desert. There you will join one of the many Gorban caravans that travel to the Zaagote fortress of Keldac where the citadel of high sacrifices is located." Both he and Ipec opened their mouths to speak at the same time, but Takal put his finger on his lips to stop them and continued.

"The Gorbans belong to a tribe that maintains its independent status by taking no sides in the Zaagote war against us. They also supply the

Zaagotes with the desert salt that the virus affecting them causes their bodies to crave. In return for Gorban neutrality, and for the salt, the Zaagotes allow the Gorbans and those who travel with them into the citadel to trade. Once you are with the caravan, you will blend in with pilgrims who go to the citadel to watch the sacrifices or with the strange traders who go there to do business."

"But we cannot go as we are," Ipec said. "Everyone is hunting for us."

"True," Takal said. "That is where one of the bold moves I spoke of comes in, and now to initiate that bold move, it is time to try the special drinks that I have created." As Takal spoke, Mentor saw sparks of excitement in his teacher's eyes, but he also saw concern. "When I took apart my first Zaagote and my first tracker," Takal said, "I knew that someday someone would need the blood and the body fluids that I drained and preserved from each and every one. I hoped that someday all of my hard work would help somebody. I did not know there would be two somebodies or that they would be my very own assistant and his friend," Takal said giving them a serious look.

"Ipec," Takal said without pausing long enough to allow either of them to interject, "because your size and shape are already similar to a Zaagote's size and shape you will be the Zaagote master, and Mentor, my young protégé, will be your tracker." Mentor stiffened.

"I do not want to be the tracker," he said. "Trackers are slaves to their Zaagote masters. I have been Ipec's slave long enough."

"Ipec is larger and a more experienced fighter than you," Takal said. "You must make an impression in the challenges that precede the sacrifices if you want to be invited to them, so he must be the Zaagote, but as his tracker you will have special abilities that Ipec will not have. You will be stronger than a bull and you will be fast, very fast. You will also be able to see, hear, and smell things from greater distances than he can. When Takal finished, an enormous grin had spread itself across Ipec's face.

"Since I am not only bigger, but better looking than you are," Ipec said, "you are the logical choice for a tracker," he added pointing to

Mentor. "Making you ugly will not be a problem. Takal already has a lot to work with. Making you a tracker with special ability to find and kill whatever you track will be the challenge."

Though Mentor had been worried about whether or not Ipec really would be his true self again, the Ayan's sarcastic comments about the tracker role that his slave would have to play convinced him that he already was.

In spite of the disappointment over his repugnant role in Takal's plan and Ipec's sarcasm, Mentor felt like laughing. He carefully concealed his happiness over Ipec's recovery, especially the fact that the master he had once resented was also someone he now cared about. To cover the sense of relief and joy that Mentor felt over Ipec's return to life, he decided to respond with a jibe of his own.

"Some Zaagotes are uglier than the trackers who serve them," he said making his tone as nasty as he could. "Do not be too sure about which one of us gives Takal a real opportunity to make someone a monstrosity," he added. He was determined not to give Ipec the last word, but he was not surprised when Takal put an end to their insults.

"Do not joke about what you are about to do," Takal said solemnly. "Transformations are serious business. If you transform too often, you will die. If you are in a transformed state too long, you may remain that way and never be able to change back. Do you still want to go to Zaeg as a Zaagote and a tracker? Do you still want to attempt this rescue?" Takal paused and waited for Ipec and Mentor to nod their assent. As Mentor did, he decided it would be a good time to ask the all-important question.

"How do we change back to our true forms?"

"When you drink the special mixture that I have created, you will sleep," Takal replied. "While you are sleeping, I will sew sacs into the gum lining above your teeth and all around the insides of your mouth.

When you want to transform from a Zaagote state or a tracker state to a human state, you will use the sharp tips of your new and pointed tongues to puncture the sacs on the right sides of your mouths. When you want to change from your true forms into your foreign bodies, you will puncture the sacs on the left with a finger." After Takal finished speaking, he paused for a long time and waited for them to change their minds. When they didn't, he spoke again.

"Before you drink," Takal said with a worried look, "understand how life-changing and life- threatening what you are about to do really is. Ayans were never meant to be Zaagotes and humans were never meant to be trackers. It has taken years to perfect the fluids that will change you into a Zaagote and a tracker, and to perfect the antidotes that will change you back, but I have never done anything this drastic before to anyone and I am not sure exactly how these changes will work. Remember, there will be unanticipated side effects in the way your voices come out, in your senses, and in other ways that we cannot foresee. You will be risking your own lives in every way. Are you both sure you still want to try?"

After they nodded their final assent, Takal handed each of them a large wooden mug. Then he pulled open the cover of an enormous chest on which he had been sitting. When he took out impressive looking armor and handed it to Ipec, he looked proud.

"Not all Zaagotes wear armor, but this armor belonged to someone in a high ranking, royal family. I took it off one of the Zaagotes that we carried away from the battlefield to study. If you wear it, you will look formidable." Then Takal reached into the chest a second time, pulled out a huge saddled harness, and held it in front of Mentor, but this time he laughed.

"And this contraption is one I took from a giant tracker who died in the unknown lands. It is a mysterious device that I have altered. It will fit your tracker body perfectly, but when you change to a human shape, it will become light and flexible. It will wrap itself around your neck or body. It adheres and adjusts to any form and to whatever it carries. Wear it. Inside the pouches you will find firestones and provisions to nourish you. You will be able to hang quivers full of your specially prepared arrows and other weapons from the hooks. I've put my special elixir in a vial in this pocket. Use it sparingly. Too much, too often, can be lethal. There are also healing medicines inside the leather pockets sewn all the way along the bottom. You may need them."

"You cannot expect me to wear that," Mentor said inspecting the harness. "It looks heavy and uncomfortable. How will it be able to adjust? How will I be able to move fast enough in it?"

"The harness works mysteriously as I told you. Trust my words. It will adhere and adjust its shape," Takal said. "If you turn out to be as big, as strong, and as fast as I think you will be, wearing the harness and carrying the extra things you will need will feel like nothing at all and you will fly like the wind in it. Now drink up."

"This smells terrible," Mentor said as he held the mug closer to his lips.

"No worse than mine," Ipec added.

"Drink it all," Takal said first putting his hand on Mentor's shoulder, then on Ipec's, and then back to Mentor's. "Console yourself with this thought—even though Ipec will be the master and you will be the slave, he will be as hard to look at as you, and he will suffer just as much. Although transformations are my specialty, they are never easy, especially transformations I have never done before."

"You should become the ugliest Zaagote that ever was," Mentor said as he faced Ipec, pinched his nose shut, and drank. Lowering the cup from his lips, he added, "someone with looks like yours has a head start on the road to becoming a truly repulsive beast. No female, Zaagote or otherwise, will ever admire your body. You will achieve a true keep away status no matter what you are."

"Compared to me, slave," Ipec retorted, "you have no looks at all. When it comes to a keep away status, all will make a wide path around the spot where you stand so they don't get close enough to smell you."

"For both of your sakes, I hope you are right," Takal said in a somber tone. "I hope that you will both be the most magnificent forms of each specimen. I also hope that you will return to this mountain before it's too late to change you back to your true forms. If you don't return here in time, you will never be free from these great and terrible transformations."

Chapter Twenty

⌘

The City

Except for some initial trouble breathing, they survived Takal's life threatening transformations very well. Though they had left Takal only three days ago, they were already approaching the desert. Just beyond the horizon was the caravan that would take them to the Zaagote high citadel where the sacrifices were to be made.

Mentor could not yet see the caravan, but he knew they were getting closer to it. With the wind blowing in the right direction, he could hear the malars grunting, or listen to the caravaners talking about the demon signs that they had seen in the desert, indicators that they said could be seen in the swirl of every dune. According to all of the desert travelers that he had listened in on, omens everywhere pointed to a terrible event that was about to occur in the desert.

From bits and pieces of conversation among the caravaners, Mentor had also learned many other things. The Zaagotes were still planning to kill Ben Zarek, Adamis, and Ipec's family. They also planned to torture Mentor and Ipec in front of Ben Zarek and Ganta if they found them before his grandfather and Ipec's father were slaughtered on the day of sacrifice.

With this torture the Zaagotes hoped to secure specific information from his grandfather and Ipec's father. They wanted Ben Zarek to tell them secrets about the war effort; they wanted Ganta to tell them the name of the Ayan most likely to unite the tribes against the Zaagotes after Ipec and his brother, Yola, were out of the way. About Oliphar, the rumors were vague. That he had escaped and no one seemed to know his location was certain. Everything else was also a rumor or an unfounded prediction.

As Mentor spotted the caravan in the distance, he put what he had learned from these conversations out of his mind. He understood how critical it was for everyone on the caravan to believe that Ipec really was a Zaagote and that he really was a tracker. He was proud of the speed that his new tracker's body had given him, but he hated his new appearance.

He was enormous and ugly. His body was powerful but ungainly. It was larger and bulkier than a horse's body. In many places where a horse's mane would have been, there were black and brown spots. Gray lumps also covered his tan-colored body and black, spike-like hairs protruded from these like sharp knives. According to Ipec, he had the tail and jaws of a wild boar. He also had huge horns, but when he had first looked at himself in the lake just below Takal's mountain, what he really despised was his face.

Rough with warts, his visage was distorted. His head stuck out from the rest of his body on a thick neck. On that same face was a long, protruding, hooked nose. With this nose he could smell almost anything, even when it was a great distance away. Inside his dark purple eye sockets were two white eyes ringed with indigo circles. With these eyes he could see great distances. Under thick eyebrows, these piercing eyes could see equally well during the day and at night. They often fixed themselves on objects without blinking and could discern the smallest of details. His ears were even better. They could detect the slightest sounds. They did this by moving side to side or up and down involuntarily, as if they were in a search mode until whatever was being searched for was detected.

His mouth was as strange as his eyes and ears. Ipec had told him how it lolled open as if he was ready to chew on something in his dreams. When he was awake, his mouth also snapped open unpredictably, ready to devour anything he came upon at any time. These spontaneous behaviors were even more bizarre than the way he looked.

Based on what he had experienced so far, he hoped other behaviors might be closer to normal than his looks were. He felt the same emotions that he had always felt, but he was sure that other involuntary reactions, reflexes, and things that he knew nothing about yet, would eventually pop up and surprise him.

In the present moment, he was worrying about the way he looked more than the way he felt or acted because his body was so different from the one he once had. The only places on his large frame that in any way resembled parts of his once human form were the handless stubs that had replaced his arms. These stubs were above his front legs and were covered with thick dense fur, except for one place on his right stub. This place was bare and had a light layer of human-like hair under which was a patch of human skin.

On this skin a blood red birthmark which he'd had since he was a baby was visible. If hair did not cover the birthmark in just the right way, he knew others would see it, but Ipec combed the hair over this birthmark to make sure that no one noticed it. Somehow the hidden birthmark comforted him. It reminded him that someday he would be human again.

As they approached the Gorban caravan his attention turned away from what he had become, and from the birthmark, and moved toward what he and Ipec were about to do. When he looked at Ipec, he saw the most imposing Zaagote that he had seen thus far, with the exception of the one Zaagote he would never forget—Fade.

Though some Zaagote warriors had chosen to embrace their animal-like states and wore no armor at all, or cast their armor away in the beastlike frenzy that sometimes seemed to overtake them, others chose to wear impressive armor.

Some Zaagotes could not wear the mysterious, shell-like armor due to the thickness of their skin or the scales that protected much of their bodies, but the armor that Takal had given to Ipec before they'd left his mountain hideaway clearly indicated that Ipec was not one of these and that his rank was of the highest order.

The armor proved that he belonged to a noble Zaagote family, part of a royal house. With his helmet, his coat of heavy mail, and the large shield he carried, Ipec was impressive. A battle ax and a spiked ball and chain dangled from the heavy gold weapons' belt that Takal had fastened around the Ayan's waist. An enormous sword protruded from his jeweled sheath. He held a spear in his huge right hand. He looked more imposing than any real Zaagote Mentor had ever seen. Ipec's prowess as a Zaagote could not be disputed. Only one exception challenged him—Fade.

Like Fade, Ipec was a giant. He did not need armor to be impressive. His massive head, his thick arms, his broad chest, and his long, muscled legs gave him the tremendous size that dwarfed most Zaagotes. He did have high ridges on his forehead extending to the back of his neck, and rippling indigo colored rings around his large gray eyes, but these features made his face riveting rather than revolting. Thick hair hung past his shoulders and grew over the top of his enormous chest where even larger ridges were. In many ways those who saw him might have assumed he was one of those Zaagotes in whom the virus had run rampant for many years, but there was something about him that separated him from these horrifying mutations, something that made him magnificent rather than mangled—a quality that Fade also shared.

With every inch of Ipec's newly transformed body declaring his identity to be that of one of the most terrifying Zaagote princes who had ever lived, and with Mentor's own hideous but powerful body declaring him to be not just any tracker, but the most hideous and powerful predator that had ever hunted on their planet, he felt confident about their disguises. He was certain that when they reached the caravan, no one would discover their true identities unless they did something stupid.

In spite of the apparent successes of their transformations, he understood that drawing undue attention to themselves when they joined the caravan would be a bad idea. Immediate attention would only cause other Zaagotes and trackers to challenge them right away. Takal had told him that such challenges often took place when any Zaagote and his tracker joined a caravan because Zaagotes and trackers liked to test their powerful skills against each other in combat. He also knew that Zaagotes made large bets on their favorites in such challenges and that these contests often ended in death.

Though part of him wanted to prove that he and Ipec could win in any type of combat that came their way, he was aware of how foolish it would be to take such a chance. As thrilling as winning such a challenge might be, no thrill was worth the lives of the people they loved and had come so far to save. For that reason he and Ipec decided to join the caravan in the cool shadows of morning when the caravaners would be too sleepy to notice them.

At dawn they quietly joined the end of the line of beasts that were tethered tail to tail waiting for the signal from the caravan leader. Mentor lowered his head so that no one would see it or think that he was challenging anyone. In front of them the caravan boss raised his staff, jerked the rope hard on the lead malorda, and shouted "forward." Pans and bowls clanged and clattered. This cacophony mixed with the "ma gaaa" of the malordas and the sounds of other animals. This was how their desert journey began.

As the long noisy line of Gorban tribesmen, beasts, Zaagotes, trackers, and traders lurched forward, Ipec called Mentor names in the Zaagote tongues which Takal had taught him. He also kicked his sides and shoulders with a thorny stick to blend in with other Zaagote masters who had joined the caravan to make the pilgrimage to the Zaagote high citadel for the sacrifices. It was a common practice for Zaagote masters to beat their trackers to demonstrate their superiority. Competitions in cruelty were frequent and expected.

"Move, filthy beast," Ipec said, always kicking Mentor's sides in the same spots, but each time that Ipec's feet connected with Mentor's sides, the slave shook his body enough to make his master slide into one of the spiky hairs that grew from his back. The thick hide that covered Mentor's sides prevented any serious pain from Ipec's kicks, but he enjoyed it when one of the spikes managed to pierce Ipec's thick

Zaagote skin and he was able to make his Zaagote rider wince. Each time he succeeded, he whispered the word "master" loud enough for Ipec to hear and chortled a chuckle.

"Gologa," Ipec replied. He grunted a Zaagote curse in response to the discomfort caused by his tracker's spikes. The familiar insult made Mentor's thick black lips grin with satisfaction. He recognized the word for what it really was—a disguised form of ouch.

As Ipec slid into one of his spikes again, he wondered if his master had noticed the Zaagote who had been watching them. Now the giant was strutting towards them. Though he realized how intelligent Ipec was, he hoped the Ayan would remember the simple form of the Zaagote high tongue that Takal had taught him before they joined the caravan.

"Is your tracker as strong as he looks?" the stranger said. While the Zaagote circled Mentor's tracker body to inspect it, every hair stiffened. Then the giant studied them both. For a moment Mentor thought he was Fade, but when he did not see the necklace that he had seen in the forest, he knew he was wrong. He did, however, recognize an unmistakable pattern of brown and white markings across the Zaagote's forehead—a pattern common to members of Fade's family—and a familiar scar that ran down the left side of the Zaagote's face. From the descriptions that had been passed on to him by his grandfather and by other scouts with whom he had spoken from time to time, Mentor recognized the Zaagote as Kol Tar, Fade's brother.

"Stronger," Ipec said, giving Mentor the hardest kick that he had given so far before he dismounted. At the same time he gave Kol Tar a fearless look.

Fade's brother nodded approvingly. "Who are you? What is your tracker's name?" Kol Tar sneered while he waited for the response.

"I am Zakar," Ipec replied. "My tracker is Gorig. Who are you and what do you call your tracker?" Ipec spoke arrogantly to further demonstrate his boldness.

"I am Kol Tar. My tracker is Rol."

Knowing that Zaagotes liked to pick on anyone who appeared to be timid, Mentor stomped on the ground, growled, and dipped his head up and down violently as if he was about to attack Kol Tar and Rol.

"Your tracker wants to show how strong he is," Kol Tar said flicking his long tongue in Ipec's direction. He did this until he lobbed a huge glob of spit on each of Ipec's cheeks before he pulled his tongue back. Realizing how his bluff had failed to send the "Leave us alone message" across, Mentor prepared himself for the worst.

Ipec sneered, flicked his tongue just short of Kol Tar's nose, and returned the challenge by spitting back. When the spit landed on only one of Kol Tar's cheeks, he roared savagely. He also drew his spear, but before he could stab Ipec's chest with it, Mentor lunged at him, bit his spear in half, and shoved him back. With the spear still in his mouth, Mentor positioned himself between Kol Tar and Ipec, bellowed, and snorted. Rol, charged, rammed him, and knocked the spear out of his mouth.

Mentor and Rol butted heads and shoved against each other. Rol could not budge him, but the stench from Rol's teeth made Mentor want to throw up. Rol was a huge beast. His extensive horns, his spiked tail, and his protruding spine were not the only features that gave the beast his unique appearance. His gaping jaws, his enormous fangs, and his powerful legs also made him unique. Rol was a nasty opponent. With a growing crowd gathering around them, Kol Tar mounted Rol while Ipec mounted Mentor.

Kol Tar tossed his head back and roared before he spoke again. "I cannot remember the last time that someone returned my challenge with only one glob of spit," he said. "The stakes will have to be higher now. If I win I get to torture your tracker until he dies," the Zaagote said nonchalantly before he roared again. "After that I will kill you." Kol Tar waved the Korban caravan leader over.

"Homur, we are going to fight," the Zaagote said as the leader came to his side. "They," he said pointing at Ipec and Mentor, "will withdraw to that dune. My tracker and I will withdraw to the other one, over there." He indicated two huge mounds of sand. "On your signal we will charge each other. If we survive the charge, we will fight to the death.

Summon the other Korbans. They may want to make bets, as will the other Zaagotes who are with me. Before them my honor was insulted. Before them my honor will be avenged. Agreed?"

"It is not agreed," Homur said calmly.

"Why not?" Kol Tar replied.

"Because we do not have time for this," Homur answered. "There are unknown dangers nearby. Demon signs are everywhere. Some caravans have been completely destroyed. We must keep moving. Your brother gave strict orders to get the salt that we are carrying to the citadel on time. If we are attacked, we will be delayed. Your brother will not be pleased."

Although Homur said nothing more, Mentor felt sure that Kol Tar would not go against his brother's command. He was stunned when Kol Tar picked Homur up with one hand, held him in the air above his head, and thundered at him in a voice that shook the bystanders.

"If we are attacked, we may die, but if you do not agree to my demands, you definitely will. As I recall you also have a wife, sons, grandchildren, and an only daughter who can be made to suffer," he quickly added. Then he pointed to a young girl robed in pink. Her lacy veil covered everything, but her dark blue eyes. Kol Tar paused briefly before he went on, but Mentor could see how much he was looking forward to the next threat.

"I could use more slaves," Kol Tar said, "and I could definitely use a wife," he added in a slightly calmer tone. "So far no one seems to want me, but you dared to defy me and that is why your only daughter will be part of my prize if you fail to comply, or if they lose." After Kol Tar finally lowered the man to the ground, Homur pointed to Mentor and Ipec. Then he pointed to the dune from which they would make their charge before he blew the horn to let the betting begin.

Glad that the dune was as far away as it was, Mentor thundered towards it right away. He could not wait to speak to Ipec, but he delayed until he was sure that no one could hear. "I thought we were going to stay unnoticed a little longer than this," Mentor said.

"We did what any Zaagote or tracker would have done," Ipec replied. "Others were watching."

"Like *you* were watching that girl?" Mentor said, making no effort to keep the jibe about the girl in pink out of his voice.

"I was not watching her. She was watching me—the way all girls of all breeds watch me," Ipec said arrogantly.

"If we win we will save that girl, but she is not your type," Mentor said, hoping to draw Ipec's opinion of Homur's daughter to the surface.

"I do not have a type," Ipec said. "I like all the girls and all the girls like me." Mentor recognized the conceited tone the Ayan sometimes used to hide what he was really thinking.

"The way you look at this girl is different," Mentor said. "Have you, perhaps, seen her without the veil over her face? Is she as beautiful as the gossip on the caravan says she is?"

Ipec kicked him hard, but did not curse him. The Korban priest was approaching. Mentor recognized the insignia on his dark purple robe and on the golden staff he pointed at them when he reached them.

"By the way," the priest said, "the appropriate Zaagote custom of insulting is to lob a glob of spit on each cheek, not on one. By spitting on only one of Kol Tar's cheeks, you announced that he was not only unworthy to fight you, but also that he was unworthy to eat your tracker's dung." Before Ipec could respond, the priest held his hand up to silence him. "My name is Val Azar. I am a seer," he said quietly. "So you do not have to say anything. You do not have to convince me that you are who you pretend to be. I know better."

Before Ipec or Mentor could respond, the priest put his hand up again. "I travel with the caravan to pray a blessing upon it, but now I must bless you so that you will not die. It is against Korban custom to fight until death in the light of the full moons. Our people believe that breaking this custom will bring evil upon us. Zaagotes have no respect for our customs. Also, Kol Tar has refused my blessing. Whoever you both are, whatever you are, will you do the same?"

"We will take all the help we can get," Ipec said dismounting.

As the priest raised his staff, he gave Mentor a penetrating look and spoke. "You must kneel. It is a sign of humility before God. After they knelt, Val Azar began the blessing.

"Whoever would please God and get His blessing must believe that He exists and that He is a rewarder of those who diligently seek him. In the name of God, the benevolent, the compassionate," he said in a deep voice that challenged the silence of the black desert around them, "may you who have come here with a pure heart live long enough to find what you are searching for. May you be guided on the straight path, the path of those blessed, not the path of those who have gone astray."

Mentor and Ipec remained in their kneeling posture, but the priest raised his hands above them and continued praying. While he did this, the howling of the desert wind increased. In spite of Mentor's continuing doubts about a divine protector, he found himself wondering if God was trying to make himself known in yet another critical moment in his life. Was the increasingly strong desert wind His voice? Was the voice telling them God was on their side?

While Mentor considered whether or not the howling wind was a divine and benevolent sign, he heard a hissing sound somewhere near them in the sand. He wondered if Ipec and the priest had heard it, but he did not wonder for long.

"The demons are here," Val Azar said. "You can hear them in the air. If you are victorious over these demons and this Zaagote, some good will come to my people and other people because of you. I know this." Then Homur blew the horn.

"Ah, that is my signal and yours," the priest said. "The bets have been made. The challenge is about to begin. At the next sound of the horn, you must make your charge." Ipec climbed on Mentor's back.

"Wait," Ipec said. "Before you go, can you tell us about the demons?"

"Of the demons I can only tell you that no one seems to know exactly who or what they are. When they come, they kill everyone and everything—malordas, Zaagotes, Korbans, and humans. It does not matter. We have seen the swollen, blackened bodies of whatever they leave behind. I cannot tell you how to protect yourselves from them or how to defeat them. All I can do for you today, I have already done," Val Azar said, but as he started to walk away he stopped, turned around, and shouted back, "but if you ever want to ask my advice in the future, I am only a deep thought away." Before he had time to think about what Val Azar meant by this, Mentor heard the hissing sound again.

The hissing came from more than one direction. He wondered how many demons were there, but when he spotted two large, dome shaped bumps moving just under the sand towards them, he wondered if the hissers always traveled in pairs. In the distance he saw Kol Tar sitting proudly on his tracker, waiting for the final starting horn to blow.

When Mentor heard it, his charge began. Though he had seen others charge both on foot and by riding into battle on all sorts of animals, he had always imagined that his first experience in real combat would be as a man not as a beast carrying a fighter into battle.

As he thundered towards Rol and his master, he readied himself for the collision. He knew their only chance for survival depended on the accuracy of his strike. He had to penetrate Rol's chest with both of his massive horns to protect himself and Ipec. If he lowered his head too soon, he would not be able to see where to strike the chest wall and puncture the heart. For the Ayan's sake, for his own sake, and for the sake of Homur's only daughter, he had to hit the target.

Determined to keep his head up until the last possible moment so that he could see where to thrust, he pounded over the sand at full speed until the distance between him and the other tracker closed, but before he could lower his head and strike, two large worms shot out of the sand and blocked his assault.

The worms opened their mouths to expose fangs with which to strike them, but two large animals with barrel-like bodies shot out of burrows and attacked the worms. As the worms and burrow animals fought, they came between Koltar's tracker and him.

Trying to avoid the battle between these creatures, Mentor thudded to the left, but before he could lower his head in a charge, the wailing sound of a Zaagote horn echoed in the distance. Remembering what the wailing horn meant, he turned and raced Kol Tar's tracker back to the caravan. There many other worms and burrow animals menaced each other and surrounded the caravan. To protect themselves, the Korbans, the Zaagotes, the traders, and the other travelers lit torches. With these flaming torches the defenders formed a wall of fire around the caravan as it inched forward.

Mentor leapt over the flaming ring and landed inside of it. At the same time Kol Tar and his tracker landed next to Ipec and him, but they did not fight. They turned away from each other and fought off the army of worms and burrow animals that were battling each other.

Although more animals from the burrows attacked the worms that had surrounded the caravan, it was clear that the worms far outnumbered them and that the Zaagotes and other caravaners could not expect their assistance to secure a victory.

While Ipec hacked off worms' heads, Mentor kicked the worms and trampled them. Next to them, Kol Tar and his tracker did the same. When morning came and it became clear that the Zaagotes, the Korbans, and the other travelers had won the battle, Kol Tar approached them.

"Your tracker is as fierce in battle as you are," Kol Tar said. "Come to the formal challenge in the temple. If you survive, you can attend the sacrifice as an honored guest." He spoke in a deep rolling voice. "It would be good to kill you with Emperor Vorg and my brother, Fade, looking on." The braggart finished his invitation with a snarling laugh. Then he reached into his battle vest, pulled out a small dagger, and handed it to Ipec as he stood beside Mentor and adjusted his harness.

"Just give this to the guards at the citadel entrance. The dagger will identify you as my chosen opponent and admit you to the innermost part of the temple grounds where the high sacrifices will be offered." Ipec nodded his acceptance, took the dagger, and climbed on Mentor's back. Together they entered the city.

Chapter Twenty-One

⌘

Time to Die

As the caravan trudged closer to Keldac, the Zaagote fortress and high temple, Mentor thought about what it would be like to fight Kol Tar with the Zaagote Emperor, Vorg, and his best assassin, Fade, looking on. He had seen Kol Tar and his tracker in action against the worms. They would be hard to defeat. Would he and Ipec win the combat against this Zaagote and his tracker? If they did, this victory would put them in a position to do what they had come to do—rescue their families.

While the sun was close to setting, he studied the towering stone walls that surrounded the high temple of the citadel. Where, inside of those walls, Ben Zarek and Adamis were being held, he did not know, and though he could not see Ipec's face because the Ayan was riding on his back, he knew that the chief was wondering the same thing about his father, Ganta, and his younger brother, Yola.

The orange sky changed to deep purple as they approached the outer gate, but at the very instant Mentor carried Ipec past the gaping, fanged mouth that formed the outer portal entrance, the purple sky and the pink desert sand that partially reflected the violet color above were swallowed in black. He was grateful for the moonlight and the starlight above, but the darkness made him jumpy.

Ipec was sleeping. His heavy body was spread over Mentor's back. As he trudged forward, Ipec snored loudly. Because Ipec was asleep, he knew he had to stay alert. He forced himself to concentrate by translating the love song that a Zaagote warrior in front of him was singing.

"Kalar Zin, sebut a larna, Kalar Zin avian zewar," the warrior sang over and over. Mentor translated the words as "Come back to me, come back to me, love of my life." The words surprised him. Although meeting Oliphar had made him realize that at least one Zaagote might be capable of feeling something other than hate, the idea that any Zaagote could feel love struck him as impossible.

As he trekked on and the soft melody of the Zaagote's love song echoed through the canyon, he realized something that he had never realized before. No matter how hideous Zaagotes looked on the outside, no matter how cruel some of them were, each one he had had more than a surface contact with was unique and different. Oliphar, Fade, Kol Tar, and now this singer, they all surprised him, but what shocked him more than anything else about them was this—in addition to their brutal ways, they seemed to be capable of other feelings.

How could they have feelings? He pondered this as he carried Ipec down through the deep canyon. Here he noticed many tombs carved into the dry rock. Beyond these tombs he saw walls of stone rising steeply on the left and on the right until a narrow cleft, called the Sar by Zaagotes, revealed the path to the sacred core.

Ahead the Sar narrowed. On each side the walls towered above him. As the Sar twisted and turned, its high walls shut out all of the light except the light from the torchbearers who walked in front of him. Then, abruptly, through another cleft in the rocks, he saw light from huge bonfires illuminating the middle gateway to the Zaagote high temple. Carved out of stone, the ornate pillars of this gate jutted out from the cliff faces into which the temple was carved. They sparkled in glittering shades of rose-colored crystal stones.

From Takal's map of the Sar, Mentor knew that there was only one path from the opening of the outer gateway to the middle gateway; he also remembered that the middle gateway led to the city surrounding the citadel as well as to the temple. While he watched most of the traders, travelers, and Zaagotes who came to observe the sacrifice or to enjoy the festivities move through this dual access point, it was the portal on the left that held his attention. That portal led to the inner citadel and to the arena where he would fight Kol Tar. Perhaps it was also close to the dark cells where the prisoners who were to be sacrificed were kept.

Apart from the emperor's family or invited guests, only Zaagote warriors who identified themselves as combatants passed through this opening. Determined to look as fierce as he could, Mentor pounded toward the entrance in slow ponderous steps and snorted loudly.

"You must be the fighters the rumors have told us of," the Zaagote commander said as he inspected the symbols on Ipec's shield. "We have heard about the challenge between you and Kol Tar. Fade's brother is a great champion and Rol, his tracker, is undefeated so far. Your tracker must be strong and ferocious if you are going to face him. Can I take a closer look?"

When the commander moved around Mentor and smacked his behind, he bared his teeth and growled menacingly. Deliberately allowing a glob of saliva to collect in his mouth, he waited for the Zaagote to pull his lips back and inspect his teeth before he drooled all over his hands, spat on his feet, and bared his teeth again.

The commander shook the excess drool from his hands before he wiped them with a cloth that hung from his belt. Mentor wanted to laugh out loud, but he controlled the urge and stared at the drool on the Zaagote's heavy boots. After that, the Zaagote took a step back.

"Where is the dagger that identifies you as Kol Tar's challenger?" he said suspiciously.

When Ipec handed the dagger to the Zaagote, he laughed. "You get to keep it, but only if you live."

The commander was still laughing while Mentor paused and stared into the dark tunnel in front of him. Ahead he saw a huge arena surrounded by torches and bonfires. Ipec rubbed the back of his right ear and nudged him gently forward. Lifting his head higher, Mentor wondered if his master had developed some type of positive feeling about his slave. Then Ipec bent down and whispered in his ear.

"If we work together, we can win," Ipec said. He dipped his head twice to acknowledge Ipec's words. He also snorted and pawed the ground to demonstrate his readiness. Then he moved from the darkness of the corridor entrance into the blazing light of the arena.

Kol Tar dropped on top of Ipec from somewhere just above the entrance. During the struggle, he tried to knock Ipec off Mentor's back. After Ipec threw him off and he bolted out of the way, Rol thudded toward them from the other side of the arena. He charged with great speed and rammed them two more times before he slowed, turned around, and dipped long enough to allow Kol Tar to get back on. Again the trackers and their riders collided, but Fade's brother and his tracker could not knock Mentor out or knock Ipec off his back.

Rol plowed toward them once more, but this time when he came within striking distance, Mentor bit Rol's right side. Then he rammed the beast the way the beast had butted him. He tried to gore Rol with his horns, but the tracker's hide was thick. Pulling back he thudded toward the far wall of the ring before he turned to attack.

This time as Mentor charged Rol and Rol charged him, Ipec leapt from his place on Mentor's back before the collision. He yanked Kol Tar off his tracker and wrestled him to the ground. Smashing into Rol several times, Mentor turned and thudded closer to the wall behind him. When Rol regained his footing he charged again, but the speed with which Mentor moved out of the way made Rol ram into the stone barrier behind him.

Mentor prepared for another charge while Kol Tar and Ipec hacked away at each other with clavegs, but Rol's horn was so firmly embedded in a huge crack in the stone wall that he could not pull himself out.

Ipec's claveg clanged against Kol Tar's until a gong interrupted their fierce fight. At that moment the emperor's elite guard entered the arena to pull them apart. When a tall Zaagote with long white hair approached Kol Tar, Mentor wondered what he would say.

"I am Lor, the emperor's representative," he said addressing Kol Tar. "This fight is over. Your opponent has won. You have your weapon and you are on your feet, but your tracker is stuck in the wall. Your opponent and his tracker are the new champions." When Lor turned toward Ipec and him, Mentor hoped that what Takal had told them about the Zaagote emperor's new champions was true.

"As the winners of this challenge," Lor announced, "your special role in the sacrifice will be explained before you enter the inner part of the temple. I will see you inside." When Lor withdrew, Ipec dismounted. Kol Tar approached them.

"After the sacrifice I will kill you and your beast," Kol Tar said growling. When he raised his claveg in the air, Ipec grabbed it. He held Kol Tar's arm above his head before he could strike.

"Let us hope you can get Rol out in time to do it," Ipec said pointing to the place in the wall where Rol's horn was still stuck in the stone crevice.

The emperor's elite guard pulled Kol Tar away from Ipec for the second time. After that Ipec climbed on Mentor's back. Together they entered the inner gate. As they passed through it he saw Fade standing in the shadows of the entrance. Every one of the spiked hairs on his body stiffened.

He *did* not look at Fade directly. He carried Ipec past him and stared straight ahead. From the corner of his eye, he caught only a glimpse of Fade's dark face. As he stood next to Kol Tar, Mentor saw fires burning in Fade's eyes.

His molten gaze told Mentor one thing—if Kol Tar did not kill them, Fade would. Mentor was not a mind reader, but he knew what Kol Tar and Fade were thinking—*Soon this new champion and his tracker will pay for their insults. Soon it will be time for them to die.*

Chapter Twenty-Two

⌘

After Them

Mentor carried Ipec over the narrow path that led to the high place. There the captives were to be killed. Along this path the strange faces of Zaagote gods glowered at them under torch lights embedded in the rock walls. Though they had been traveling on the almost totally black, hairline trail for some time, Mentor finally saw a well lit opening ahead. In the middle was a glittering rock wall. Here the names of former champions were cut in the stone.

Because they were the newest champions, their Zaagote names would soon be added to the honored list. How horrified the Zaagotes would be when they realized that, Zakar, their newest champion, and Gorig, his tracker, were their enemies.

He and Ipec occupied the last place in the royal entourage. The sense of satisfaction that he felt at having come so far undetected, and at having penetrated the Zaagote citadel, was only diminished by one thought—it would all be for nothing if they failed to save the lives of those they had come so far to rescue.

In moments this rescue would be possible. Lor had told them how they would have direct access to the condemned. As the emperor's special guests, Lor had given them three distinct duties: to make the final preparations for the sacrifice, to release the catapults that would launch the sacrificial victims onto the wall of blood, and to retrieve the bodies of the victims once the sacrificial executions had been carried out.

The other members of the entourage parted to let the executioners enter a huge amphitheater lit by innumerable torches and bonfires. Ipec rubbed the back of Mentor's right ear. Was it a signal that his master was ready to do the impossible, and that he expected his slave to be ready too? Or was it a final goodbye between a master and his slave?

Mentor wanted Ipec to think of him as more than a slave. He wanted him to think of him as an equal. He had come to respect Ipec and he wanted Ipec to respect him. He had even dreamt about a day when their roles would be reversed. Ipec's size and his experience as a fighter had made him the natural choice for the Zaagote warrior's role. His own size and his own lack of experience as a combatant had made him the natural choice for the tracker's role, but he was not the novice that he had been before he met Ipec. The challenges he had encountered had forced him to grow in every way. He was no longer a beginner or just a follower. He was ready to be in charge.

In spite of his intense desire to lead, he readied himself in response to his master's ear-rubbing signal. Now he did not look to the right or to the left. He kept his eyes on the massive stone steps in front of him. He thought about what he was doing and what he would do once he had carried Ipec to the top of the sacrificial steps. There the Zaagotes expected them to execute their own families on the wall of blood.

As the chosen executioners, it was their privilege to stand next to the victims on the high stone platform where the Zaagote horde below could see them. They would then be expected to release the catapults which would hurl their victims against the wall. Now facing this wall, a wall that Mentor did not want to look at, but had come so far to reach, he held his breath. In front of him, high above the amphitheater, a flat, bloodstained, stone mountain challenged any rescue attempt.

In front of this wall, Ipec sat motionless on Mentor's back. Together they waited for the emperor's nod. While Mentor stared at the long sharp spikes that protruded from the bloody wall, Ipec's huge legs pressed tighter against his sides. The crowd began to chant. When the chanting was replaced by a frenzy of constant roaring, wild howling, and hysterical shrieking, the captives emerged from a small opening in the high rock wall on the opposite side above.

Finally, at the royal nod, four Zaagotes whom he now recognized as the emperor's elite guard, moved from their customary positions behind the black stone slab where their ruler sat. Covered in a heavy black veil that completely hid his form from view, the Zaagote wearing the dazzling golden crown, Vorg, the ruler of all the Zaagotes, stood up.

When Vorg took a few steps toward them, Mentor expected him to speak, but he remained silent. To the emperor's right an enormous Zaagote, completely dressed in golden ceremonial armor and a golden face mask stood holding a silver claveg in the air above his head. To the emperor's left, Kol Tar held a golden shield. On it was a black viper poised to strike. It was a familiar emblem, a symbol that all of the members of Fade's family carried on their shields.

Vorg finally nodded again and lifted his hand to signal the beginning of the execution. The golden giant came toward them. Although Mentor could not see any part of the form beneath the shining armor and the face mask, the tremendous height and girth of the figure told him it was Fade. At Fade's signal, four subordinates almost as large as he was, bowed before him. Mentor recognized these warriors as the elite guard under Fade's command. After bowing to their lord, Fade's warriors bowed before their new champions. Then they started to climb the steps that led to the catapults. The time to act had come. Mentor waited until the giants were a few steps in front of him before he followed.

He placed his huge feet on the broad steps that led to the four catapults from which the captives would be launched against the wall and started to climb. Ipec was still sitting on his back, but he could not feel his weight as they went up. In spite of this sudden numbness, Mentor continued their ascent.

When he finally reached what had appeared from below to be the top step, he realized that he was not standing on a step at all. He was on a broad stone platform where the catapults had been carefully positioned.

From here he saw how easy it would be to launch the victims into the spikes protruding from the wall with deadly accuracy.

While the Zaagotes fastened their captives to the catapults, Mentor's eyes filled with tears. He wanted to whisper words of comfort to Ben Zarek and Adamis, but their handlers stood beside them. Ben Zarek showed no emotion, but Adamis' eyes were filled with fear. When Ipec dismounted and approached his father and his brother, Mentor saw the same anguish in his eyes that he felt in his own heart. Like him, the Ayan also wanted to comfort his loved ones. From their bruised and battered bodies, Mentor could tell how much they had all suffered and how they were suffering now, but he realized what Ipec realized—that in this critical moment, no words of comfort could be spoken, and no form of retribution could be exacted if they wanted to complete the rescue.

They could say and do nothing if they wanted to get their loved ones away from the wall of blood alive, but Mentor understood one other thing. It was something he believed but could not prove—someday, somewhere, there would be another moment, a moment when he and Ipec would not be crippled by enforced silence or inaction, a moment when they would make the Zaagotes pay for all of the pain they had inflicted on Ipec's people, on his own people, and on all of the other inhabitants who lived in his world.

In silence Mentor and Ipec watched until all the Zaagotes withdrew from the gray stone ledge. Then they waited until the elite guards left the platform and moved back inside the opening from which the prisoners had emerged. While the Zaagote masses below them shrieked their approval, Mentor moved his enormous body until his massive form stood between the sharp eyes of the powerful guards and the catapults.

He was keenly aware that his huge body would prevent the guards from seeing anything. He was directly in front of the opening into which they had withdrawn to watch the executions. While Ipec maneuvered behind the catapults to adjust the rings that controlled the angle at which the prisoners would be propelled into the air, he did not move.

In this blocking position, Mentor turned his head toward the opening directly behind him to make sure that the handlers were still inside. Everything was going the way they had planned it until the ring that controlled the angle on the last catapult jammed. While Ipec frantically tried to budge it from its stuck position, the impatient guards started to emerge to see what was going on.

To keep the guards from coming out, Mentor jammed his rear end against the opening. In spite of fierce jabbing from the ceremonial spears that the guards carried, he stayed where he was until Ipec inched the jammed ring into the slot where it needed to be. Some of the spears were starting to penetrate Mentor's thick skin, but he did not move his body out of the way. Grateful for the thick scales that grew over the tough hide on his posterior, he winced when the guards jabbed deeper to get him to step aside, but he maintained his protective position. His massive body totally blocked their exit.

Now he felt pain from the spears stabbing him. Their sharp points broke through the scales. The guards who wanted to come out and check on the progress of the execution were incensed. When the torture reached the point where he thought he could stand it no longer, he wondered how long he could keep these Zaagotes from emerging. The bloody spikes protruding from the wall reminded him that he had to hold on. He had to keep the guards sealed inside of the opening. He did not want them to discover the adjustments that Ipec had made until it was too late for them to do anything about it.

Ben Zarek, Adamis, Ganta, and Yola would not survive if he did not hold his blocking posture. If the Ayan failed to correctly adjust the rings that controlled the catapults, his family and Ipec's family would die. They would hit the wall and be smashed to pieces or speared on spikes instead of landing in the dammed lake behind the great stone barrier. Mentor took one last look at Ben Zarek and Adamis. Then he turned his head in the direction of the emperor's throne and waited for Fade to light the ceremonial fire.

The flame from the torch ignited the tall wooden pyre in front of Vorg. Ipec released the rings. As Mentor watched the captives catapult high above the bloody wall and over it, his heart throbbed in the first uncontrollable thrill of victory. Anxiously, he waited for Ipec to remount. Then he charged away from the opening.

He thundered up the narrow steps that connected the sacrificial ledge with the top of the wall. He had to see if those they had come so far to save had survived. At first he saw no one. Fearfully, he scanned the surface of the lake again, but this time he searched slowly. When he spotted four people bobbing on the surface of the water his heart soared, but the attackers were already coming.

He turned and lowered his head to meet the onslaught. He charged the hunters who were trying to follow. With lightning speed he battered them and knocked them all down. Then, before the last aggressor's body had tumbled to the bottom of the steps, he reversed direction and pounded the rest of the way up the narrow steps with Ipec on his back.

When they reached the top of the wall, he wanted to look down at the Zaagote horde still staring up at the empty spikes in disbelief, but there was no time to gloat. Some in the crowd below definitely thought that the catapults were faulty, especially those who had not been paying enough attention to see him suddenly charge the guards who tried to follow them to the top of the wall. However, those who had seen his lightning charge already realized that they had been tricked. Fade was one of these perceptive Zaagotes. He would come after them.

Chapter Twenty-Three

⌘

Out of Sight

He kept his eyes on the four bobbing heads. He only stood on top of the wall long enough to make sure that he knew exactly where they were. His heart was beating so hard that he thought it would thump right out of his chest. He had seen how weak his grandfather, Adamis, and Ipec's father and brother were. Even if they had survived their wild toss into the lake, he wondered how long they would live in the water. He inhaled deeply before he jumped in. Without pausing for a second breath, he swam toward them as fast as he could.

For a short time he was sure that some would believe that he and Ipec had jumped into the lake to pursue the captives. But it would not be long before all their enemies understood that they were not coming back. Any moment now the Zaagotes and their trackers would appear. In fury they would hunt down the champions who had betrayed them. For the time being Mentor chose to ignore them. He swam toward the four bobbing heads and tried not to think about how fast their pursuers would be, especially Kol Tar and Fade.

Mindful of their adversaries Mentor splashed furiously to reach the swimmers. He was not surprised when they tried to escape. In their eyes he was a beast, a Zaagote tracker, with a brutal Zaagote master riding on his back. In spite of their efforts to get away, he was almost there.

Ipec shouted his father's and his brother's names in the Ayan tongue to identify himself, but they did not respond.

"Tapa, Tapee!" This time Ipec shouted his father's and brother's nicknames. Mentor decided to follow his example.

"Benza! Ada! It's me!" These were the names Mentor had called Ben Zarek and Adamis when he was younger. He had summoned his human voice, but he hadn't used it in so long. It didn't sound the way he wanted it to.

Grateful that his voice could still sound somewhat human, he cried out again. Ipec dove from his back and swam towards his father and brother. Mentor approached Adamis and Ben Zarek. He could see that they were no longer trying to swim away from him, but he panicked when he realized that they were no longer swimming at all. Before he reached them, they disappeared under the water. He dove after them.

The dive took him right where he needed to be. When he opened his eyes under the water, he saw Ben Zarek and Adamis in front of him. They were unconscious. Behind them was an enormous underwater cave. It had been turned into some kind of a holding cell. Heavy bars covered the opening. These same bars were anchored into the rock walls that bordered the cave. They separated it from the rest of the lake by forming a heavy gate. When this gate rumbled and started to inch up, he refused to let himself think about what might be on the other side.

He knew that he had to get Ben Zarek and Adamis away from the gate before whatever was on the other side of it came after them, but he understood that there was no way to pull them to the surface with a tracker's body. He needed arms and legs to do that. Realizing that the moment for transformation had come, he pierced one of the soft pellets that Takal had sewn into his gum with the sharp point of his tracker's tongue. The sweet liquid inside of the pellet trickled down his throat. A jolt of energy shocked his huge body. In the two sharp jolts that followed the first one, his body sizzled.

His eyelids snapped shut. When he forced them open he was thrilled to have a human body again. He saw Ipec beside him. Ben Zarek was wrapped in his large arms. In one long stroke Mentor reached Adamis and grabbed her. While the gate continued rumbling behind them and inched higher, two tentacles shot at them from behind the bars.

From the expression on Ipec's face, he could tell that the Ayan had seen the tall, dark, red-eyed figure staring at them from its watery holding cell. Its tentacles shot toward them again as it yanked furiously at the chain where it was anchored behind the gate, but they had already moved beyond its reach. Before the gate edged any higher, before the creature behind it could break free from the chain and swim out after them, they bolted to the surface with their loved ones and swam to the shore.

"I told my father and brother to go on ahead of us and meet us at the gorge," Ipec said. He kept breathing air into Ben Zarek's lungs until Mentor's grandfather started to breathe on his own. Mentor parted Adamis' lips and desperately, but carefully, revived her in the same way.

They were breathing again, but their hold on life was tenuous. Prior to their near drowning, they had been beaten and starved. He poured a few drops of Takal's elixir into their mouths.

"Look at the bruises and scars," Mentor said. "They are weak. They will not be able to travel away from this place fast enough to escape.

"I know what you are thinking," Ipec replied, "but transformations are too dangerous when not much time has passed between them. You just got your human form back. You should not change back to your tracker state now."

"I can make the change and you must make it too, Mentor answered. "You have to become a man again. Your Zaagote body is too heavy and too big. As a man you will be smaller, lighter, and easier to carry. I'll have to get used to looking at your other ugly face, but there will be plenty of room on my back for you and them once I revert to my tracker body again. In that form, I will be big enough and fast enough to carry all of us away from here in time. There is no other way to escape."

"Wait! We still have a little time. Zaagotes and trackers are not coming across the lake after us yet," Ipec said as he turned and looked across it.

"Not yet," Mentor said, "but they are not our immediate problem. I'm in a human body right now, but I still have a tracker's vision, and I can see something swimming toward us just under the surface of the water. Whatever was behind those bars is free. It's coming and it's fast. If it's a land traveler, our chances of fighting it and getting Adamis and Ben Zarek away from here before Fade and Kol Tar arrive are slim.

Before Ipec could say another word Mentor lifted the sharp point of his tongue until it pierced another small lump that Takal had sewn into the inside part of his cheek. Then he readied himself for the premature transition back to his tracker state. The pain started in his feet. First there was a burning sensation. Then three sharp jolts of energy pulsed upward and exited through the top of his head. As more of the same exploding current surged through his body in powerful waves, his eyes snapped shut again. When he opened them his transformation was complete; so was the Ayan's. Ipec had become a man again.

With these changes completed, Mentor looked back at the lake again. The first thing he noticed was how much closer the shadow under the water was. He did not know what it was, but he assumed that it was some type of tracker. This realization hit him hard. Prior to this he had never seen or heard of an underwater tracker.

"Hurry," he said. "Whatever it is has almost reached the shore." Ipec lifted Ben Zarek and Adamis and fastened them into the harness on Mentor's back. Then he climbed up behind them. As soon as the Ayan secured the straps, Mentor pounded away.

While the dizziness from the transformation subsided, Mentor thudded down a steep path. It led to one of the narrow gorges that Takal had pointed out to him on the map. Because of the precious time they had lost at the lake, their pursuers would soon catch up with them.

Above him, on each side of the path, the boulder-studded hills rose higher. Ahead Ipec's father and brother were waiting for them at the rim of the gorge opening. He hurried toward it. Though his tracker's eyes could see the smallest of details, he could not see around the many rocky bends that curved into the mouth of the gorge when he looked back.

While he was still glancing behind, at the bend closest to them, his legs began to tingle. Somehow this transformation had affected them. Something was happening, but he did not know what. There was no time to think about it. At least his hearing was sharper than it normally was. He could hear the Zaagotes coming. They were still hidden from view, but he knew who was leading the pack. Side by side Kol Tar and Fade were barreling toward them, and perhaps with them, a strange new enemy would arrive, a tracker with water and land capabilities would also descend upon them. He would know soon. They were just out of sight.

Chapter Twenty-Four

⌘

The Constant Sound of Fade's Howling

Mentor expected many Zaagotes and trackers to hunt for them with Kol Tar and Fade, but he eyed the narrow gorge ahead with relief. No one was there ahead of them. He also saw no sign of the strange underwater creature coming after them on land. As he studied the narrow opening between the two rock masses that formed the gorge entrance, he saw that this irregularly shaped aperture would be hard to get through.

In addition to the narrow entrance, the sliver-like, winding route that led beyond thrilled him. The unusual rocky portal and the path on the other side would severely limit the size and number of hunters who could pass through, and it would slow them down, but when he reached the craggy opening and found that *he* was unable to squeeze by, he was stymied. It was too soon to change back to his human form without risk and Ipec refused to go without him. "I'm staying with you," he said.

When Ipec pulled the semi-conscious Ben Zarek from Mentor's back and helped him through the gorge opening where his father and brother waited, a weakened but conscious Adamis slid off her ride and sank to the ground. She sat there without saying a word until Ipec pulled her up and pointed to the opening. Ben Zarek was disoriented. He stumbled, but Ipec's father and brother supported him and helped him move forward. Adamis did not follow them.

"You must go with them," Ipec said. He helped Adamis get to her feet and led her toward the opening. "Mentor and I will climb to the boulders nearby and cover your escape."

"Where is he?" Adamis asked. When Ipec pointed to Mentor's tracker body, she was speechless. She had to sit down again. While she stared at him incredulously, he collapsed and gasped for breath. As convulsions ripped through his body and he became paralyzed, Ipec wrapped his arms around Adamis and held her back.

"Takal gave us the power to change forms," he said still holding her; he transformed too soon, but his seizures should pass." After the convulsions started to subside and she calmed down, Ipec released her and pointed to the hills above. "Mentor and I can fight from there as soon as he can climb again," he said. As Adamis sat beside Mentor and stroked the thick skin on the right side of his enormous tracker body, he wondered if she had heard a word the Ayan had just said.

As soon as Ipec had her attention again, he pointed to the opening of the gorge. "He cannot fit through there now, but it's much too soon for him to become a man again. Another premature transformation could cripple or kill him. While we are waiting for him to recover enough to change once more, I will shower our enemies with arrows from above until you have time to get away."

He pointed to the opening again and tried to pull her toward it, but she kept her hand on Mentor's thick hide and kept stroking his massive side. Mentor tried to speak. He wanted to reassure her, but when no sound came he didn't know if or how his voice would come back. A moment later as his sight, hearing, and strength returned, he shuddered with relief and stood up. She stared at him, but he still could not speak. She looked dazed, but her mind was clear. "I am staying with the two of you," she said. There was no time to argue. Kol Tar and Fade charged around the sharp rocky shoulder of the ravine and headed toward them. Behind the shouts of the two brothers, Mentor could hear more trackers and Zaagotes coming. Ipec jumped on Mentor's back and pulled Adamis up in front of him where he could steady her. Mentor thundered upwards on a high path to the right and shot behind the boulders.

By the time the three of them were looking down from the massive rocks above the narrow opening, Kol Tar and Fade had almost reached the entrance. He knew what he had to do. With all of the strength that his huge tracker's body possessed, he pushed against the largest of the boulders. It did not move. He pushed again. This time the massive stone crashed down from the cliff adjacent to the gorge and landed right in front of the entrance. Half of the rocky precipice came down with it. This landslide sealed the opening shut.

With the gorge opening effectively sealed off by the landslide, relief swept over him. No one would be able to follow BenZarek, Ganta, and Yola that way, but his relief was short-lived. Kol Tar's tracker, Rol, and Fade's tracker were climbing up the narrow side path toward them. In hot pursuit, Kol Tar and Fade took cover behind their beasts and ascended to attack.

Behind Mentor's huge body, Adamis fainted before the attackers could reach them, but Ipec knelt in a firing position. One arrow after the other whirred from his bow, but with no results. Every poison-tipped arrow that he fired hit some place on each of the tracker bodies, but none penetrated their thick hides. Hidden by the bulky forms of their thick-skinned trackers, Kol Tar and Fade were unscathed. As long as the two Zaagotes remained behind their trackers, Ipec could not stop them. Kol Tar and Fade kept coming. They did not take time to stop and fire back.

The Zaagote strategy was clear. It was one that Mentor had heard about. Old warriors had told him stories about trackers unaffected by arrows. They had told him how Zaagotes used such trackers as shields. Trackers with the thickest hides and the thickest scales provided complete protection.

In spite of the poison arrows that Mentor and Ipec had gone through so much trouble to create, Kol Tar's and Fade's trackers were invincible. Mentor could not see either brother's face, but he imagined their cold smiles as the two climbed closer.

Kol Tar was in front of Fade. Although Fade was the highest ranking one in the emperor's elite command and also its leader, Mentor was sure that he had temporarily relinquished his command to his brother to give him a chance to recover from the humiliating defeat he had suffered in emperor's ring.

Mentor imagined the look of satisfaction on Fade's face as he anticipated a victorious return to the capital where he and Kol Tar would execute their new sacrificial offerings. There Fade would place a new jalar around Kol Tar's neck—a jalar made with the hair of his next victims—Ipec, Mentor, and Adamis.

Just when he thought the situation could get no worse, he spotted more Zaagotes on foot behind the boulders at the bottom of the rock avalanche. Moving slowly from rock to rock, these others were also pursuing. They had managed to survive the landslide, but their trackers had not gotten through. These trackerless survivors were approaching from the left on a narrow incline that had not been destroyed. Kol Tar and Fade were still climbing on the path they had taken to the right.

Fade roared victoriously and shouted several quick commands at his subordinates. Mentor understood every order. When the attack came, it would be from opposite directions at the same time. It would force Ipec to use his remaining arrows to respond on two fronts.

Fade's long arm emerged from behind his tracker's enormous rump to initiate the dual onslaught. When the giant pointed his subordinates uphill toward Ipec, Adamis, and him, Mentor knew he could not protect his friends. Even if he charged, he could only move in one direction. He could not take all the Zaagotes down at the same time.

For a moment he was overwhelmed by discouragement, but only for a moment. He remembered all that he had been through. He rememberd that he had never given up and that he had survived. Once more he refused to surrender. He started looking for another way to win the battle. Suddenly an idea hit him. If he could send another rocky avalanche down on the brothers and their reinforcements, he might still be able to defeat them and rescue his loyal companions.

He pushed on another boulder. It did not move. Kol Tar and Fade continued to climb using their trackers as shields; the Zaagotes without trackers were still approaching cautiously from the opposite direction.

All the attackers were drawing nearer at the same time. He scanned the area around him until he spotted two other boulders just above and behind the ledge where he was. Another climb more winding than the first led to them. His tracker body was big and heavy, but he negotiated the narrow path ferociously, pushed the boulders down, and caused another landslide to fall on the unshielded Zaagotes. Before he could move again his tingling legs collapsed. He crashed to the ground until the seizure passed.

When the seizure was over, four legs were under him once more. Praying that the convulsion would not return, he charged further up the hairline trail. When he reached other boulders, Fade and Kol Tar were within striking distance of Adamis and Ipec. As Fade directed the last two remaining hunters on foot toward Ipec and Adamis, it was clear that these survivors were ready to sacrifice their lives to aid their leaders.

The two stubborn survivors and their Zaagote commanders charged up the cliff firing arrows at Ipec and Adamis. He saw everything happening below him. While Adamis woke up, Ipec's arrows flew in two directions—at Kol Tar and Fade hidden behind their trackers and at the other two hunting them without cover.

Ipec's arrows struck the exposed warriors in quick succession, but before the second one fell, one of his arrows struck Ipec's shooting arm. Ipec did not look seriously wounded, but when he pulled the arrow out, it was clear that the tip contained something powerful. Mentor shuddered when Ipec dropped to the ground.

Was the Ayan unconscious or dead? He did not know. What he did know was that Adamis was alone now except for him. He had always admired her bravery, but he had never admired her more than he did now. Somehow, she had come out of her faint. When she saw Ipec drop, she grabbed his bow, crouched in a firing position, and prepared to fight to the end.

Without arms to use a weapon or legs that he could depend on to hold him up, he was helpless to defend her unless he could move another boulder. He pushed against a large, irregulary shaped one with all of his might, but it refused to budge. Spotting yet another pile of rocks, he crawled toward them, rammed his shoulder against the largest, and started shoving.

At that moment Adamis fired an arrow. It flew into the eye of Kol Tar's tracker. Rol rolled back and over his master's body. He was about to collide with Fade's tracker when Mentor dislodged the pile of rocks. Fade darted out of the way to avoid the collision with Rol, but in the darting motion that he made to keep his brother's tracker from rolling over him, he lost his balance and tumbled into the landslide until he reached the bottom of the ravine.

In the silence that followed the rock slide, Mentor heard something stirring below. At first it sounded like a few rocks shifting, but it soon became a waterfall of small pebbles and bigger stones. He stretched his huge form into a lying down position to make his body appear as if it was one of the irregularly shaped boulders on the rock ledge.

From there he peered into the ravine. There Fade's massive form rose slowly from the rubble. In the brightness of the full twin moons, he heard a wild shriek. He watched Fade wrap his enormous hand around a pointed rock shard protruding from his neck and listened to his groans as he tried to pull it out.

During Fade's second and third attempts to remove the shard in his neck, he heard the same piercing sounds of pain, but when Fade saw his brother's motionless body, his shrieks stopped. In the rock-covered ravine only one sound followed the silent pause—the spine chilling sound of Fade's howling.

Chapter Twenty-Five

⌘

The Right Blood

Fade's body shot up from the ground like a giant black thunderbolt streaking into the sunset sky on the evening of the next day. Against the crimson of the setting sun, he looked like an enormous black spider. As the giant crawled over the white rocks tinted orange by the last rays of the sun, even the silence trembled.

He's coming, was Mentor's only thought, but even as it passed through his mind, he did not believe what he was seeing. In spite of the rock fragment lodged in Fade's neck and the terrible pain that it had to be causing, the Zaagote climbed up the mountain on the other side of the ravine with amazing speed.

He was in awe of Fade's power, but for her sake he forced himself to stay calm and willed himself to speak. This time intelligible words came out. "He is going to circle around and come down on us from above."

"I do not see him," Adamis said. She looked across the ravine, but she was dizzy. She had to sit.

"He's there," Mentor replied. He hoped his voice would not leave him again. He wanted to talk to her, to be with her. He could see how much she wanted to help him watch for Fade's inevitable approach, but he was not surpised by her inability to spot him. She was exhausted. She shook herself to stay alert.

"Look! There are torches in the gorge, coming this way," Ipec said. As the Ayan stood up and nursed his wounded arm, Mentor wondered if he missed his tougher Zaagote body, a body that might have prevented the arrow from piercing his skin in the first place. Though Mentor's real body was human and much more vulnerable than his present bulky tracker form, he could not wait to be himself again, but it was still too soon for him to change back safely, or for Ipec to risk the convulsions that might end his life if he tried to become a Zaagote again.

"Go, Ipec," Mentor said, "but stay in your present state. Don't change to your Zaagote form to fight Fade. Look what has happened to me; another transformation now might paralyze or end your life. If it does, you'll have no chance at all and she'll have no chance. So climb just as you are, as fast as you can, before Fade is on us. I will follow when I can."

"Explain what you mean by 'When I can,'" Adamis cried hysterically. "Just how long will it be before you can become yourself again and come with us without risking your life?"

"The tingling sensation that lingers after the transformation is subsiding, but it is still there, so there is no way to tell how long it might be before I can follow you."

"If you value his life," Ipec said, "you must let him stay here as he is for now, but we must go. Come," Ipec said again, but he was unsteady. He had to sit down. He was still affected by whatever it was that the Zaagote had put on his arrow tip. The Ayan would have to climb slowly. Mentor was desperate to help him, but he needed human arms and legs for that.

"Go, Adamis," Mentor said. This time he stared into her eyes while he made his plea. "Fade wants the captives and the Zaagote who helped the captives more than he wants the tracker. When he gets here and sees an animal, he will be chasing you and Ipec. If you lead him away, you will give me the time I need to get arms and legs again so I can climb out of here."

"I am staying," Adamis said. Mentor recognized "the look," but he knew what he had to say to convince her to leave.

"Whatever was on the arrow weakened Ipec. He needs your help—and what about me? If you do not go, if you do not draw Fade away, I have no chance. The tingling is starting to subside. Start moving. I will be able to transform soon and I will be right behind you."

"He is right," Ipec said. "It is our only chance. It is his only chance." Ipec pointed to the crevice in the ravine that was closest to them, grabbed her hand, and pulled her up next to him with his good arm.

They were halfway up the ravine when the sound of rocks crumbling beneath their feet echoed around them. On the other side of the gorge, directly across from the high ledge where Mentor crouched behind the remaining boulders, Fade stopped climbing and put his hand on the point of the sharp fragment sticking out of his neck. He did not try to pull it out again. He just listened. As the sound of more stones cascaded down the rocky mountain where Ipec and Adamis stood above Mentor, Fade roared. After the sound disappeared Fade started moving.

Once more, the twin moons bathed the ravine in bright light. In their glow Fade's form stood out clearly, but this time he was almost to the top. The black shape of his massive body contrasted starkly against the white rocks in the moonlit canyon, so starkly that Mentor spotted him easily as the Zaagote completed his ascent. The longer he watched the powerful giant, the more he realized that his friends would never be fast enough to escape, or strong enough to fight their stalker in their weakened conditions. He had to do something to help them.

He placed the sharp point of his tracker's tongue against the last pouch sewn into his gum line and pierced it to start the transformation. The smooth, bitter liquid slid down his throat once more. The tingling sensations started in his feet, but when he felt them he knew that they were different from any sensations that he had ever experienced before. This tingling turned to shooting pains that ran all the way up his legs. He wanted to scream. He fell to the ground and gasped for breath. Convulsions shook him.

The pains spread through the upper part of his body until they became a raging fire. He had never been in this much agony before. He bit his tongue. He prayed that the shooting pains would pass. Suddenly he was paralyzed and there was nothing that he could do to reverse it. He had to wait for the fire in his body to burn itself out. He had not heeded Takal's warning, but he hoped he would live through this transformation. He had to save Adamis and Ipec.

How much time passed before the shooting pains stopped, he did not know. After the fire from the premature change had finished ravaging his body and his skin had stopped burning, he began to move again. When he finally opened his eyes he realized that he had regained the body parts that he needed to climb—hands and feet.

He had always taken his hands and feet for granted, but not tonight. Tonight, he was grateful for them and thankful to be alive. He saw that he no longer had a tracker's body, but he had not returned to his human form either. His hands and arms were not those of a man, or of a monster, but of something in between. He glanced down at his legs and feet. They too were not quite human. What his face looked like he had no time to consider. Everything went black.

When the twin moons rose above him yet again, he was stunned. Another full day had passed. His metamorphosis had gone on for hours. It was night again and too much precious time had already been lost in the transformation.

He realized that Fade might have already caught up with his friends, but he forced himself to believe that the giant would not kill them right away, that there would still be time to save them. With this hope he started climbing furiously.

He used his strange legs with some difficulty, but he finally reached the top of the ravine. He was not surprised when he saw no signs of his friends or Fade. However slow they might have traveled, Adamis and Ipec were far ahead of him, as was the giant. What frightened him more than the distance he had to travel to reach them was his last glimpse of Fade. He had never seen anyone filled with such incredible power or so fueled by revenge.

As these thoughts passed through his mind, he ran faster than he had ever run before. It came to him now, in the aftermath of this last transformation, that he too was filled with incredible speed and strength. While he ran, new energy powered his transformed body.

He glanced at his new hands again. They were much larger and much stronger than human hands could ever be and he was much stronger. His speed was so great that his legs barely touched the ground as he flew over it. Were his legs powerful enough to catch up with Fade before Fade did something terrible to his friends? That was the burning question. Suddenly, he recalled his grandfather's most repeated advice—"You have to have faith, boy, faith! You have to understand that some things are just part of God's plan, and that His plan always works out better than ours would. Some things you cannot change. They are just meant to be."

Were these new limbs just meant to be? In addition to the words "meant to be," his grandfather had also told him to take one day at a time, to do the best that he could with each day, and to trust God with the future because the future often turned out to be far different than we thought it would. In spite of Ben Zarek's wise counsel, he had never understood the phrases "meant to be" or "one day at a time." He had always worried about the future. How senseless! The future that he had worried about had never included these powerful hands or these amazing legs.

With these legs, he was faster than he had ever been on his best day as a courier. While he ran, he thought about the many times he had twisted and turned in nightmares about Fade. All of these foreshadowed confrontations had ended badly. In these horrible dreams he had seen himself overpowered by Fade, but circumstances had changed. Fade was wounded, and in his present form, Mentor was more powerful than he had ever been as a human.

Such were his ideas as he sped toward the future, but as he reached the edge of the forest and approached the mountains ahead, nothing could have prepared him for what he saw. Upside down, dangling at the end of two ropes tied around trees at the edge of a mountain cliff, Adamis and Ipec hung helplessly suspended. Fade hovered above them.

The giant was moving back and forth between his two captives. The ropes were close to each other, but far enough apart to avoid collision.

He swung the rope from which Adamis hung with sadistic, methodical cruelty. First he swung it horizontally across the face of the cliffside. Then he raised the rope and let it drop suddenly as if he intended to let her plunge all the way to her death at the bottom, but he yanked the rope up before she hit. He tortured Ipec in the same way.

Almost directly under his tortured friends, a turbulent river crashed along the bed of the gorge. The water roared over the rocks, but he could hear the sound of Fade's rolling laughter above it. The Zaagote's brutality filled him with rage. Though he wanted to punish the maniac without delay, he knew he had to control his ire. In order to rescue his friends he had to think clearly.

His first thought was to climb up the face of the cliff, surprise Fade, and push him off before he could cut the ropes that kept his friends from plunging to their deaths, but he did not obey his first impulse. Fade had been weakened by his neck wound, but Mentor did not know if he could get close enough to the giant to give him a shove that would send him over the side, or if he was strong enough to do it.

Whether to climb up or not was a difficult decision. *Should I go up to confront Fade or should I confront him somewhere here below?* The question kept repeating itself in his mind; he was surprised when the answer came from the same place, but in his grandfather's voice.

Suddenly Ben Zarek was beside him in the forest, invisible but audible, helping him plan his strategy. "Consider the place where you will face your adversary and the way he thinks," his grandfather said. "Then decide the best moment to do it and how."

He considered the place first. He looked up at his friends where they dangled helplessly. Then he looked at their captor on the cliff above. As he studied the river that flowed beneath the cliff and listened to the tumbling water, he tried to think the way Fade would think about prisoners and visualize the best course of action. He was sure that Fade would not kill Adamis and Ipec quickly; he would extend the torture as long as he could before he ended their lives, or he would keep them alive and take them back to the citadel to sacrifice them there. He hated to see his friends being tortured, but Fade's intense desire to prolong the suffering of his victims would give him a chance to face the giant here alone, without an army of other Zaagotes and trackers around. He also knew that his friends had no chance at all if he faced Fade and lost—that their best hope for survival was an escape on the river, not a confrontation on a cliff.

Escape was the answer; now was the time. As he scanned the riverbank, the how became clear when he spotted two rafts—one that looked as if it had been built with new wood, and one that bore the symbol of another Zaagote who had left his raft here for another purpose and time. He had not noticed these rafts before. They were perfect for the escape he had in mind, but he decided to wait until he heard Fade's rolling laughter no more before he did anything. He had seen Fade touch the shard sticking out of his neck each time he swung the rope that held his prisoners. He was sure that the Zaagote was exhausted by pain, and that he would soon withdraw from the cliff to regain his strength.

Edging closer to the riverbank behind some thick shrubs, he gazed up at the rim of the cliff and waited until the pained exhaustion became silence. When there were no further sounds from the giant, and he did not appear at the cliff edge to repeat the swinging, dropping torture, he surmised that Fade was asleep or resting. Even if the giant was awake and watching, the ropes would appear to be anchored firmly in place at the top where Fade had tied them to trees.

The moment to execute his plan had come. With his incredibly powerful new body, he scrambled up the face of the cliff effortlessly. He was careful not to move either rope. If Fade was eyeing the ropes he would see them dangling where they were. He cut the first rope well below the rim of the cliffside to avoid detection. Wrapping his left arm tightly around Adamis, he used the other arm and hand to hold on to strategic places. He navigated his descent with her by placing his feet in safe niches. Then he climbed back up and cut the second rope. He repeated the same steps for Ipec with even greater speed.

His two ascents and descents on the cliffside had been fast, but not fast enough. His heart stopped when he saw Fade. He was almost all the way down the cliffside, coming after them. He had planned to cut the other raft free so that Fade could not follow them that way, but it was too far to go. If he took the time to run to it, cut it away from the shore, and return to his helpless companions, they would never get away.

He tied his unconscious friends to the center of the raft to keep them from falling off and pushed away from the riverbank. Fade ran to the other raft, shoved it into the middle of the river, and paddled after them. Just ahead of Fade, Mentor's raft twisted and turned in the wild water. In front of him a churning whirlpool swirled around a rocky mountain spine that divided the strong current in two.

As Mentor headed toward the stony divider, he shoved the raft away from the rocks. So far he had kept the raft from crashing, but he could tell by the way the water was turning the raft that he would have no control over which direction it would take. He did not know on which side of the split river the raft would go down.

Finally, an unexpected spin sent the raft tumbling down on the right side of the rocky divider and flung it into calmer water there. When he glanced back his racing heart began to pump even harder. Fade was crashing down the river right behind them. After the giant's raft hit one of the rocky points that he had barely missed, Mentor's heart soared, but Fade leapt into the water and swam to the shore. There he flew along the narrow trail parallel to the river and kept up with the raft as it moved more slowly through less turbulent water.

In front of him was a large rock formation that projected itself over and above the middle of the river in a very low bridge. He knew that Fade saw it too. As the giant sprinted toward the bridge that conveniently hung out just above the river, Mentor knew that it was the spot from which he would jump onto the raft. When Fade suddenly put his hand on the rock shard that was still impaled in his neck again, he hoped that the pain would slow the assassin down, but the killer kept coming.

He held his sword in readiness for Fade's attack. Grasping his own blade, Fade climbed onto the rock that stretched itself over the water, but before he could jump onto the raft, two barbed tentacles shot out of the river. One struck Mentor's leg. The other struck Fade's.

"Zing lot tera! Zing lot tera," Fade shouted commands from where he lay on the stone bridge. As fire from the wound shot through Mentor's leg, he collapsed on the raft that was now stuck on some rocks, but he held on to his sword and gasped for breath. He had never felt such pain. His eyes blurred, but he could clearly hear Fade shouting orders again.

"Zing lot tera! Zing lot tera." In spite of the pain Mentor translated the words easily, but he did not understand why the tracker did not respond to his master.

"Zing lot tera! Zing lot tera," Fade kept shouting. As a tall black creature rose from the water, Mentor recognized it. The fiery red eyes were unmistakable. It was the creature that he had seen behind the bars under the lake, but why had this tracker attacked Fade?

Fade kept repeating "Strike your enemy not your master," but there was no pause between Fade's last command and the tracker's next strike. Once more the creature projected two barbed tentacles; one at Mentor, his enemy, and one at Fade, his master, but this time the man and the Zaagote were ready for the attack.

Mentor sliced through the heavy long projectile that whipped at him. In one fluid movement, he chopped off the barb. As the sharp projectile which had flown at him fell into the water next to the raft, he heard another splash and looked up. The other barb was floating in the river by Fade who had cut if off with his sword.

Before the barbless creature sank below the surface of the river, Mentor imagined that he saw the beginning of new tentacles growing where the old ones had been. He thought he was hallucinating from the poison in the barb, but he was sure that he saw the creature's thick black lips curve in a smile before it disappeared.

Though Zaagotes were supposed to be able to control trackers, it was clear that no Zaagote controlled this one. It was equally clear that if Mentor saw what he thought he had seen before this tracker disappeared under the water, the creature was quickly regenerating. If the raft stayed where it was, the tracker would rise from the river and strike again.

Fade stirred restlessly where he was lying. Mentor was not surprised when the giant did not get up. The throbbing pain in his own leg prevented him from standing, but when he saw Fade struggle to sit up and heard the shrill vibration that Zaagotes used to call other Zaagotes and trackers, he realized that Fade understood the threat to himself. In his wounded condition, the giant was in as much danger of being killed by the rebellious tracker as they were.

While Fade dragged himself away and crawled into the heavy bushes bordering the river to escape the disobedient tracker, Mentor pushed the raft away from the rocks that kept it from moving until it floated free again. He remembered that the stony peaks dividing the river in two went on for miles.

There were many watery channels and passes through which Fade or the horrific tracker might have been able to go to follow them to the other side of the rocky spine, but it would take the injured giant or his out-of-control hunter time to recover and time to locate these channels and passes. It would take even longer to inspect the routes, pick up their scent, and decide which way they had gone.

He hoped that Fade would die from his injury, and that the tracker would fail to regenerate, but he was sure that these hopes were vain. Somehow he knew that a day would come when he would face the giant and this unpredictable tracker again. For now he decided to banish Fade and the tracker from his mind. While the raft moved over the gentle, but strong, current in the shaded waterway, he could see that the passage was widening. He felt confident that it would take them all the way to the other side of the mountains.

Although days would pass before they reached that other side, they were safer than they had been in a long time. When he finally brought the raft to a stop, he drank some of the elixir that Takal had given him and ate a piece of Oliphar's bark. As soon as the pain in his leg subsided, he carried his injured friends to a dry niche protected by rocks above and all around. He quickly built a large fire from dry twigs. Now it was time to concentrate on the desperate matter at hand—saving his friends' lives.

He tried to recall everything that Takal had taught him about healing. Although his friends' breathing patterns were shallow and irregular, their chests were moving. In spite of the fire he had built, they were still icy cold; so much water had washed over them in their tumultuous escape on the raft. They had also lost a lot of blood from the wounds that they had suffered. How many times their bodies had collided with the rocky cliffside over which Fade had been swinging them, he could only imagine.

They were in grave condition. They could not chew Oliphar's bark, but he was grateful for all of the medicines that Takal had tucked inside the tracker's harness. The strange device that had once fitted his tracker body, that was now wrapped around his neck, was amazing. He was also grateful for Takal's elixir. He planned to use the remaining drops cautiously. He would also use the other cures to nurse Adamis and Ipec back to health. He had to get them away from this river before Fade or the rebellious tracker caught up with them.

In the warmth of the firelight Mentor pounded the medicines and the bark until they dissolved in the water that he boiled from the river. As he dripped this cooled liquid into each of his friend's mouths from a spoon he had made, he wanted to shout when Ipec opened his eyes. Although Ipec stared at him for several moments without a word, relief swept over him when the Ayan finally recognized him and smiled.

"You are not as ugly as you were when you were a tracker," Ipec said pausing, "but you look different. A slave should ask his master's permission before he changes the way he looks. I will get used to your new body, but it will take time."

Before he could answer Ipec, he heard Adamis murmur his name. Would she feel the same way? For her, he knew his latest transformation would be harder to accept, especially if he could never change back. When she whispered his name a second time, he summoned every ounce of courage. Then he turned around and knelt by her side in the firelight where she could see him.

"Some things change," she said finally after studying his face for a long time. The longer she stared at him the more he wanted to run away, but she grabbed one of the enormous fingers on his huge hand before he could leave. She held his finger tightly and spoke to him softly.

"But some things never change," she added as she lifted his hand up, turned it over, and put her small one inside of his.

"You have always loved to fish," she said, "with this hand you will catch many. You will not need a pole. You have better equipment." He could not speak. He thought if he did he might cry. He saw tears in her eyes, but she went on. "Another thing that won't change is that you still like taking care of me. You saved my life and you saved the Ayan." She paused for a moment before she continued and squeezed his finger again. "You know I never agreed with Tal. You never had to prove anything to me. On the outside you are very different, but on the inside you are still the same. You've always had power running through those arteries and veins; you just didn't know it."

As he bent down to kiss her cheek, he knew beyond any doubt that it would take every ounce of this power to keep them alive. Perhaps Fade or this wild tracker, or both, had already recovered. Perhaps the two hunters were already on their way, traveling closer to them on one of the waterways, or over the rocky spine that divided one river into two, or on another mountainous path he knew nothing about. Would they appear before Adamis and Ipec were strong enough to travel?

Holding her hand, Mentor stared into the darkness outside. He tried to convince himself that the rebel tracker's wounds were too serious, that it would either die from them or take a long time to heal and regenerate weapons with which to stab them again. He tried to persuade himself that Fade would also die from his wounds. He told himself that the Zaagote would never recover, that he would never complete the revenge that Mentor was sure he had planned for all three of them, but he did not believe any of these things.

Fade would hunt for them until his brother's death was avenged, and the tracker he had first seen behind bars in the lake near the Zaagote temple would hunt them all. He was sure that it lived to find and strike whoever or whatever might have temporarily escaped from it.

This tracker was a more dangerous, more versatile type of hunter than any of the others. It was a more determined predator. It had followed them all the way from the lake where it had been imprisoned under the water. It was also extremely intelligent and evil, and with regenerating powers—perhaps invincible. He had seen the malevolent grin on its face before it sank into the water, a grin that hinted at the threat of an evil power too great to be killed. Beyond these frightening characteristics, there was one other trait that could not be denied. It was violently rebellious. It would not allow itself to be commanded by any Zaagote, even one as formidable as Fade. It was an uncontrolled, focused, and relentless predator bent upon executing the prey that had eluded it in the lake and the master who had once commanded it. There was no doubt about its intentions.

About Fade personally executing those he held responsible for his brother's death, there was also no doubt. Even with life-threatening injuries, Fade would not give up. He was still the fiercest, most powerful Zaagote Mentor had ever seen. When he regained his full strength, Fade would confront the rebellious tracker. He would also search for those who had escaped his wrath and give each one a long, torturous death.

In spite of the unexpected new threat which the rebel tracker posed, and in spite of Fade's determination to destroy him and everyone he loved, Mentor was not as afraid as he had been before this hunt had begun. He could not explain his new confidence. He wondered if it came from the prayers that had been answered by his grandfather's God.

Though his father would have said that the help he had prayed for came by accident or by coincidence, he did not believe this was true. Outwardly the circumstances of his life were still the same. His world was more dangerous than ever. He was pursued by Zaagotes and trackers—one Zaagote in particular and one new tracker far more dangerous than any he had ever encountered before. He was hunted by his own people for an act of treason he had never committed and he looked like a cross between a man and a monster. He might never be able to change back to his true form again.

Still he had survived all of these challenges, and someone seemed to be watching over him. Another good thing was that Adamis and Ipec accepted him the way he was in spite of his odd appearance. Above all, he accepted himself.

Through all of the trials and the heartaches that Mentor had endured and overcome, he had discovered two truths. The first was that he would be able to face the dangers ahead bravely, whatever they might be. The second was that he had the right blood.

About the Author

Cris Pfeil earned a bachelor of arts and a master in education degree at Bridgewater State College. She also completed a master of fine arts degree in creative writing and publishing at Emerson College in Boston, Massachusetts. After a fulfilling career in public school education, Cris retired. Cris is the author of *A Shepherd's Rod*, a biblically-based fiction thriller; *Outside the Box*, a non-fiction book about miracles, and *Miracles Happen: Outside the Box*. Cris lives in Rhode Island.

More Titles by Cris Pfeil

A Shepherd's Rod

ISBN: 978-1-60911-731-3

A Shepherd's Rod demonstrates three life-changing messages. The first is that we find the meaning of life in unexpected places. The second is that destiny comes to us through trials. The third is that challenges are not accidental; they come to change us into the people we are meant to be through the divinely appointed touches of *A Shepherd's Rod.*

Of her first book Cris says "*A Shepherd's Rod* is a biblically based, romantic adventure. I believe audiences will love it because of its unusual point of view. The story of Exodus has never been told by the daughter of the magician who failed to defeat Moses."

A Shepherd's Rod is available through www.strategicpublishinggroup.com, Amazon or Barnes and Noble.

Outside the Box

ISBN: 978-1-926831-04-6

In her second book, *Outside the Box*, the title clearly communicates its message: You will not see God act how, when, or where you expect Him to be. In these pages God lives, works, heals, and performs miracles where He loves to do them---*Outside the Box.*

Of her second book Cris says "In *Outside the Box* I wanted to share my experiences and the experiences of others to encourage people. I wanted them to know that God does answer each cry for help with an unusual and amazing response, one uniquely designed to fit each individual, situation, or need.

Outside the Box is available at www.navaronebooks.com, Amazon and select locations.

More Titles by 5 Fold Media

45 Minutes
by Kristen Young
$15.00
ISBN: 978-1-936578-10-8

45 Minutes by Kristen Young is the undeniable journey of Anthony Michaels' life, which is oddly typical until he faces an encounter with eternity. Readers will relate to the characters as they read about painful life lessons, true forgiveness, answered prayers and the love of God that can change any situation.

45 Minutes was written with the purpose of helping readers see the unfailing love of God. The author hopes that this book will draw people into a relationship with their Savior as they see themselves through the eyes of the characters.

Sling Shot Circuit Rider
by Randy Pogue
$15.00
ISBN: 978-1-936578-25-2

SLING SHOT CIRCUIT RIDER by Randy Pogue is the tale of an ordinary man who accepts the extraordinary call of God to become a Methodist itinerant preacher during the early 1800s. While the main characters are fictional, this story depicts the true life history of Missouri's settlement days through the personal story of one young circuit rider named William Travers.

Pastor Gary Brothers of Cape First in Cape Girardeau, MO comments, "As you read this book you will find yourself riding the trails side-by-side with the circuit rider of a day long forgotten. This book will inform you, encourage you, and challenge you to 'ride the trail' that God has for you today."

Visit www.5foldmedia.com to sign up for 5 Fold Media's FREE email update. You will get notices of our new releases, sales, and special events such as book signings and media conferences.

5 Fold Media, LLC is a Christ-centered media company. Our desire is to produce lasting fruit in writing, music, art, and creative gifts.

"To Establish and Reveal"

For more information visit:

www.5foldmedia.com

Use your mobile device to scan the tag above and visit our website.
Get the free app: http://gettag.mobi

CPSIA information can be obtained at www.ICGtesting.com
Printed in the USA
LVOW13s2131210514

386854LV00001B/167/P

9 781936 578368